WRITER OF THE
PURPLE RAGE

WRITER OF THE PURPLE RAGE

Joe R. Lansdale

CARROLL & GRAF PUBLISHERS, INC.
New York

Copyright © 1994 by Joseph R. Lansdale

First Carroll & Graf edition 1997

Carroll & Graf Publishers, Inc.
260 Fifth Avenue
New York, NY 10001

ISBN 0-7867-0389-X

Manufactured in the United States of America

Writer of the Purple Rage is dedicated to my good friends, Ruth and Neal Barrett, Jr., with great love and respect, and a sincere hope that Ruth will only allow Neal out in public for short periods of time while under intense supervision.

CONTENTS

INTRODUCTION

These stories represent the best of my short work these last few years. They are a mixed bag, ranging from the Southern Gothic to the comic, with way stations in between.

Some of the stories are obviously of the ilk of those in my collection *By Bizarre Hands*. Some have the echo of my earlier work, collected in *Stories By Mama Lansdale's Youngest Boy*, and later retitled, *Bestsellers Guaranteed*, and cursed with a stupid dragon cover that had absolutely nothing to do with my writing, but hey, stock art is cheap.

Bestsellers also had an added story, "The Events Concerning A Nude Fold-Out Found In A Harlequin Romance," which actually should have been included here, as it is of recent vintage. But that's how it goes sometimes. I wanted the readers of *Stories By Mama Lansdale's Youngest Boy* to have something else in their stocking should they decide to purchase the *Bestsellers Guaranteed* version.

But all of the stories here, in my view, are transitional. They're not quite the same as any that have gone before, though they may at times carry the echoes of earlier stories.

Maybe bounce a new note or two off the wall to show you where I'm going next.

What may be different about future stories is perhaps I've said all I have to say about the extremes of the dark side. It's getting so taking that trip is too painful, and I feel I'm getting beyond exploring the mystery of it, using it to understand myself and human nature. I'm no longer shining a glaring light on those shadows, making the things that live there scuttle for cover.

I'm becoming too familiar with them. They're starting to yawn when I show up. Sometimes they invite me down there in the cool darkness with them, want me to sit around and drink a Co-Cola and talk about dismemberment and child molestation and all the evils of the world. Maybe watch a little TV, throw a steak on the grill.

I don't like being that friendly with the wet, waltzing shadows. I keep it up, these dark trips will no longer be exploratory expeditions. Most likely I'll just be visiting darkness to visit darkness, slumming, and for me, when you start doing that, it's time to quit. I do not want to be one of those writers who is always looking to out-gross the other. Nothing wrong with gross. It's as legitimate a technique as any other. But enough is enough, and for that to be the entire point of a work is to tire one out. That has never been my attitude, and I do not want to become that sort of writer.

That is a poor parlor game. Darkness should be there to deliver a point, an insight, or give a reader a chance to explore some horrible mystery, something to satisfy the innate curiosity of human beings. But if you find yourself getting off primarily on the graphic details, and you're past puberty, out of your early twenties, then maybe you ought to find another hobby. Stretch out. Read a variety of things. I'm not saying what you need now is "Gilligan's Island" and a tonic for the bowels, but a little more mental stimulation might not be bad for you. Masturbate less. Watch your diet. Expand your horizons. Well, get some exercise too, least you expand your hind-end.

These comments should not be construed as apology of my past work or an interest in your hind-end. I'm very proud of my early work, as well as my hind-end, which I've nearly worked off a couple of times. So, no apology.

Nor is it veiled criticism of the good work of this nature done by others. I'm merely stating that perhaps I've had my say. I say "perhaps," because who knows when I might return to the shadows with a brighter light and bigger club. I never say never, least I end up having to eat my words and smile between bites.

I do not mean to imply that my work from here on out will have a Pollyanna nature. I've always been varied. But it seems to me it is time to move into new avenues. Or even alleys. Ones that may not be brightly lit, but are at least equipped with one lonesome, bug-swarmed street light. Too much darkness after a time is just darkness.

Enough of that.

Of the stories included, several have seen print a few times, been reprinted more than once. Though one of my best, and most powerful, "Drive-In Date," perhaps due to the subject matter, has only been reprinted once in this country, and there was a play version of it printed in *Cemetery Dance* for the special Joe R. Lansdale issue.

Other stories, like "Everybody Plays The Fool" and "Man With Two Lives" appeared either in an obscure magazine or an anthology that got about as much exposure as a nun's ass at high mass.

Others, like "In The Cold Dark Time" and "Love Doll" were better exposed, but not so frequently I feel like everyone that picks up this collection will have read them.

Also, one novelette, "Bubba Ho-tep," and a short story, "Godzilla's Twelve Step Program," are brand new, and appear here for the first time. Or should. I always leave room for snafus of publishing beyond which I have no control.

But, if all goes well, they should provide well over 15,000 words of original material.

Also, there's an article, "A Hard-On For Horror." A number of readers of my fiction might enjoy it, but may well have missed it, as it appeared in a fun book on horror films titled *Cut.* It deals with the subject matter of my *Drive-In* novels, as well as a few of the short stories I've written. Drive-in movies, late night movies, and low budget movies, are in my blood, and therefore, pop up repeatedly in my fiction.

Lastly, I've included one of my plays, "By Bizarre Hands." Though based on the story of the same name, and faithful to it in many ways, it also contains some differences. Primarily in the ending. For that reason, and the fact that I'm proud of the different types of writing I do, I have included it here, and will comment more on it when I introduce it.

Okay, another introduction finished. Another stall until you get to the fiction. I believe it was John Steinbeck who spoke of Prologues as being written after a book is finished as a sort of apology for everything that the writer didn't do right.

Perhaps it's the same way with Introductions to collections. I hope not. I hope I'm just opening the door and smiling and inviting you in.

Then, I'm gonna trip you.

MISTER
WEED-EATER

Mr. Job Harold was in his living room with his feet on the couch watching "Wheel of Fortune" when his five-year-old son came inside covered in dirt. "Daddy," said the boy dripping dirt, "there's a man outside want to see you."

Mr. Harold got up and went outside, and there standing at the back of the house next to his wife's flower bed, which was full of dead roses and a desiccated frog, was, just like his boy had said, a man.

It was over a hundred degrees out there, and the man, a skinny sucker in white T-shirt and jeans with a face red as a baboon's ass, a waterfall of inky hair dripping over his forehead and dark glasses, stood with his head cocked like a spaniel listening for trouble. He had a bright-toothed smile that indicated everything he heard struck him as funny.

In his left hand was a new weed-eater, the cutting line coated in greasy green grass the texture of margarita vomit, the price tag dangling proudly from the handle.

In the other hand the man held a blind man's cane, the tip of which had speared an oak leaf. His white T-shirt, stained pollen-yellow under the arms, stuck wetly to his chest and little pot belly tight as plastic wrap on a fish head. He had on dirty white socks with played-out elastic and they had fallen over the tops of his tennis shoes as if in need of rest.

The man was shifting his weight from one leg to the other. Mr. Harold figured he needed to pee and wanted to use the bathroom and the idea of letting him into the house with a weed-eater and pointing him at the pot didn't appeal to Mr. Harold cause there wasn't any question in Mr. Harold's mind the man was blind as a peach pit, and Mr. Harold figured he got in the bathroom, he was gonna pee from one end of the place to the other trying to hit the commode, and then Mr. Harold knew he'd have to clean it up or explain to his wife when she got home from work how on his day off he let a blind man piss all over their bathroom. Just thinking about all that gave Mr. Harold a headache.

"What can I do for you?" Mr. Harold asked.

"Well, sir," said the blind man in a voice dry as Mrs. Harold's sexual equipment, "I heard your boy playin' over here, and I followed the sound. You see, I'm the grounds keeper next door, and I need a little help. I was wonderin' you could come over and show me if I've missed a few spots?"

Mr. Harold tried not to miss a beat. "You talking about the church over there?"

"Yes, sir. Just got hired. Wouldn't want to look bad on my first day."

Mr. Harold considered this. Cameras could be set in place somewhere. People in trees waiting for him to do something they could record for a TV show. He didn't want to go on record as not helping a blind man, but on the other hand, he didn't want to be caught up in no silliness either.

Finally, he decided it was better to look like a fool and a samaritan than a cantankerous asshole who wouldn't help a poor blind man cut weeds.

"I reckon I can do that," Mr. Harold said. Then to his five-year-old who'd followed him outside and was sitting in the dirt playing with a plastic truck: "Son, you stay right here and don't go off."

"Okay, Daddy," the boy said.

The church across the street had been opened in a building about the size of an aircraft hanger. It had once been used as a liquor warehouse, and later it was called Community Storage, but items had a way of disappearing. It was a little too community for its renters, and it went out of business and Sonny Guy, who owned the place, had to pay some kind of fine and turn up with certain items deemed as missing.

This turn of events had depressed Mr. Guy, so he'd gotten religion and opened a church. God wasn't knocking them dead either, so to compensate, Sonny Guy started a Gospel Opry, and to advertise and indicate its location, beginning on their street and on up to the highway, there was a line of huge orange Day-glo guitars that pointed from highway to Opry.

The guitars didn't pull a lot of people in though, bright as they were. Come Sunday the place was mostly vacant and when the doors were open on the building back and front, you could hear wind whistling through there like it was blowing through a pipe. A special ticket you could cut out of the newspaper for five dollars off a fifteen dollar buffet of country sausages and sliced cantaloupe hadn't rolled them in either. Sonny and God most definitely needed a more exciting game plan. Something with titties.

Taking the blind man by the elbow, Mr. Harold led him across the little street and into the yard of the church. Well, actually, it was more than a yard. About four acres. On the front acre sat Sonny Guy's house, and out to the right of it was

17

a little music studio he'd built, and over to the left was the metal building that served as the church. The metal was aluminum and very bright and you could feel the heat bouncing off of it like it was an oven with bread baking inside.

Behind the house were three more acres, most of it weeds, and at the back of it all was a chicken wire fence where a big black dog of undetermined breed liked to pace.

When Mr. Harold saw what the blind man had done, he let out his breath. The fella had been all over that four acres, and it wasn't just a patch of weeds now, but it wasn't manicured either. The poor bastard had tried to do the job of a lawn mower with a weed-eater, and he'd mostly succeeded in chopping down the few flowers that grew in the midst of brick-lined beds, and he'd chopped weeds and dried grass here and there, so that the whole place looked as if it were a head of hair mistreated by a drunk barber with an attitude.

At Mr. Harold's feet, he discovered a mole the blind man's shoe had dislodged from a narrow tunnel. The mole had been whipped to death by the weed-eater sling. It looked like a wad of dirty hair dipped in red paint. A lasso loop of guts had been knocked out of its mouth and ants were crawling on it. The blind had slain the blind.

"How's it look?"

"Well," Mr. Harold said, "you missed some spots."

"Yeah, well they hired me cause they wanted to help the handicapped, but I figure it was just as much cause they knew I'd do the job. They had 'em a crippled nigger used to come out and do it, but they said he charged too much and kept making a mess of things."

Mr. Harold had seen the black man mow. He might have been crippled, but he'd had a riding mower and he was fast. He didn't do such a bad job either. He always wore a straw hat pushed up on the back of his head, and when he got off the mower to get on his crutches, he did it with the style of a rodeo star dismounting a show horse. There hadn't been a thing wrong with the black man's work. Mr. Harold figured Sonny guy wanted to cut a few corners. Switch a crippled nigger for a blind honky.

"How'd you come to get this job?" Mr. Harold asked. He tried to make the question pleasant, as if he were asking him how his weekend had been.

"References," the blind man said.

"Of course," said Mr. Harold.

"Well, what do I need to touch up? I stayed me a line from the building there, tried to work straight, turn when I got to the fence and come back. I do it mostly straight?"

"You got off a mite. You've missed some pretty good-sized patches."

Mr. Harold, still holding the blind man's elbow, felt the blind man go a little limp with disappointment. "How bad is it?"

"Well . . . "

"Go on and tell me."

"A weed-eater ain't for this much place. You need a mower."

"I'm blind. You can't turn me loose out here with a mower. I'd cut my foot off."

"I'm just saying."

"Well, come on, how bad is it? It look worse than when the nigger did it?"

"I believe so."

"By much?"

"When he did it, you could look out here and tell the place had been mowed. Way it looks now, you might do better just to poison the weeds and hope the grass dies."

The blind man really slumped now, and Mr. Harold wished he'd chosen his words more carefully. It wasn't his intention to insult a blind man on his lawn skills in a hundred degree heat. He began to wish the fella had only wanted to wet on the walls of his bathroom.

"Can't even do a nigger's job," the blind man said.

"It ain't so bad if they're not too picky."

"Shit," said the blind man. "Shit, I didn't have no references. I didn't never have a job before, really. Well, I worked out at the chicken processing plant tossing chicken heads in a metal drum, but I kept missing and tossin' them on this lady worked by me. I just couldn't keep my mind on the drum's location. I think I might actually be more artistic than mechanical. I got one side of the brain works harder, you know?"

"You could just slip off and go home. Leave 'em a note."

"Naw, I can't do that. Besides, I ain't got no way home. They picked me up and brought me here. I come to church last week and they offered me the job, and then they come and got me and brought me here and I made a mess of it. They'll be back later and they won't like it. They ain't gonna give me my five dollars, I can see that and I can't see nothing."

"Hell, man," Mr. Harold said, "that black fella mowed this lawn, you can bet he got more than five dollars."

"You tryin' to say I ain't good as a nigger?"

"I'm not trying to say anything 'cept you're not being paid enough. A guy ought to get five dollars an hour just for standing around in this heat."

"People charge too much these days. Niggers especially will stick you when they can. It's that civil rights business. It's gone to their heads."

"It ain't got nothing to do with what color you are."

"By the hour, I reckon I'm making 'bout what I got processing chicken heads," the blind man said. "Course, they had a damn fine company picnic this time each year."

"Listen here. We'll do what we were gonna do. Check the spots you've missed. I'll lead you around to bad places, and you chop 'em."

"That sounds all right, but I don't want to share my five dollars. I was gonna get me something with that. Little check I get from the government just covers my necessities, you know?"

"You don't owe me anything."

Mr. Harold took the blind man by the elbow and led him around to where the grass was missed or whacked high, which was just about everywhere you looked. After about fifteen minutes, the blind man said he was tired. They went over to the house and leaned on a tree in the front yard. The blind man said, "You seen them shows about those crop circles, in England, I think it is?"

"No," said Mr. Harold.

"Well, they found these circles in the wheat. Just appeared out there. They think it's aliens."

"Oh yeah, I seen about those," Mr. Harold said, suddenly recalling what it was the man was talking about. "There ain't no mystery to that. It's some guys with a stick and a cord. We used to do that in tall weed patches when we were kids. There's nothing to it. Someone's just making jackasses out of folks."

The blind man took a defiant posture. "Not everything like that is a bunch of kids with a string."

"I wasn't saying that."

"For all I know, what's wrong with that patch there's got nothing to do with me and my work. It could have been alien involvement."

"Aliens with weed-eaters?"

"It could be what happened when they landed, their saucers messin' it up like that."

"If they landed, why didn't they land on you? You was out there with the weed-eater. How come nobody saw or heard them?"

21

"They could have messed up the yard while I was coming to get you."

"Kind of a short visit, wasn't it?"

"You don't know everything, Mister-I-Got-Eyeballs. Those that talk the loudest know less than anybody."

"And them that believe every damn thing they hear are pretty stupid, Mister Weed-Eater. I know what's wrong with you now. You're lazy. It's hot out there and you don't want to be here, so you're trying to make me feel sorry for you and do the job myself, and it ain't gonna work. I don't feel sorry for you cause you're blind. I ain't gonna feel sorry at all. I think you're an asshole."

Mr. Harold went across the road and back to the house and called his son inside. He sat down in front of the TV. "Wheel of Fortune" wasn't on anymore. Hell, it was a rerun anyway. He changed the channel looking for something worth watching but all that was on was midget wrestling, so he watched a few minutes of that.

Those little guys were fast and entertaining and it was cool inside with the air-conditioner cranked up, so after a couple minutes Mr. Harold got comfortable watching the midgets sling each other around, tumble up together and tie themselves in knots.

However, time eroded Mr. Harold's contentment. He couldn't stop thinking about the blind man out there in the heat. He called to his son and told him to go outside and see if the blind man was still there.

The boy came back a minute later. He said, "He's out there, Daddy. He said you better come on out and help him. He said he ain't gonna talk about crop circles no more."

Mr. Harold thought a moment. You were supposed to help the blind, the hot and the stupid. Besides, the old boy might need someone to pour gas in that weed-eater. He did it himself he was liable to pour it all over his shoes and later get around

22

someone who smoked and wanted to toss a match. An accident might be in the making.

Mr. Harold switched the channel to cartoons and pointed them out to his son. The boy sat down immediately and started watching. Mr. Harold got the boy a glass of Kool-Aid and a stack of chocolate cookies. He went outside to find the blind man.

The blind man was in Mr. Harold's yard. He had the weed-eater on and was holding it above his head whacking at the leaves on Mr. Harold's red-bud tree; his wife's favorite tree.

"Hey, now stop that," Mr. Harold said. "Ain't no call to be malicious."

The blind man cut the weed-eater and cocked his head and listened. "That you, Mister-I-Know-There-Ain't-No Aliens?"

"Now come on. I want to help you. My son said you said you wasn't gonna get into that again."

"Come on over here," said the blind man.

Mr. Harold went over, cautiously. When he was just outside of weed-eater range, he said, "What you want?"

"Do I look all right to you? Besides being blind?"

"Yeah. I guess so. I don't see nothing wrong with you. You found the leaves on that tree good enough."

"Come and look closer."

"Naw, I ain't gonna do it. You just want to get me in range. Hit me with that weed-eater. I'll stay right here. You come at me, I'll move off. You won't be able to find me."

"You saying I can't find you cause I'm blind?"

"Come after me, I'll put stuff in front of you so you trip."

The blind man leaned the weed-eater against his leg. His cane was on a loop over his other hand, and he took hold of it and tapped it against his tennis shoe.

"Yeah, well you could do that," the blind man said, "and I bet you would too. You're like a guy would do things to the handicapped. I'll tell you now, sir, they take roll in heaven you ain't gonna be on it."

"Listen here. You want some help over there, I'll give it but I ain't gonna stand here in this heat and take insults Midget wrestling's on TV and it's cool inside and I might jus go back to it."

The blind man's posture straightened with interes "Midget wrestling? Hell, that's right. It's Saturday. Was Little Bronco Bill and Low Dozer McGuirk?"

"I think it was. They look alike to me. I don't know on midget from another, though one was a little fatter and had haircut like he'd got out of the barber chair too soon."

"That's Dozer. He trains on beer and doughnuts. I hear him talk about it on the TV."

"You watch TV?"

"You tryin' to hurt my feelings?"

"No. I mean, it's just, well, you're blind."

"What? I am? I'll be damned! I didn't know that. Gla you was here to tell me."

"I didn't mean no harm."

"Look here, I got ears. I listen to them thumping on tha floor and I listen to the announcer. I listen so good I ca imagine, kinda, what's goin' on. I 'specially like them littl scudders, the midgets. I think maybe on a day I've had enoug to eat, and I had on some pants weren't too tight, I'd like t get in a ring with one of 'em."

"You always been blind? I mean, was you born that way?"

"Naw. Got bleach in my eyes. My mama told me a nigge done it to me when I was a baby, but it was my daddy. I know that now. Mama had a bad eye herself, then the cancer go her good one. She says she sees out of her bad eye way you' see if you seen something through a Coke bottle with dirt o the bottom."

Mr. Harold didn't really want to hear about the blind man's family history. He groped for a fresh conversation handle. Before he could get hold of one, the blind man said, "Let's go to your place and watch some of that wrestlin' and cool off, then you can come out with me and show me them places I missed."

Mr. Harold didn't like the direction this conversation was taking. "I don't know," he said. "Won't the preacher be back in a bit and want his yard cut?"

"You want to know the truth?" the blind man said, "I don't care. You're right. Five dollars ain't any wages. Them little things I wanted with that five dollars I couldn't get no how."

Mr. Harold's mind raced. "Yeah, but five dollars is five dollars, and you could put it toward something. You know, save it up till you got some more. They're planning on making you a permanent grounds keeper, aren't they? A little time, a raise could be in order."

"This here's kinda a trial run. They can always get the crippled nigger back."

Mr. Harold checked his watch. There probably wasn't more than twenty minutes left of the wrestling program, so he took a flyer. "Well, all right. We'll finish up the wrestling show, then come back and do the work. You ain't gonna hit me with that weed-eater if I try to guide you into the house, are you?"

"Naw, I ain't mad no more. I get like that sometimes. It's just my way."

Mr. Harold led him into the house and onto the couch and talked the boy out of the cartoons, which wasn't hard; it was some kind of stuff the boy hated. The blind man had him crank the audio on the TV up a notch and sat sideways on the couch with his weed-eater and cane, taking up all the room and leaving Mr. Harold nowhere to sit. Dirt and chopped grass dripped off of the blind man's shoes and onto the couch.

Mr. Harold finally sat on the floor beside his boy and tried to get the boy to give him a cookie, but his son didn't play that way. Mr. Harold had to get his own Kool-Aid and cookies, and he got the blind man some too.

The blind man took the Kool-Aid and cookies and didn't say thanks or kiss my ass. Just stretched out there on the couch listening, shaking from side to side, cheering the wrestlers on. He was obviously on Low Dozer McGuirk's side, and Mr. Harold figured it was primarily because he'd heard Dozer trained on beer and doughnuts. That struck Mr. Harold as a thing the blind man would latch onto and love. That and crop circles and flying saucers.

When the blind man finished up his cookies and Kool-Aid, he put Mr. Harold to work getting more, and when Mr. Harold came back with them, his son and the blind man were chatting about the wrestling match. The blind man was giving the boy some insights into the wrestling game and was trying to get the boy to try a hold on him so he could show how easily he could work out of it.

Mr. Harold nixed that plan, and the blind man ate his next plate of cookies and Kool-Aid, and somehow the wrestling show moved into an after show talk session on wrestling. When Mr. Harold looked at his watch nearly an hour had passed.

"We ought to get back over there and finish up," Mr. Harold said.

"Naw," said the blind man, "not just yet. This talk show stuff is good. This is where I get most of my tips."

"Well, all right, but when this is over, we're out of here."

But they weren't. The talk show wrapped up, the "Beverly Hillbillies" came on, then "Green Acres," then "Gilligan's Island." The blind man and Mr. Harold's son laughed their way through the first two, and damn near killed themselves with humor when "Gilligan" was on.

Mr. Harold learned the Professor and Ginger were the blind man's favorites on "Gilligan," and he liked the pig, Ralph, on "Green Acres." No one was a particular favorite on the "Beverly Hillbillies," however.

"Ain't this stuff good?" the blind man said. "They don't make em like this anymore."

"I prefer educational programming myself," Mr. Harold said, though the last educational program he'd watched was a PBS special on lobsters. He'd watched it because he was sick as a dog and lying on the couch and his wife had put the remote across the room and he didn't feel good enough to get up and get hold of it.

In his feverish delirium he remembered the lobster special as pretty good cause it had come across a little like a science fiction movie. But that lobster special, as viewed through feverish eyes, had been the closest Mr. Harold had ever gotten to educational TV.

The sickness, the remote lying across the room, had caused him to miss what he'd really wanted to see that day, and even now, on occasion, he thought of what he had missed with a certain pang of regret; a special on how young women were chosen to wear swim suits in special issues of sports magazines. He kept hoping it was a show that would play in rerun.

"My back's hurtin' from sitting on the floor," Mr. Harold said, but the blind man didn't move his feet so Mr. Harold could have a place on the couch. He offered a pointer, though.

"Sit on the floor, you got to hold your back straight, just like you was in a wooden chair, otherwise you'll really tighten them muscles up close to your butt."

When "Gilligan" was wrapped up, Mr. Harold impulsively cut the television and got hold of the blind man and started pulling him up. "We got to go to work now. I'm gonna help you, it has to be now. I got plans for the rest of the day."

"Ah, Daddy, he was gonna show me a couple wrestling holds," the boy said.

"Not today," Mr. Harold said, tugging on the blind man, and suddenly the blind man moved and was behind him and had him wrestled to the floor. Mr. Harold tried to move, but couldn't. His arm was twisted behind his back and he was lying face down and the blind man was on top of him pressing a knee into his spine.

"Wow!" said the boy. "Neat!"

"Not bad for a blind fella," said the blind man. "I told you I get my tips from that show."

"All right, all right, let me go," said Mr. Harold.

"Squeal like a pig for me," said the blind man.

"Now wait just a goddamned minute," Mr. Harold said.

The blind man pressed his knee harder into Mr. Harold's spine. "Squeal like a pig for me. Come on."

Mr. Harold made a squeaking noise.

"That ain't no squeal," said the blind man. "Squeal!"

The boy got down by Mr. Harold's face. "Come on, Dad," he said. "Squeal."

"Big pig squeal," said the blind man. "Big pig! Big pig! Big pig!"

Mr. Harold squealed. The blind man didn't let go.

"Say calf rope," said the blind man.

"All right, all right. Calf rope! Calf rope! Now let me up."

The blind man eased his knee off Mr. Harold's spine and let go of the arm lock. He stood up and said to the boy, "It's mostly in the hips."

"Wow!" said the boy, "You made Dad squeal like a pig."

Mr. Harold, red faced, got up. He said, "Come on, right now."

"I need my weed-eater," said the blind man.

The boy got both the weed-eater and the cane for the blind man. The blind man said to the boy as they went outside, "Remember, it's in the hips."

Mr. Harold and the blind man went over to the church property and started in on some spots with the weed-eater. In spite of the fact Mr. Harold found himself doing most of the weed-eating, the blind man just clinging to his elbow and being pulled around like he was a side car, it wasn't five minutes before the blind man wanted some shade and a drink of water.

Mr. Harold was trying to talk him out of it when Sonny Guy and his family drove up in a club cab Dodge pickup.

The pickup was black and shiny and looked as if it had just come off the showroom floor. Mr. Harold knew Sonny Guy's money for such things had come from Mrs. Guy's insurance before she was Mrs. Guy. Her first husband had gotten kicked to death by a maniac escaped from the nut house; kicked until they couldn't tell if he was a man or a jelly doughnut that had gotten run over by a truck.

When that insurance money came due, Sonny Guy, a man who had antennas for such things, showed up and began to woo her. They were married pretty quick, and the money from the insurance settlement had bought the house, the aircraft hanger church, the Day-Glo guitar signs, and the pickup. Mr. Harold wondered if there was any money left. He figured they might be pretty well run through it by now.

"Is that the Guys?" the blind man asked as the pickup engine was cut.

"Yeah," said Mr. Harold.

"Maybe we ought to look busy."

"I don't reckon it matters now."

Sonny got out of the pickup and waddled over to the edge of the property and looked at the mauled grass and weeds. He walked over to the aircraft hanger church and took it all in from that angle with his hands on his ample hips. He stuck his fingers under his overall straps and walked alongside the fence with the big black dog running behind it, barking, grabbing at the chicken wire with his teeth.

The minister's wife stood by the pickup. She had a bun of colorless hair stacked on her head. The stack had the general shape of some kind of tropical ant-hill that might house millions of angry ants. Way she was built, that hair and all, it looked as if the hill had been precariously built on top of a small round rock supported by an irregular shaped one, the bottom rock wearing a print dress and a pair of black flat-heeled shoes.

The two dumpling kids, one boy, and one girl, leaned against the truck's bumper as if they had just felt the effect of some relaxing drug. They both wore jeans, tennis shoes and Disney t-shirts with the Magic Kingdom in the background. Mr. Harold couldn't help but note the whole family had up-turned noses, like pigs. It wasn't something that could be ignored.

Sonny Guy shook his head and walked across the lot and over to the blind man. "You sure messed this up. It's gonna cost me more'n I'd have paid you to get it fixed. That crippled nigger never done nothing like this. He run over a sprinkler head once, but that was it. And he paid for it." Sonny turned his attention to Mr. Harold. "You have anything to do with this?"

"I was just tryin' to help," Mr. Harold said.

"I was doin' all right until he come over," said the blind man. "He started tellin' me how I was messin' up and all and got me nervous, and sure enough, I began to lose my place and my concentration. You can see the results."

"You'd have minded your own business," Sonny said to Mr. Harold, "the man woulda done all right, but you're one of those thinks a handicap can't do some jobs."

30

"The man's blind," said Mr. Harold. "He can't see to cut grass. Not four acres with a weed-eater. Any moron can see that."

The Reverend Sonny Guy had a pretty fast right hand for a fat man. He caught Mr. Harold a good one over the left eye and staggered him.

The blind man stepped aside so they'd have plenty of room, and Sonny set to punching Mr. Harold quite regularly. It seemed like something the two of them were made for. Sonny to throw punches and Mr. Harold to absorb them.

When Mr. Harold woke up, he was lying on his back in the grass and the shadow of the blind man lay like a slat across him.

"Where is he?" asked Mr. Harold, feeling hot and sick to his stomach.

"When he knocked you down and you didn't get up, he went in the house with his wife," said the blind man. "I think he was thirsty. He told me he wasn't giving me no five dollars. Actually, he said he wasn't giving me jackshit. And him a minister. The kids are still out here though, they're looking at their watches, I think. They had a bet on how long it'd be before you got up. I heard them talking."

Mr. Harold sat up and glanced toward the Dodge club cab. The blind man was right. The kids were still leaning against the truck. When Mr. Harold looked at them, the boy, who was glancing at his watch, lifted one eye and raised his hand quickly and pulled it down, said, "Yesss!" The little girl looked pouty. The little boy said, "This time you blow me."

They went in the house. Mr. Harold stood up. The blind man gave him the weed-eater for support. He said, "Sonny says the crippled nigger will be back next week. I can't believe it. Scooped by a nigger. A crippled nigger."

Mr. Harold pursed his lips and tried to recall a couple of calming Bible verses. When he felt somewhat relaxed, he said, "Why'd you tell him it was my fault?"

"I figured you could handle yourself," the blind man said.

Mr. Harold rubbed one of the knots Sonny had knocked on his head. He considered homicide, but knew there wasn't any future in it. He said, "Tell you what. I'll give you a ride home."

"We could watch some more TV?"

"Nope," said Mr. Harold probing a split in his lip. "I've got other plans."

Mr. Harold got his son and the three of them drove over to where the blind man said he lived. It was a lot on the far side of town, outside the city limits. It was bordered on either side by trees. It was a trailer lot, scraped down to the red clay. There were a few anemic grass patches here and there and it had a couple of lawn ornaments out front. A cow and a pig with tails that hooked up to hoses and spun around and around and worked as lawn sprinklers.

Behind the sprinklers a heap of wood and metal smoked pleasantly in the sunlight.

They got out of the car and Mr. Harold's son said, "Holy shit."

"Let me ask you something," said Mr. Harold to the blind man. "Your place got a cow and a pig lawn ornament? Kind that sprinkles the yard?"

The blind man appeared nervous. He sniffed the air. He said, "Is the cow one of those spotted kind?"

"A Holstein?" asked Mr. Harold. "My guess is the pig is a Yorkshire."

"That's them."

"Well, I reckon we're at your place all right, but it's burned down."

"Oh, shit," said the blind man. "I left the beans on."

32

"They're done now," said the boy.

The blind man sat down in the dirt and began to cry. It was a serious cry. A cat walking along the edge of the woods behind the remains of the trailer stopped to watch in amazement. The cat seemed surprised that any one thing could make such noise.

"Was they pinto beans?" the boy asked.

The blind man sputtered and sobbed and his chest heaved. Mr. Harold went and got the pig sprinkler and turned it on so that the water from its tail splattered on the pile of smoking rubble. When he felt that was going good, he got the cow working. He thought about calling the fire department, but that seemed kind of silly. About all they could do was come out and stir what was left with a stick.

"Is it all gone?" asked the blind man.

"The cow's all right," said Mr. Harold, "but the pig was a little too close to the fire, there's a little paint bubbled up on one of his legs."

Now the blind man really began to cry. "I damn near had it paid for. It wasn't no double-wide, but it was mine."

They stayed that way momentarily, the blind man crying, the water hissing onto the trailer's remains, then the blind man said, "Did the dogs get out?"

Mr. Harold gave the question some deep consideration. "My guess would be no."

"Then I don't guess there's any hope for the parakeet neither," said the blind man.

Reluctantly, Mr. Harold loaded the blind man back in the car with his son, and started home.

It wasn't the way Mr. Harold had hoped the day would turn out. He had been trying to do nothing more than a good deed, and now he couldn't get rid of the blind man. He wondered if this kind of shit ever happened to Jesus. He was always doing good stuff in the Bible. Mr. Harold wondered if he'd ever had an incident misfire on him, something that hadn't been reported in the Testaments.

Once, when Mr. Harold was about eleven, he'd experienced a similar incident, only he hadn't been trying to be a good Samaritan. Still, it was one of those times where you go in with one thing certain and it turns on you.

During recess he'd gotten in a fight with a little kid he thought would be easy to take. He punched the kid when he wasn't looking, and that little dude dropped and got hold of his knee with his arms and wrapped both his legs around him, positioned himself so that his bottom was on Mr. Harold's shoe.

Mr. Harold couldn't shake him. He dragged him across the school yard and even walked him into a puddle of water, but the kid stuck. Mr. Harold got a pretty good sized stick and hit the kid over the head with it, but that hadn't changed conditions. A dog tick couldn't have been fastened any tighter. He had to go back to class with the kid on his leg, pulling that little rascal after him wherever he went, like he had an anvil tied to his foot.

The teacher couldn't get the kid to let go either. They finally had to go to the principal's office and get the principal and the football coach to pry him off, and even they had to work at it. The coach said he'd once wrestled a madman with a butcher knife, and he'd rather do that again than try and get that kid off someone's leg.

The blind man was kind of like that kid. You couldn't lose the sonofabitch.

Near the house, Mr. Harold glanced at his watch and noted it was time for his wife to be home. He was overcome with deep concerns. He'd just thought the blind man pissing on his bathroom wall would be a problem, now he had greater worries. He actually had the gentleman in tow, bringing him to the house at supper time. Mr. Harold pulled over at a station and got some gas and bought the boy and the blind man a Coke. The blind man seemed to have gotten over the loss of his trailer. Sadness for its contents, the dogs and the parakeet, failed to plague him.

While the boy and the blind man sat on the curb, Mr. Harold went around to a pay booth and called home. On the third ring his wife answered.

"Where in the world are you?" she said.

"I'm out here at a filling station. I got someone with me."

"You better have Marvin with you."

"I do, but I ain't talking about the boy. I got a blind man with me."

"You mean he can't see?"

"Not a lick. He's got a weed-eater. He's the grounds keeper next door. I tried to take him home but his trailer burned up with his dogs and bird in it and I ain't got no place to take him but home for supper."

A moment of silence passed as Mrs. Harold considered. "Ain't there some kinda home you can put him in?"

"I can't think of any. I suppose I could tie a sign around his neck said 'Blind Man' and leave him on someone's step with his weed-eater."

"Well, that wouldn't be fair to whoever lived in that house, just pushing your problems on someone else."

Mr. Harold was nervous. Mrs. Harold seemed awfully polite. Usually she got mad over the littlest thing. He was trying to figure if it was a trap when he realized that something about all this was bound to appeal to her religious nature. She went to church a lot. She read the *Baptist Standard* and watched a couple of Sunday afternoon TV shows with preaching in them. Blind people were loved by Baptists. Them and cripples. They got mentioned in the Bible a lot. Jesus had a special affection for them. Well, he liked lepers too, but Mr. Harold figured that was where even Mrs. Harold's dedicated Baptist beliefs might falter.

A loophole presented itself to Mr. Harold. He said, "I figure it's our Christian charity to take this fella in, honey. He can't see and he's lost his job and his trailer burned down with his pets in it."

"Well, I reckon you ought to bring him on over then. We'll feed him and I'll call around and see what my ladies' charities can do. It'll be my project. Wendy Lee is goin' around gettin' folks to pick up trash on a section of the highway, but I figure helping out a blind man would be Christian. Jesus helped blind people, but I don't never remember him picking up any trash."

When Mr. Harold loaded his son and the blind man back into the car, he was a happier man. He wasn't in trouble. Mrs. Harold thought taking in the blind man was her idea. He figured he could put up with the bastard another couple hours, then he'd find him a place to stay. Some homeless shelter with a cot and some hot soup if he wanted it. Maybe some preaching and breakfast before he had to hit the road.

At the house, Mrs. Harold met them at the door. Her little round body practically bounced. She found the blind man's hand and shook it. She told him how sorry she was, and he dropped his head and looked sad and thanked her. When they were inside, he said, "Is that cornbread I smell?"

"Yes it is," Mrs. Harold said, "and it won't be no time till it's ready. And we're having pinto beans with it. The beans were cooked yesterday and just need heating. They taste best when they've set a night."

"That's what burned his trailer down," the boy said. "He was cooking some pinto beans and forgot 'em."

"Oh my," said Mrs. Harold, "I hope the beans won't bring back sad memories."

"No ma'am, them was limas I was cookin'."

"There was dogs in there and a parakeet," said the boy. "They got burned up too. There wasn't nothing left but some burnt wood and a piece of a couch and old bird cage."

"I have some insurance papers in a deposit box downtown," the blind man said. "I could probably get me a couple of double wides and have enough left over for a vacation with the money I'll get. I could get me some dogs and a bird easy enough too. I could even name them the same names as the ones burned up."

They sat and visited for a while in the living room while the cornbread cooked and the beans warmed up. The blind man and Mrs. Harold talked about religion. The blind man knew her favorite gospel tunes and sang a couple of them. Not too good, Mr. Harold thought, but Mrs. Harold seemed almost swoony.

The blind man knew her Sunday preaching programs too, and they talked about a few highlighted TV sermons. They debated the parables in the Bible and ended up discussing important and obscure points in the scripture, discovered the two of them saw things a lot alike when it came to interpretation. They had found dire warnings in Deuteronomy that scholars had overlooked.

Mrs. Harold got so lathered up with enthusiasm, she went into the kitchen and started throwing an apple pie together. Mr. Harold became nervous as soon as the pie pans began to rattle. This wasn't like her. She only cooked a pie to take to relatives after someone died or if it was Christmas or Thanksgiving and more than ten people were coming.

While she cooked, the blind man discussed wrestling holds with Mr. Harold's son. When dinner was ready, the blind man was positioned in Mr. Harold's chair, next to Mrs. Harold. They ate, and the blind man and Mrs. Harold further discussed scripture, and from time to time, the blind man would stop the religious talk long enough to give the boy a synopsis of some wrestling match or another. He had a way of cleverly turning the conversation without seeming to. He wasn't nearly as clever about passing the beans or the cornbread. The apple pie remained strategically guarded by his elbow.

After a while, the topic switched from the Bible and wrestling to the blind man's aches and miseries. He was overcome with them. There wasn't a thing that could be wrong with a person he didn't have.

Mrs. Harold used this conversational opportunity to complain about hip problems, hypoglycemia, overactive thyroids, and out-of-control sweat glands.

The blind man had a tip or two on how to make living with each of Mrs. Harold's complaints more congenial. Mrs. Harold said, "Well, sir, there's just not a thing you don't know something about. From wrestling to medicine."

The blind man nodded. "I try to keep up. I read a lot of braille and listen to the TV and the radio. They criticize the TV, but they shouldn't. I get lots of my education there. I can learn from just about anything or anyone but a nigger."

Mrs. Harold, much to Mr. Harold's chagrin, agreed. This was a side of his wife he had never known. She had opinions and he hadn't known that. Stupid opinions, but opinions.

When Mr. Harold finally left the table, pieless, to hide out in the bathroom, the blind man and Mrs. Harold were discussing a plan for getting all the black folk back to Africa. Something to do with the number of boats necessary and the amount of proper hygiene needed.

And speaking of hygiene, Mr. Harold stood up as his bottom became wet. He had been sitting on the lid of the toilet and dampness had soaked through his pants. The blind man had been in the bathroom last and he'd pissed all over the lowered lid and splattered the wall.

Mr. Harold changed clothes and cleaned up the piss and washed his hands and splashed his face and looked at himself in the mirror. It was still him in there and he was awake.

About ten P.M. Mrs. Harold and the blind man put the boy to bed and the blind man sang the kid a rockabilly song, told him a couple of nigger jokes and one kike joke, and tucked him in.

Mr. Harold went in to see the boy, but he was asleep. The blind man and Mrs. Harold sat on the couch and talked about chicken and dumpling recipes and how to clean squirrels properly for frying. Mr. Harold sat in a chair and listened, hoping for some opening in the conversation into which he could spring. None presented itself.

Finally Mrs. Harold got the blind man some bedclothes and folded out the couch and told him a pleasant good night, touching the blind man's arm as she did. Mr. Harold noted she left her hand there quite a while.

In bed, Mr. Harold, hoping to prove to himself he was still man of the house, rolled over and put his arm around Mrs. Harold's hip. She had gotten dressed and gotten into bed in record time while he was taking a leak, and now she was feigning sleep, but Mr. Harold decided he wasn't going to go for it. He rubbed her ass and tried to work his hand between her legs from behind. He touched what he wanted, but it was as dry as a ditch in the Sahara.

Mrs. Harold pretended to wake up. She was mad. She said he ought to let a woman sleep, and didn't he think about anything else? Mr. Harold admitted that sex was a foremost thought of his, but he knew now nothing he said would matter. Neither humor nor flattery would work. He would not only go pieless this night, he would go assless as well.

Mrs. Harold began to explain how one of her mysterious headaches with back pain had descended on her. Arthritis might be the culprit, she said, though sometimes she suspicioned something more mysterious and deadly. Perhaps something incurable that would eventually involve large leaking sores and a deep coma.

Mr. Harold, frustrated, closed his eyes and tried to go to sleep with a hard-on. He couldn't understand, having had so much experience now, why it was so difficult for him to just forget his boner and go to bed, but it was, as always, a trial.

Finally, after making a trip to the bathroom to work his pistol and plunk its stringy wet bullet into the toilet water, he was able to go back to bed and drift off into an unhappy sleep.

A few hours later he awoke. He heard a noise like girlish laughter. He lay in bed and listened. It was in fact, laughter, and it was coming from the living room. The blind man must have the TV on. But then he recognized the laughter. It hadn't come to him right away, because it had been ages since he had heard it. He reached for Mrs. Harold and she was gone.

He got out of bed and opened the bedroom door and crept quietly down the hall. There was a soft light on in the living room; it was the lamp on the TV muted by a white towel.

On the couch-bed was the blind man, wearing only his underwear and dark glasses. Mrs. Harold was on the bed too. She was wearing her nightie. The blind man was on top of her and they were pressed close. Mrs. Harold's hand sneaked over the blind man's back and slid into his underwear and cupped his ass.

Mr. Harold let out his breath, and Mrs. Harold turned her head and saw him. She gave a little cry and rolled out from under the blind man. She laughed hysterically. "Why, honey, you're up."

The blind man explained immediately. They had been practicing a wrestling hold, one of the more complicated, and not entirely legal ones that involved grabbing the back of an opponent's tights. Mrs. Harold admitted, that as of tonight, she had been overcome with a passion for wrestling and was going to watch all the wrestling programs from now on. She thanked the blind man for the wrestling lesson and shook his hand and went past Mr. Harold and back to bed.

Mr. Harold stood looking at the blind man. He was on the couch on all fours looking in Mr. Harold's direction. The muted light from the towel-covered lamp hit the blind man's dark glasses and made them shine like the eyes of a wolf. His bared teeth completed the image.

Mr. Harold went back to bed. Mrs. Harold snuggled close. She wanted to be friendly. She ran her hand over his chest and down his belly and held his equipment, but he was as soft as a sock. She worked him a little and finally he got hard in spite of himself. They rolled together and did what he wanted to do earlier. For the first time in years, Mrs. Harold got off. She came with a squeak and thrust of her hips, and Mr. Harold knew that behind her closed eyes she saw a pale face and dark glasses, not him.

Later, he lay in bed and stared at the ceiling. Mrs. Harold's pussy had been as wet as a fish farm after her encounter with the blind man, wetter than he remembered it in years. What was it about the blind man that excited her? He was a racist cracker asshole who really knew nothing. He didn't have a job. He couldn't even work a weed-eater that good.

Mr. Harold felt fear. What he had here at home wasn't all that good, but he realized now he might lose it, and it was probably the best he could do. Even if his wife's conversation was as dull as the Republican convention and his son was as interesting as needlework, his home life took on a new and desperate importance. Something had to be done.

Next day, Mr. Harold got a break. The blind man made a comment about his love for snow cones. It was made while they were sitting alone in the kitchen. Mrs. Harold was in the shower and the boy was playing Nintendo in the living room.

The blind man was rattling on like always. Last night rang no guilty bells for him.

"You know," said Mr. Harold, "I like a good snow cone myself. One of those blue ones."

"Oh yeah, that's coconut," said the blind man.

"What you say you and me go get one?"

"Ain't it gonna be lunch soon? I don't want to spoil my appetite."

"A cone won't spoil nothing. Come on, my treat."

The blind man was a little uncertain, but Mr. Harold could tell the idea of a free snow cone was strong within him. He let Mr. Harold lead him out to the car. Mr. Harold began to tremble with anticipation. He drove toward town, but when he got there, he drove on through.

"I thought you said the stand was close?" said the blind man. "Ain't we been driving a while?"

"Well, it's Sunday, and that one I was thinking of was closed. I know one cross the way stays open seven days a week during the summer."

Mr. Harold drove out into the country. He drove off the main highway and down a red clay road and pulled over to the side near a gap where irresponsibles dumped their garbage. He got out and went around to the blind man's side and took the blind man's arm and led him away from the car toward a pile of garbage. Flies hummed operatic notes in the late morning air.

"We're in luck," Mr. Harold said. "Ain't no one here but us."

"Yeah, well it don't smell so good around here. Somethin' dead somewheres?"

"There's a cat hit out there on the highway."

"I'm kinda losin' my appetite for a cone."

"It'll come back soon as you put that cone in your mouth. Besides, we'll eat in the car."

Mr. Harold placed the blind man directly in front of a bag of household garbage. "You stand right here. Tell me what you want and I'll get it."

"I like a strawberry. Double on the juice."

"Strawberry it is."

Mr. Harold walked briskly back to his car, cranked it, and drove by the blind man who cocked his head as the automobile passed. Mr. Harold drove down a ways, turned around and drove back the way he had come. The blind man still stood by the garbage heap, his cane looped over his wrist, only now he was facing the road.

Mr. Harold honked the horn as he drove past.

Just before reaching the city limits, a big black pickup began to make ominous maneuvers. The pickup was behind him and was riding his bumper. Mr. Harold tried to speed up, but that didn't work. He tried slowing down, but the truck nearly ran up his ass. He decided to pull to the side, but the truck wouldn't pass.

Eventually, Mr. Harold coasted to the emergency lane and stopped, but the truck pulled up behind him and two burly men got out. They looked as if the last bath they'd had was during the last rain, probably caught out in it while pulp wooding someone's posted land.

Mr. Harold assumed it was all some dreadful mistake. He got out of the car so they could see he wasn't who they thought he must be. The biggest one walked up to him and grabbed him behind the head with one hand and hit him with the other. The smaller man, smaller because his head seemed under-sized, took his turn and hit Mr. Harold. The two men began to work on him. He couldn't fall down because the car held him up, and for some reason he couldn't pass out. These guys weren't as fast as Sonny Guy, and they weren't knocking him out, but they certainly hurt more.

"What kinda fella are you that would leave a blind man beside the road?" said the bigger man just before he busted Mr. Harold a good one in the nose.

Mr. Harold finally hit the ground. The small-headed man kicked him in the balls and the bigger man kicked him in the mouth, knocking out what was left of his front teeth; the man's fist had already stolen the others. When Mr. Harold was close to passing out, the small-headed man bent down and got hold of Mr. Harold's hair and looked him in the eye and said, "We hadn't been throwing out an old stray dog down that road, that fella might have got lost or hurt."

"He's much more resourceful than you think," Mr. Harold said, realizing who they meant, and then the small-headed man hit him a short chopping blow.

"I'm glad we seen him," said the bigger man, "and I'm glad we caught up with you. You just think you've took a beating. We're just getting started."

But at that moment the blind man appeared above Mr. Harold. He had found his way from the truck to the car, directed by the sound of the beating most likely. "No, boys," said the blind man, "that's good enough. I ain't the kind holds a grudge, even 'gainst a man would do what he did. I've had some theology training and done a little Baptist ministering. Holding a grudge ain't my way."

"Well, you're a good one," said the bigger man. "I ain't like that at all. I was blind and I was told I was gonna get a snow cone and a fella put me out at a garbage dump, I'd want that fella dead, or crippled up at the least."

"I understand," said the blind man. "It's hard to believe there's people like this in the world. But if you'll just drive me home, that'll be enough. I'd like to get on the way if it's no inconvenience. I have a little Bible lesson in braille I'd like to study."

They went away and left Mr. Harold lying on the highway beside his car. As they drove by, the pickup tires tossed gravel on him and the exhaust enveloped him like a foul cotton sack.

Mr. Harold got up after five minutes and got inside his car and fell across the seat and lay there. He couldn't move. He spat out a tooth. His balls hurt. His face hurt. For that matter, his kneecaps where they'd kicked him didn't feel all that good either.

After an hour or so, Mr. Harold began to come around. An intense hatred for the blind man boiled up in his stomach. He sat up and started the car and headed home.

When he turned on his road, he was nearly sideswiped by a yellow moving van. It came at him so hard and fast he swerved into a ditch filled with sand and got his right rear tire stuck. He couldn't drive the car out. More he worked at it, the deeper the back tire spun in the sand. He got his jack out of the trunk and cranked up the rear end and put debris under the tire. Bad as he felt, it was quite a job. He finally drove out of there, and off the jack, leaving it lying in the dirt.

When he got to his house, certain in his heart the blind man was inside, he parked next to Mrs. Harold's station wagon. The station wagon was stuffed to the gills with boxes and sacks. He wondered what that was all about, but he didn't wonder too hard. He looked around the yard for a weapon. Out by the side of the house was the blind man's weed-eater. That would do. He figured he caught the blind man a couple of licks with that, he could get him down on the ground and finish him, stun him before the sonofabitch applied a wrestling hold.

He went in the house by the back door with the weed-eater cocked, and was astonished to find the room was empty. The kitchen table and chairs were gone. The cabinet doors were open and all the canned goods were missing. Where the stove had set was a greasy spot. Where the refrigerator had set was a wet spot. A couple of roaches, feeling brave and free to roam, scuttled across the kitchen floor as merry as kids on skates.

The living room was empty too. Not only of people, but furniture and roaches. The rest of the house was the same. Dust motes spun in the light. The front door was open.

Outside, Mr. Harold heard a car door slam. He limped out the front door and saw the station wagon. His wife was behind the wheel, and sitting next to her was the boy, and beside him the blind man, his arm hanging out the open window.

Mr. Harold beckoned to them by waving the weed-eater, but they ignored him. Mrs. Harold backed out of the drive quickly. Mr. Harold could hear the blind man talking to the boy about something or another and the boy was laughing. The station wagon turned onto the road and the car picked up speed. Mr. Harold went slack and leaned on the weed-eater for support.

At the moment before the station wagon passed in front of a line of high shrubs, the blind man turned to look out the window, and Mr. Harold saw his own reflection in the blind man's glasses.

For Neal Barrett, Jr.

STEPPIN' OUT,
SUMMER, '68

Buddy drank another swig of beer and when he brought the bottle down he said to Jake and Wilson, "I could sure use some pussy."

"We could all use some," Wilson said, "problem is we don't never get any."

"That's the way I see it too," Jake said.

"You don't get any," Buddy said. "I get plenty, you can count on that."

"Uh huh," Wilson said. "You talk pussy plenty good, but I don't ever see you with a date. I ain't never even seen you walking a dog, let alone a girl. You don't even have a car, so how you gonna get with a girl?"

"That's the way I see it too," Jake said.

"You see what you want," Buddy said. "I'm gonna be getting me a Chevy soon. I got my eye on one."

"Yeah?" Wilson said. "What one?"

"Drew Carrington's old crate."

"Shit," Wilson said, "that motherfucker caught on fire at a streetlight and he run it off in the creek."

"They got it out," Buddy said.

"They say them flames jumped twenty feet out from under the hood before he run it off in there," Jake said.

"Water put the fire out," Buddy said.

"Uh huh," Wilson said, "after the motor blowed up through the hood. They found that motherfucker in a tree out back of Old Maud Page's place. One of the pistons fell out of it and hit her on the head while she was picking up apples. She was in the hospital three days."

"Yeah," Jake said. "And I hear Carrington's in Dallas now, never got better from the accident. Near drowned and some of the engine blew back into the car and hit him in the nuts, castrated him, fucked up his legs. He can't walk. He's on a wheeled board or something, got some retard that pulls him around."

"Them's just stories," Buddy said. "Motor's still in the car. Carrington got him a job in Dallas as a mechanic. He didn't get hurt at all. Old Woman Page didn't get hit by no piston either. It missed her by a foot. Scared her so bad she had a little stroke. That's why she was in the hospital."

"You seen the motor?" Wilson asked. "Tell me you've seen it."

"No," Buddy said, "but I've heard about it from good sources, and they say it can be fixed."

"Jack it up and drive another car under it," Wilson said, "it'll be all right."

"That's the way I see it too," Jake said.

"Listen to you two," Buddy said. "You know it all. You're real operators. I'll tell you morons one thing, I line up a little of the hole that winks and stinks, like I'm doing tonight, you won't get none of it."

Wilson and Jake shuffled and eyed each other. An unspoken, but clear message passed between them. They had never known Buddy to actually get any, or anyone else to know of him getting any, but he had a couple of years on them, and he might have gotten some, way he talked about it, and they damn sure knew they weren't getting any, and if there was a chance of it, things had to be patched up.

"Car like that," Wilson said, "if you worked hard enough, you might get it to run. Some new pistons or something . . . What you got lined up for tonight?"

Buddy's face put on some importance. "I know a gal likes to do the circle, you know what I mean?"

Wilson hated to admit it, but he didn't. "The circle?"

"Pull the train," Buddy said. "Do the team. You know, fuck a bunch a guys, one after the other."

"Oh," Wilson said.

"I knew that," Jake said.

"Yeah," Wilson said. "Yeah sure you did." Then to Buddy: "When you gonna see this gal?"

Buddy, still important, took a swig of beer and pursed his lips and studied the afternoon sky. "Figured I'd walk on over there little after dark. It's a mile or so."

"Say she likes to do more than one guy?" Wilson asked.

"Way I hear it," Buddy said, "she'll do 'em till they ain't able to do. My cousin, Butch, he told me about her."

Butch. The magic word. Wilson and Jake eyed each other again. There could be something in this after all. Butch was twenty, had a fast car, could play a little bit on the harmonica, bought his own beer, cussed in front of adults, and most importantly, he had been seen with women.

Buddy continued. "Her name's Sally. Butch said she cost five dollars. He's done her a few times. Got her name off a bathroom wall."

"She costs?" Wilson asked.

"Think some gal's going to do us all without some money for it?" Buddy said.

Again, an unspoken signal passed between Wilson and Jake. There could be truth in that.

"Butch gave me her address, said her pimp sits on the front porch and you go right up and negotiate with him. Says you talk right, he might take four."

"I don't know," Wilson said. "I ain't never paid for it."

"Me neither," said Jake.

"Ain't neither one of you ever had any at all, let alone paid for it," Buddy said.

Once more, Wilson and Jake were struck with the hard and painful facts.

Buddy looked at their faces and smiled. He took another sip of beer. "Well, you bring your five dollars, and I reckon you can tag along with me. Come by the house about dark and we'll walk over together."

"Yeah, well, all right," Wilson said. "I wish we had a car."

"Keep wishing," Buddy said. "You boys hang with me, we'll all be riding in Carrington's old Chevy before long. I've got some prospects."

It was just about dark when Wilson and Jake got over to Buddy's neighborhood, which was a long street with four houses on it widely spaced. Buddy's house was the ugliest of the four. It looked ready to nod off its concrete blocks at any moment and go crashing into the unkempt yard and die in a heap of rotting lumber and squeaking nails. Great strips of graying Sherwin Williams flat-white paint hung from it in patches, giving it the appearance of having a skin disease. The roof was tin and loved the sun and pulled it in and held it so that the interior basked in a sort of slow simmer until well after sundown. Even now, late in the day, a rush of heat came off the roof and rippled down the street like the last results of a nuclear wind.

Wilson and Jake came up on the house from the side, not wanting to go to the door. Buddy's mother was a grumpy old bitch in a brown bathrobe and bunny rabbit slippers with an ear missing on the left foot. No one had ever seen her wearing anything else, except now and then she added a shower cap to her uniform, and no one had ever seen her, with or without the shower cap, except through the screenwire door. She wasn't thought to leave the house. She played radio contests and had to be near the radio at strategic times throughout the day so she could phone if she knew the answer to something. She claimed to be listening for household tips, but no one had ever seen her apply any. She also watched her daughter's soap operas, though she never owned up to it. She always pretended to be reading, kept a *Reader's Digest* cracked so she could look over it and see the TV.

She wasn't friendly either. Times Wilson and Jake had come over before, she'd met them at the screen door and wouldn't let them in. She wouldn't even talk to them. She'd call back to Buddy inside, "Hey, those hoodlum friends of yours are here."

Neither Wilson or Jake could see any sort of relationship developing between them and Buddy's mother, and they had stopped trying. They hung around outside the house under the open windows until Buddy came out. There were always interesting things to hear while they waited. Wilson told Jake it was educational.

This time, as before, they sidled up close to the house where they could hear. The television was on. A laugh track drifted out to them. That meant Buddy's sister LuWanda was in there watching. If it wasn't on, it meant she was asleep. Like her mother, she was drawing a check. Back problems plagued the family. Except for Buddy's pa. His back was good. He was in prison for sticking up a liquor store. What little check he was getting for making license plates probably didn't amount to much.

Now they could hear Buddy's mother. Her voice had a quality that made you think of someone trying to talk while fatally injured; like she was lying under an overturned refrigerator, or had been thrown free of a car and had hit a tree.

"LuWanda, turn that thing down. You know I got bad feet."

"You don't listen none with your feet, Mama," LuWanda said. Her voice was kind of slow and lazy, faintly squeaky, as if hoisted from her throat by a hand-over pulley.

"No," Buddy's mother said. "But I got to get up on my old tired feet and come in here and tell you to turn it down."

"I can hear you yelling from the bedroom good enough when your radio ain't too high."

"But you still don't turn it down."

"I turn it down anymore, I won't be able to hear it."

"Your old tired mother, she ought to get some respect."

"You get about half my check," LuWanda said, "ain't that enough. I'm gonna get out of here when I have the baby."

"Yeah, and I bet that's some baby, way you lay up with anything's got pants."

"I hardly never leave the house to get the chance," LuWanda said. "It was Pa done it before he tried to knock-over that liquor store."

"Watch your mouth, young lady. I know you let them in through the windows. I'll be glad to see you go, way you lie around here an watch that old TV. You ought to do something educational. Read the *Reader's Digest* like I do. There's tips for living in those, and you could sure profit some."

"Could be something to that all right," LuWanda said. "Pa read the *Reader's Digest* and he's over in Huntsville. I bet he likes there better than here. I bet he has a better time come night."

"Don't you start that again, young lady."

"Way he told me," LuWanda said, "I was always better with him than you was."

"I'm putting my hands right over my ears at those lies. I won't hear them."

"He sure had him a thrust, didn't he Mama?"

"Ooooh, you . . . you little shit, if I should say such a thing. You'll get yours in hell, sister."

"I been getting plenty of hell here."

Wilson leaned against the house under the window and whispered to Jake. "Where the hell's Buddy?"

This was answered by Buddy's mother's shrill voice. "Buddy, you are *not* going out of this house wearing them nigger shoes."

"Oh, Mama," Buddy said, "these ain't nigger shoes. I bought these over at K-Woolens."

"That's right where the niggers buy their things," she said.

"Ah Mama," Buddy said.

"Don't you Mama me. You march right back in there and take off them shoes and put on something else. And get you a pair of pants that don't fit so tight people can tell which side it's on."

A moment later a window down from Wilson and Jake went up slowly. A hand holding a pair of shoes stuck out. The hand dropped the shoes and disappeared.

Then the screen door slammed and Wilson and Jake edged around to the corner of the house for a peek. It was Buddy coming out, and his mother's voice came after him, "Don't you come back to this house with a disease, you hear?"

"Ah, Mama," Buddy said.

Buddy was dressed in a long-sleeved paisley shirt with the sleeves rolled up so tight over his biceps they bulged as if actually full of muscle. He had on a pair of striped bell-bottoms and tennis shoes. His hair was combed high and hard and it lifted up on one side; it looked as if an oily squirrel were clinging precariously to the side of his head.

When Buddy saw Wilson and Jake peeking around the corner of the house, his chest got full and he walked off the porch with a cool step. His mother yelled from inside the house, "And don't walk like you got a corncob up you."

That cramped Buddy's style a little, but he sneered and went around the corner of the house trying to look like a man who knew things.

"Guess you boys are ready to stretch a little meat," Buddy said. He paused to locate an almost flat half-pack of Camels in his back pocket. He pulled a cigarette out and got a match from his shirt pocket and grinned and held his hand by his cheek and popped the match with his thumb. It sparked and he lit the cigarette and puffed. "Those things with filters, they're for sissies."

"Give us one of those," Wilson said.

"Yeah, well, all right, but this is it," Buddy said. "Only pack I got till I collect some money owed me."

Wilson and Jake stuck smokes in their faces and Buddy snapped another match and lit them up. Wilson and Jake coughed some smoke clouds.

"Sshhhh," Buddy said. "The old lady'll hear you."

They went around to the back window where Buddy had dropped the shoes and Buddy picked them up and took off the ones he had on and slipped on the others. They were smooth and dark and made of alligator hide. Their toes were pointed. Buddy wet his thumb and removed a speck of dirt from one of them. He put his tennis shoes under the house, brought a flat little bottle of clear liquid out from there.

"Hooch," Buddy said, and winked. "Bought it off Old Man Hoyt."

"Hoyt?" Wilson said. "He sells hooch?"

"Makes it himself," Buddy said. "Get you a quart for five dollars. Got five dollars and he'll sell to bottle babies."

Buddy saw Wilson eyeing his shoes appreciatively.

"Mama don't like me wearing these," he said. "I have to sneak them out."

"They're cool," Jake said. "I wish I had me a pair like 'em."

"You got to know where to shop," Buddy said.

As they walked the night became rich and cool and the moon went up and it was bright with a fuzzy ring around it. Crickets chirped. The streets they came to were little more than clay, but there were more houses than in Buddy's neighborhood, and they were in better shape. Some of the yards were mowed. The lights were on in the houses along the street, and the three of them could hear televisions talking from inside houses as they walked.

They finished off the street and turned onto another that was bordered by deep woods. They crossed a narrow wooden bridge that went over Mud Creek. They stopped and leaned on the bridge railing and watched the dark water in the moonlight. Wilson remembered when he was ten and out shooting birds with a BB gun, he had seen a dead squirrel in the water, floating out from under the bridge, face down, as if it were snorkeling. He had watched it sail on down the creek and out of sight. He had popped at it and all around it with his BB gun for as long as the gun had the distance. The memory made him nostalgic for his youth and he tried to remember what he had done with his old Daisy air rifle. Then it came to him that his dad had probably pawned it. He did that sort of thing now and then, when he fell off the wagon. Suddenly a lot of missing items over the years began to come together. He'd have to get him some kind of trunk with a lock on it and nail it to the floor or something. It wasn't nailed down, it and everything in it might end up at the pawn shop for strangers to paw over.

They walked on and finally came to a long street with houses at the end of it and the lights there seemed less bright and the windows the lights came out of much smaller.

"That last house before the street crosses," Buddy said, "that's the one we want."

Wilson and Jake looked where Buddy was pointing. The house was dark except for a smudgy porch light and a sick yellow glow that shone from behind a thick curtain. Someone was sitting on the front porch doing something with their hands. They couldn't tell anything about the person or about what the person was doing. From that distance the figure could have been whittling or masturbating.

"Ain't that nigger town on the other side of the street?" Jake said. "This gal we're after, she a nigger? I don't know I'm ready to fuck a nigger. I heard my old man say to a friend of his that Mammy Clewson will give a hand job for a dollar and a half. I might go for that from a nigger, but I don't know about putting it in one."

"House we want is on this side of the street, before nigger town," Buddy said. "That's a full four foot difference. She ain't a nigger. She's white trash."

"Well . . . all right," Jake said. "That's different."

"Everybody take a drink," Buddy said, and he unscrewed the lid on the fruit jar and took a jolt. "Wheee. Straight from the horse."

Buddy passed the jar to Wilson and Wilson drank and nearly threw it up. "Goddamn," he said. "Goddamn. He must run that stuff through a radiator hose or something."

Jake took a turn, shivered as if in the early throes of an epileptic fit. He gave the jar back to Buddy. Buddy screwed the lid on and they walked on down the street, stopped opposite the house they wanted and looked at the man on the front porch, for they could clearly see now it was a man. He was old and toothless and he was shelling peas from a big paper sack into a little white wash pan.

"That's the pimp," Buddy whispered. He opened up the jar and took a sip and closed it and gave it to Wilson to hold. "Give me your money."

They gave him their five dollars.

"I'll go across and make the arrangements," Buddy said. "When I signal, come on over. The pimp might prefer we go in the house one at a time. Maybe you can sit on the porch. I don't know yet."

The three smiled at each other. The passion was building.

Buddy straightened his shoulders, pulled his pants up, and went across the street. He called a howdy to the man on the porch.

"Who the hell are you?" the old man said. It sounded as if his tongue got in the way of his words.

Buddy went boldly up to the house and stood at the porch steps. Wilson and Jake could hear him from where they stood, shuffling their feet and sipping from the jar. He said, "We come to buy a little pussy. I hear you're the man to supply it."

"What's that?" the old man said, and he stood up. When he did, it was obvious he had a problem with his balls. The right side of his pants looked to have a baby's head in it.

"I was him," Jake whispered to Wilson, "I'd save up my share of that pussy money and get me a truss."

"What is that now?" the old man was going on. "What is that you're saying, you little shit?"

"Well now," Buddy said cocking a foot on the bottom step of the porch like someone who meant business, "I'm not asking for free. I've got fifteen dollars here. It's five a piece, ain't it? We're not asking for anything fancy. We just want to lay a little pipe."

A pale light went on inside the house and a plump, blonde girl appeared at the screen door. She didn't open it. She stood there looking out.

"Boy, what in hell are you talking about?" the old man said. "You got the wrong house."

"No one here named Sally?" Buddy asked.

The old man turned his head toward the screen and looked at the plump girl.

"I don't know him, Papa," she said. "Honest."

"You sonofabitch," the old man said to Buddy, and he waddled down the step and swung an upward blow that hit Buddy under the chin and flicked his squirrel-looking hair-do out of shape, sent him hurtling into the front yard. The old man got a palm under his oversized balls and went after Buddy, walking like he had something heavy tied to one leg. Buddy twisted around to run and the old man kicked out and caught him one in the seat of the pants, knocked him stumbling into the street.

"You little bastard," the old man yelled, "don't you come sniffing around here after my daughter again, or I'll cut your nuts off."

Then the old man saw Wilson and Jake across the street. Jake, unable to stop himself, nervously lifted a hand and waved.

"Git on out of here, or I'll let Blackie out," the old man said. "He'll tear your asses up."

Buddy came on across the street, trying to step casually, but moving briskly just the same. "I'm gonna get that fucking Butch," he said.

The old man found a rock in the yard and threw it at them. It whizzed by Buddy's ear and he and Jake and Wilson stepped away lively.

Behind them they heard a screen door slam and the plump girl whined something and there was a whapping sound, like

58

a fan belt come loose on a big truck, then they heard the plump girl yelling for mercy and the old man cried "Slut" once, and they were out of there, across the street, into the black side of town.

They walked along a while, then Jake said, "I guess we could find Mammy Clewson."

"Oh, shut up," Buddy said. "Here's your five dollars back. Here's both your five dollars back. The both of you can get her to do it for you till your money runs out."

"I was just kidding," Jake said.

"Well don't," Buddy said. "That Butch, I catch him, right in the kisser, man. I don't care how big and mean he is. Right in the kisser."

They walked along the street and turned left up another. "Let's get out of boogie town," Buddy said. "All these niggers around here, it makes me nervous."

When they were well up the street and there were no houses, they turned down a short dirt street with a bridge in the middle of it that went over the Sabine River. It wasn't a big bridge because the river was narrow there. Off to the right was a wide pasture. To the left a church. They crossed into the back church yard. There were a couple of wooden pews setting out there under an oak. Buddy went over to one and sat down.

"I thought you wanted to get away from the boogies?" Wilson said.

"Naw," Buddy said. "This is all right. This is fine. I'd like for a nigger to start something. I would. That old man back there hadn't been so old and had his balls fucked up like that, I'd have kicked his ass."

"We wondered what was holding you back," Wilson said.

Buddy looked at Wilson, didn't see any signs of sarcasm.

"Yeah, well, that was it. Give me the jar. There's some other women I know about. We might try something later on, we feel like it."

But a cloud of unspoken resignation, as far as pussy was concerned, had passed over them, and they labored beneath its darkness with their fruit jar of hooch. They sat and passed the jar around and the night got better and brighter. Behind them, off in the woods, they could hear the Sabine River running along. Now and then a car would go down or up the street, cross over the bridge with a rumble, and pass out of sight beyond the church, or if heading in the other direction, out of sight behind trees.

Buddy began to see the night's fiasco as funny. He mellowed. "That Butch, he's something, ain't he? Some joke, huh?"

"It was pretty funny," Jake said, "seeing that old man and his balls coming down the porch after you. That thing was any more ruptured, he'd need a wheel barrow to get from room to room. Shit, I bet he couldn't have turned no dog on us. He'd had one in there, it'd have barked."

"Maybe he calls Sally Blackie," Wilson said. "Man, we're better off she didn't take money. You see that face. She could scare crows."

"Shit," Buddy said sniffing at the jar of hooch. "I think Hoyt puts hair oil in this. Don't that smell like Vitalis to you?"

He held it under Wilson's nose, then Jake's.

"It does," Wilson said. "Right now, I wouldn't care if it smelled like sewer. Give me another swig."

"No," Buddy said standing up, wobbling, holding the partially filled jar in front of him. "Could be we've discovered a hair tonic we could sell. Buy it from Hoyt for five, sell it to guys to put on their heads for ten. We could go into business with Old Man Hoyt. Make a fortune."

Buddy poured some hooch into his palm and rubbed it into his hair, fanning his struggling squirrel-do into greater disarray. He gave the jar to Jake, got out his comb and sculptured his hair with it. Hooch ran down from his hair-line and along his nose and cheeks. "See that," he said, holding out his arms as if he were styling. "Shit holds like glue."

Buddy seemed an incredible wit suddenly. They all laughed. Buddy got his cigarettes and shook one out for each of them. They lipped them. They smiled at one another. They were great friends. This was a magnificent and important moment in their lives. This night would live in memory forever.

Buddy produced a match, held it close to his cheek like always, smiled and flicked it with his thumb. The flaming head of the match jumped into his hair and lit the alcohol Buddy had combed into it. His hair flared up, and a circle of fire, like a halo for the devil, wound its way around his scalp and licked at his face and caught the hooch there on fire. Buddy screamed and bolted berserkly into a pew, tumbled over it and came up running. He looked like the Human Torch on a mission.

Wilson and Jake were stunned. They watched him run a goodly distance, circle, run back, hit the turned over pew again and go down.

Wilson yelled, "Put his head out."

Jake reflexively tossed the contents of the fruit jar at Buddy's head, realizing his mistake a moment too late. But it was like when he waved at Sally's pa. He couldn't help himself.

Buddy did a short tumble, came up still burning; in fact, he appeared to be more on fire than before. He ran straight at Wilson and Jake, his tongue out and flapping flames.

Wilson and Jake stepped aside and Buddy went between them, sprinted across the church yard toward the street.

"Throw dirt on his head!" Wilson said. Jake threw down the jar and they went after him, watching for dirt they could toss.

Buddy was fast for someone on fire. He reached the street well ahead of Wilson and Jake and any discovery of available dirt. But he didn't cross the street fast enough to beat the dump truck. Its headlights hit him first, then the left side of the bumper clipped him on the leg and he did a high complete flip, his blazing head resembling some sort of wheeled fireworks display. He landed on the bridge railing on the far side of the street with a crack of bone and a barking noise. With a burst of flames around his head, he fell off the bridge and into the water below.

The dump truck locked up its brakes and skidded.

Wilson and Jake stopped running. They stood looking at the spot where Buddy had gone over, paralyzed with disbelief.

The dump truck driver, a slim white man in overalls and a cap, got out of the truck and stopped at the rear of it, looked at where Buddy had gone over, looked up and down the street. He didn't seem to notice Wilson and Jake. He walked briskly back to the truck, got in, gunned the motor. The truck went away fast, took a right on the next street hard enough the tires protested like a cat with its tail in a crack. It backfired once, then there was only the distant sound of the motor and gears being rapidly shifted.

"Sonofabitch!" Wilson yelled.

He and Jake ran to the street, paused, looked both ways in case of more dump trucks, and crossed. They glanced over the railing.

Buddy lay with his lower body on the bank. His left leg was twisted so that his shoe pointed in the wrong direction. His dark, crisp head was in the water. He was straining his neck to lift his blackened, eyeless face out of the water; white wisps of smoke swirled up from it and carried with it the smell of barbecued meat. His body shifted. He let out a groan.

"Goddamn," Wilson said. "He's alive. Let's get him."

But at that moment there was splashing in the water. A log came sailing down the river, directly at Buddy's head. The log opened its mouth and grabbed Buddy by the head and jerked him off the shore. A noise like walnuts being cracked and a muffled scream drifted up to Wilson and Jake.

"An alligator," Jake said, and noted vaguely how closely its skin and Buddy's shoes matched.

Wilson darted around the railing, slid down the incline to the water's edge. Jake followed. They ran alongside the bank.

The water turned extremely shallow, and they could see the shadowy shape of the gator as it waddled forward, following the path of the river, still holding Buddy by the head. Buddy stuck out of the side of its mouth like a curmudgeon's cigar. His arms were flapping and so was his good leg.

Wilson and Jake paused running and tried to get their breath. After some deep inhalations, Wilson said, "Gets in the deep water, it's all over." He grabbed up an old fence post that had washed onto the bank and began running again, yelling at the gator as he went. Jake looked about, but didn't see anything to hit with. He ran after Wilson.

The gator, panicked by the noisy pursuit, crawled out of the shallows and went into the high grass of a connecting pasture, ducking under the bottom strand of a barb wire fence. The wire caught one of Buddy's flailing arms and ripped a flap of flesh from it six inches long. Once on the other side of the wire his good leg kicked up and the fine shine on his alligator shoes flashed once in the moonlight and fell down.

Wilson went through the barb wire and after the gator with his fence post. The gator was making good time, pushing Buddy before it, leaving a trail of mashed grass behind it.

Wilson could see its tail weaving in the moonlight. Its stink trailed behind it like fumes from a busted muffler.

Wilson put the fence post on his shoulder and ran as hard as he could, managed to close in. Behind him came Jake, huffing and puffing.

Wilson got alongside the gator and hit him in the tail with the fence post. The gator's tail whipped out and caught Wilson's ankles and knocked his feet from under him. He came down hard on his butt and lost the fence post.

Jake grabbed up the post and broke right as the gator turned in that direction. He caught the beast sideways and brought the post down on its head, and when it hit, Buddy's blood jumped out of the gator's mouth and landed in the grass and on Jake's shoes. In the moonlight it was the color of cough syrup.

Jake went wild. He began to hit the gator brutally, running alongside it, following its every twist and turn. He swung the fence post mechanically, slamming the gator in the head. Behind him Wilson was saying, "You're hurting Buddy, you're hurting Buddy," but Jake couldn't stop, the frenzy was on him. Gator blood was flying, bursting out of the top of the reptile's head. Still, it held to Buddy, not giving up an inch of head. Buddy wasn't thrashing or kicking anymore. His legs slithered along in the grass as the gator ran; he looked like one of those dummies they throw off cliffs in old cowboy movies.

Wilson caught up, started kicking the gator in the side. The gator started rolling and thrashing and Jake and Wilson hopped like rabbits and yelled. Finally the gator quit rolling. It quit crawling. Its sides heaved.

Jake continued to pound it with the post and Wilson continued to kick it. Eventually its sides quit swelling. Jake kept hitting it with the post until he staggered back and fell down in the grass exhausted. He sat there looking at the gator and Buddy. The gator trembled suddenly and spewed gator shit into the grass. It didn't move again.

After a few minutes, Wilson said, "I don't think Buddy's alive."

Just then, Buddy's body twitched.

"Hey, hey, you see that?" Jake said.

Wilson was touched with wisdom. "He's alive, the gator might be too."

Wilson got on his knees about six feet from the gator's mouth and bent over to see if he could see Buddy in there. All he could see were the gator's rubbery lips and the sides of its teeth and a little of Buddy's head shredded between them, like gray cheese on a grater. He could smell both the sour smell of the gator and the stink of burnt meat.

"I don't know if he's alive or not," Wilson said. "Maybe if we could get him out of its mouth, we could tell more."

Jake tried to wedge the fence post into the gator's mouth, but that didn't work. It was as if the great jaw was locked with a key.

They watched carefully, but Buddy didn't show any more signs of life.

"I know," Wilson said. "We'll carry him and the gator up to the road, find a house and get some help."

The gator was long and heavy. The best they could do was get hold of its tail and pull it and Buddy along. Jake managed this with the fence post under his arm. He didn't trust the gator and wouldn't give it up.

They went across an acre of grass and came to a barb wire fence that bordered the street where Buddy had been hit by the dump truck. The bridge was in sight.

They let go of the gator and climbed through the wire. Jake used the fence post to lift up the bottom strand, and

Wilson got hold of the gator's tail and tugged the beast under, along with Buddy.

Pulling the gator and Buddy alongside the road, they watched for house lights. They went past the church on the opposite side of the road and turned left where the dump truck had turned right and backfired. They went alongside the street there, occasionally allowing the gator and Buddy to weave over into the street itself. It was hard work steering a gator and its lunch.

They finally came to a row of houses. The first one had an old Ford pickup parked out beside it and a lot of junk piled in the yard. Lawn mowers, oily rope, overturned freezers, wheels, fishing reels and line, bicycle parts, and a busted commode. A tarp had been pulled half-heartedly over a tall stack of old shop creepers. There was a light on behind one window. The rest of the houses were dark.

Jake and Wilson let go of the gator in the front yard, and Wilson went up on the porch, knocked on the door, stepped off the porch and waited.

Briefly thereafter, the door opened a crack and a man called out, "Who's out there? Don't you know it's bed time?"

"We seen your light on," Wilson said.

"I was in the shitter. You trying to sell me a brush or a book or something this time of night, I won't be in no good temper about it. I'm not through shitting either."

"We got a man hurt here," Wilson said. "A gator bit him."

There was a long moment of quiet. "What you want me to do? I don't know nothin' about no gator bites. I don't even know who you are. You might be with the Ku Kluxers."

"He's . . . He's kind of hung up with the gator," Wilson said.

"Just a minute," said the voice.

Moments later a short, fat black man came out. He was shirtless and barefooted, wearing overalls with the straps off his shoulders, dangling at his waist. He had a ball bat in his hand. He came down the steps and looked at Wilson and Jake carefully, as if expecting them to spring. "You stand away from me with that fence post, hear?" he said. Jake took a step back and this seemed to satisfy the man. He took a look at the gator and Buddy.

He went back up the porch and reached inside the door and turned on the porch light. A child's face stuck through the crack in the door, said, "What's out there, papa?"

"You get your ass in that house, or I'll kick it," the black man said. The face disappeared.

The black man came off the porch again, looked at the gator and Buddy again, walked around them a couple of times, poked the gator with the ball bat, poked Buddy too.

He looked at Jake and Wilson. "Shit," he said. "You peckerwoods is crazy. That motherfucker's dead. He's dead enough for two men. He's deader than I ever seen anybody."

"He caught on fire," Jake offered suddenly, "and we tried to put his head out, and he got hit by a truck, knocked in the river, and the gator got him . . . . We seen him twitch a little a while back . . . . The fella, Buddy, not the gator, mean."

"Them's nerves," the black man said. "You better dig a hole for this man-jack, skin that ole gator out and sell his hide. They bring a right smart price sometimes. You could probably get something for them shoes too, if'n they clean up good."

"We need you to help us load him up into your pickup and take him home," Jake said.

"You ain't putting that motherfucker in my pickup," the black man said. "I don't want no doings with you honkey motherfuckers. They'll be claiming I sicked that gator on him."

"That's silly," Wilson said. "You're acting like a fool."

"Uh-huh," said the black man, "and I'm gonna go on acting like one here in my house."

He went briskly up the porch steps, closed the door and turned out the light. A latch was thrown.

Wilson began to yell. He used the word nigger indiscriminately. He ran up on the porch and pounded on the door. He cussed a lot.

Doors of houses down the way opened up and people moved onto their front porches like shadows, looked at where the noise was coming from.

Jake, standing there in the yard with his fence post, looked like a man with a gun. The gator and Buddy could have been the body of their neighbor. The shadows watched Jake and listened to Wilson yell a moment, then went back inside.

"Goddamn you," Wilson yelled. "Come on out of there so I can whip your ass, you hear me? I'll whip your black ass."

"You come on in here, cocksucker," came the black man's voice from the other side of the door. "Come on in, you think you can. You do, you'll be trying to shit you some twelve gauge shot, that's what you'll be trying to do."

At mention of the twelve gauge, Wilson felt a certain calm descend on him. He began to acquire perspective. "We're leaving," he said to the door. "Right now." He backed off the porch. He spoke softly so only Jake could hear: "Boogie motherfucker."

"What we gonna do now?" Jake said. He sounded tired. All the juice had gone out of him.

"I reckon," Wilson said, "we got to get Buddy and the gator on over to his house."

"I don't think we can carry him that far," Jake said. "My back is hurting already."

Wilson looked at the junk beside the house. "Wait a minute." He went over to the junk pile and got three shop creepers out from under the tarp and found some hunks of rope. He used the rope to tie the creepers together, end to end. When he looked up, Jake was standing beside him, still holding the fence post. "You go on and stay by Buddy," Wilson said. "Turn your back too long, them niggers will be all over them shoes."

Jake went back to his former position.

Wilson collected several short pieces of rope and a twist of wire and tied them together and hooked the results to one of the creepers and used it as a handle. He pulled his contraption around front by Buddy and the gator. "Help me put 'em on there," he said.

They lifted the gator onto the creepers. He fit with only his tail overlapping. Buddy hung to the side, off the creepers, causing them to tilt.

"That won't work," Jake said.

"Well, here now," Wilson said, and he got Buddy by the legs and turned him. The head and neck were real flexible, like they were made of chewing gum. He was able to lay Buddy straight out in front of the gator. "Now we can pull the gator down a bit, drag all of its tail. That way we got 'em both on there."

When they got the gator and Buddy arranged, Wilson doubled the rope and began pulling. At first it was slow going, but after a moment they got out in the road and the creepers gained momentum and squeaked right along. Jake used his fence post to punch at the edges of the creepers when they swung out of line.

An ancient, one-eyed Cocker Spaniel with a foot missing, came out and sat at the edge of the road and watched them pass. He barked once when the alligator's tail dragged by in the dirt behind the creepers, then he went and got under a porch.

They squeaked on until they passed the house where Sally lived. They stopped across from it for a breather and to listen. They didn't hear anyone screaming and they didn't hear any beatings going on.

They started up again, kept at it until they came to Buddy's street. It was deadly quiet, and the moon had been lost behind a cloud and everything was dark.

At Buddy's house, the silver light of the TV strobed behind the living room curtains. Wilson and Jake stopped on the far side of the street and squatted beside the creepers and considered their situation.

Wilson got in Buddy's back pocket and pulled the smokes out and found that though the package was damp from the water, a couple of cigarettes were dry enough to smoke. He gave one to Jake and took the other for himself. He got a match from Buddy's shirt pocket and struck it on a creeper, but it was too damp to light.

"Here," Jake said, and produced a lighter. "I stole this from my old man in case I ever got any cigarettes. It works most of the time." Jake clicked it repeatedly and finally it sparked well enough to light. They lit up.

"We knock on the door, his mom is gonna be mad," Jake said. "Us bringing home Buddy and an alligator, and Buddy wearing them shoes."

"Yeah," Wilson said. "You know, she don't know he went off with us. We could put him in the yard. Maybe she'll think the gator attacked him there."

"What for," Jake said, "them shoes? He recognized his aunt or something?" He began laughing at his own joke, but if Wilson got it he didn't give a sign. He seemed to be thinking. Jake quit laughing, scratched his head and looked off down the street. He tried to smoke his cigarette in a manful manner.

"Gators come up in yards and eat dogs now and then," Wilson said after a long silence. "We could leave him, and if his Mama don't believe a gator jumped him, that'll be all right. The figuring of it will be a town mystery. Nobody would ever know what happened. Those niggers won't be talking. And if they do, they don't know us from anybody else anyway. We all look alike to them."

"I was Buddy," Jake said, "that's the way I'd want it if I had a couple friends involved."

"Yeah, well," Wilson said, "I don't know I really liked him so much."

Jake thought about that. "He was all right. I bet he wasn't going to get that Chevy though."

"If he did," Wilson said, "there wouldn't have been no motor in it, I can promise you that. And I bet he never got any pussy neither."

They pulled the creepers across the road and tipped gator and Buddy onto the ground in front of the porch steps.

"That'll have to do," Wilson whispered.

Wilson crept up on the porch and over to the window, looked through a crack in the curtain and into the living room. Buddy's sister lay on the couch asleep, her mouth open, her huge belly bobbing up and down as she breathed. A half-destroyed bag of Cheetos lay beside the couch. The TV light flickered over her like saintly fire.

Jake came up on the porch and took a look.

"Maybe if she lost some pounds and fixed her hair different," he said.

"Maybe if she was somebody else," Wilson said.

They sat on the porch steps in the dark and finished smoking their cigarettes, watching the faint glow of the television through the curtain, listening to the tinny sound of a late night talk show.

When Jake finished his smoke, he pulled the alligator shoes off Buddy and checked them against the soles of his own shoes. "I think these dudes will fit me. We can't leave 'em on him. His Mama sees them, she might not consent to bury him."

He and Wilson left out of there then, pulling the creepers after them.

Not far down the road, they pushed the creepers off in a ditch and continued, Jake carrying the shoes under his arm. "These are all right," he said. "I might can get some pussy wearing these kind of shoes. My Mama don't care if I wear things like this."

"Hell, she don't care if you cut your head off," Wilson said.

"That's the way I see it," Jake said.

For Gary Raisor

LOVE DOLL:
A FABLE

I buy a plastic love doll because I want something to fuck that I don't have to talk to. Right on the box it says Love Doll. I take her home and blow her up. She looks pretty and sexy and innocent.

I fuck her. I sit with her on the couch and watch TV and put an arm around her plastic shoulders and hold my dick with my other hand.

I fuck her some more. In the morning I let the air out of her and fold her up and put her in a drawer.

When I come home from work at night, I give her a blow job and she is full and stiff again. I take her into the bedroom and fuck her. I watch TV with my arm around her, one hand on my dick.

This goes on for a while.

I start to talk to the doll. I never wanted to talk to a woman, but I talk to the doll. I name her Madge. I had a dog named Madge that I liked.

I stop letting the air out of her in the mornings. I leave her in bed. I fix breakfast on a tray, enough for two. I come in and eat beside her on the bed. There's plenty of food left when I stop and get ready for work.

When I come home the tray is where it was and the doll is gone. There's no food left on the tray.

I find Madge in the shower. She smiles at me when I slide the shower door back.

"I was going to clean up for you," she said. "Be sexy. I'm sorry the house isn't clean and dinner isn't ready. It won't happen again."

I get in the shower with her. We have sex and soap each other. We dry off and go to bed and have sex again. We lie in bed and talk afterward. She talks some about girl things. She talks about me mostly. She has good things to say about my sexual prowess. We have sex again.

Next day she drives me to work, picks me up at the end of the day. All the fellas are jealous when they see her, she's such a good-looking piece.

She always looks nice. Wears frilly things, short skirts. For bop-around she wears tight sweaters and T-shirts and jeans. She smells good. She puts her hands on me a lot. The house is clean when I get home. Dinner is ready in a jiffy.

A year passes. Quite happily. Life couldn't be better. Lots of sex. A clean house. Food when I need it. Conversation. She tells me I'm a real man when I mount her, that she needs me, calls me her stallion, makes good noises beneath me and scratches at my back, she makes a lalala noise when she comes. She likes my muscles, the scruffiness of my beard. We watch movies on the couch, my arm around her. She holds my dick in her hand. When I tell her to, she gives me a blow job while I watch the movie. She always swallows my load.

One night we're laying in bed and she says, "I think maybe I should go to school."

"What for?" I ask.

"To bring in more money. We could buy some things."

"I make enough money."

"I know. You're a hard-working man. But I want to help."

"You help enough. You be here for me at night, keep the house clean and the meals ready. That's a woman's place."

"Whatever you want, dear."

But she doesn't mean it. It comes up now and again, her going to school. Finally I think, so what? She goes off to school. The house isn't quite so clean. The meals aren't always ready on time. I drive myself to work. Some nights she doesn't feel like sex. I jack off in the bathroom a lot. We sit on the couch and watch movies. She sits on one end, I sit on the other. We wear our clothes. I have a beer in one hand, the remote control in the other. We argue about little things. She doesn't like the way I spend my money.

She gets a degree. She gets a job in business. She wears suits. For bop-around the stuff she wears is less tight. She doesn't wear makeup or perfume around the house. She keeps her hands to herself. No kissing goodbye and hello anymore. We have sex less. When we have it, she seems distracted. She doesn't call me her King, her Big Man like she used to. After sex she'll sometimes stay up late reading books by people called Sartre or Camus. She's writing something she calls a business manifesto. She sits at the typewriter for hours. She goes to business parties, and I go with her, but I can tell they think I'm boring. I don't know what they're talking about. They talk about business and books and ideas. I hear Madge say a woman has to make her own way in the world. That she shouldn't depend on a man, even if she has one. Thing to do is to be your own person. She tells a man that. Guy in a three-piece blue suit with hairspray on his hair. He agrees with her. I feel sick.

I tell her so in the car on the way home. She calls me a prick. We don't fuck that night.

I watch a lot of movies alone. She yells from the bedroom for me to turn them down, and why don't I watch something else other than car chase movies, and why don't I read a book, even a stupid one?

I feel small these days. I go to the store and look at the love dolls. They all look so sexy and innocent. I think I might buy one, but find I can't. I don't feel man enough. I can't control the one I have. I get a new one, she might change, too. Course, a new one I could let the air out of when I finished fucking her, never let her have a day alone full blown.

I go home. Madge is there. She's writing her book. I get angry. I tell her I've been patient long enough. I'm the man around here. I tell her to stop that typing, get her clothes off, and get in bed and grab her ankles. I'm going to fuck her unconscious.

She laughs. "You skinny, little, stupid pencil-dick, you couldn't fuck a gnat unconscious. You're about as manly as a Kotex."

I feel as if I've been hit in the face with a fist. I go into the bedroom and close the door. I sit on the edge of the bed. I can hear her typing in there. I get up and go over to the dresser and open the bottom drawer. I take off all my clothes and find the air spigot on the head of my dick and pull it open and listen to the air go out of me. I crumple into the open drawer, and lay there like a used prophylactic.

An hour or so later the typing stops. I hear her come into the room. She looks in the drawer. No expression. I try to say something manly, but nothing will come. I have no air and no voice. She moves away.

I hear the water running while she takes a shower. She comes out naked. I can see her pubic hair above me. I note how firm and full of air her thighs are. She opens the top drawer. She takes out panties. She puts them on. She goes away. I hear her sit on the bed. She dials the phone. She tells someone to come on over, that her thing with me is finished.

Time passes. The doorbell rings. Madge gets up and goes past me. I get a glimpse of her, her hair combed out long and pretty, a robe on.

I hear her laugh in the other room. She comes back with a man. As they go by the drawer I see it's the man in the business suit from the party. I hear them sit on the bed. They laugh a lot. She says something rude about me and my sexual abilities. I can tell she has his dick out of his pants because they're laughing about something. I realize they're laughing about sex. He's making fun of his equipment. I never like being laughed at when it's about sex. I don't like being laughed at at all, especially by a woman.

The bathrobe flies across the room and lands in the drawer on top of me and everything is dark. I hear the bedsprings squeak. They squeak for hours. They talk while they screw. After a while they stop talking. He grunts like a hog. She sings like a lark. Afterward I hear them talking. He asks her if she came. She says only a little. He says let me help you. I can't be sure, but I think he's doing something to her with his hand. I can't believe it. She doesn't seem to mind this at all.

I hear her sing again, this time louder than ever. Then they talk again. She tells him she never really came for me, that she always faked it. That I was a lousy fuck. That I didn't care if she came. That I got on and did it and got off.

A little air caught at the top of my head floats down and out of my open mouth.

They talk some more. They don't talk about him. She doesn't talk girl things. They talk about ideas. Politics. History. The office. Movies—films they call them—and books.

In the middle of the night the robe is lifted off of me. It's Madge. She's down on her knees looking in the drawer. She smiles at me. She picks me up and folds me gently. She has a box with her. It's the box she came in. The one that says Love Doll on it. The words Love Doll have been marked through with a magic marker and Fuck Toy has been written in above it. She puts me in the box and seals the lid and puts me back in the drawer and closes it.

BUBBA HO-TEP

by Joe R. Lansdale

Elvis dreamed he had his dick out, checking to see if the bump on the head of it had filled with pus again. If it had, he was going to name the bump Priscilla, after his ex-wife, and bust it by jacking off. Or he liked to think that's what he'd do. Dreams let you think like that. The truth was, he hadn't had a hard-on in years.

That bitch, Priscilla. Gets a new hairdo and she's gone, just because she caught him fucking a big tittied gospel singer. It wasn't like the singer had mattered. Priscilla ought to have understood that, so what was with her making a big deal out of it?

Was it because she couldn't hit a high note same and as good as the singer when she came?

When had that happened anyway, Priscilla leaving?

Yesterday? Last year? Ten years ago?

Oh God, it came to him instantly as he slipped out of sleep like a soft turd squeezed free of a loose asshole—for he could hardly think of himself or life in any context other than sewage, since so often he was too tired to do any thing other than let it all fly in his sleep, wake up in an ocean of piss or shit, waiting for the nurses or the aides to come in and wipe his ass. But now it came to him. Suddenly he realized it had been years ago that he had supposedly died, and longer years than that since Priscilla left, and how old was she anyway? Sixty-five? Seventy?

And how old was he?

Christ! He was almost convinced he was too old to be alive, and had to be dead, but he wasn't convinced enough, unfortunately. He knew where he was now, and in that moment of realization, he sincerely wished he were dead. This was worse than death.

From across the room, his roommate, Bull Thomas, bellowed and coughed and moaned and fell back into painful sleep, the cancer gnawing at his insides like a rat plugged up inside a watermelon.

Bull's bellow of pain and anger and indignation at growing old and diseased was the only thing bullish about him now, though Elvis had seen photographs of him when he was younger, and Bill had been very bullish indeed. Thick-chested, slab-faced and tall. Probably thought he'd live forever, and happily. A boozing, pill-popping, swinging dick until the end of time.

Now Bull was shrunk down, was little more than a wrinkled sheet-white husk that throbbed with occasional pulses of blood while the carcinoma fed.

Elvis took hold of the bed's lift button, eased himself upright. He glanced at Bull. Bull was breathing heavily and his bony knees rose up and down like he was peddling a bicycle; his kneecaps punched feebly at the sheet, making puptents that rose up and collapsed, rose up and collapsed.

Elvis looked down at the sheet stretched over his own bony knees. He thought: *My God, how long have I been here? Am I really awake now, or am I dreaming I'm awake? How could my plans have gone so wrong? When are they going to serve lunch, and considering what they serve, why do I care? And if Priscilla discovered I was alive, would she come see me, would she want to see me, and would we still want to fuck, or would we have to merely talk about it? Is there finally, and really, anything to life other than food and shit and sex?*

Elvis pushed the sheet down to do what he had done in the dream. He pulled up his gown, leaned forward, and examined his dick. It was wrinkled and small. It didn't look like something that had dive-bombed movie starlet pussies or filled their mouths like a big zucchini or pumped forth a load of sperm frothy as cake icing. The healthiest thing about his pecker was the big red bump with the black ring around it and the pus-filled white center. Fact was, that bump kept growing, he was going to have to pull a chair up beside his bed and put a pillow in it so the bump would have some place to sleep at night. There was more pus in that damn bump than there was cum in his loins. Yep. The old diddlebopper was no longer a flesh cannon loaded for bare ass. It was a peanut too small to harvest; wasting away on the vine. His nuts were a couple of darkening, about-to-rot-grapes, too limp to produce juice for life's wine. His legs were stick and paper things with over-large, vein-swollen feet on the ends. His belly was such a bloat, it was a pain for him to lean forward and scrutinize his dick and balls.

Pulling his gown down and the sheet back over himself, Elvis leaned back and wished he had a peanut butter and banana sandwich fried in butter. There had been a time when he and his crew would board his private jet and fly clean across country just to have a special made fried peanut butter and 'nanner sandwich. He could still taste the damn things.

Elvis closed his eyes and thought he would awake from a bad dream, but didn't. He opened his eyes again, slowly, and saw that he was still where he had been, and things were no better. He reached over and opened his dresser drawer and got out a little round mirror and looked at himself.

He was horrified. His hair was white as salt and had receded dramatically. He had wrinkles deep enough to conceal out-stretched earth worms, the big ones, the night crawlers. His pouty mouth no longer appeared pouty. It looked like the drop-ping waddles of a bulldog, seeming more that way because he was slobbering a mite. He dragged his tired tongue across his lips to daub the slobber, revealed to himself in the mirror that he was missing a lot of teeth.

Goddamn it! How had he gone from King of Rock and Roll to this? Old guy in a rest home in East Texas with a growth on his dick?

And what was that growth? Cancer? No one was talking. No one seemed to know. Perhaps the bump was a manifestation of the mistakes of his life, so many of them made with his dick.

He considered on that. Did he ask himself this question everyday, or just now and then? Time sort of ran together when the last moment and the immediate moment and the moment forthcoming were all alike.

Shit, when was lunch time? Had he slept through it?

Was it about time for his main nurse again? The good looking one with the smooth chocolate skin and tits like grapefruits. The one who came in and sponge bathed him and held his pitiful little pecker in her gloved hands and put salve on his canker with all the enthusiasm of a mechanic oiling a defective part?

He hoped not. That was the worst of it. A doll like that handling him without warmth or emotion. Twenty years ago, just twenty, he could have made with the curled lip smile and had her eating out of his asshole. Where had his youth gone? Why hadn't fame sustained old age and death, and why had he left his fame in the first place, and did he want it back, and could he have it back, and if he could, would it make any difference?

And finally, when he was evacuated from the bowels of life into the toilet bowl of the beyond and was flushed, would the great sewer pipe flow him to the other side where God would—in the guise of a great all-seeing turd with corn kernel eyes—be waiting with open turd arms, and would there be amongst the sewage his mother (bless her fat little heart) and father and friends, waiting with fried peanut butter and 'nanner sandwiches and ice cream cones, predigested, or course?

He was reflecting on this, pondering the afterlife, when Bull gave out with a hell of a scream, pouched his eyes damn near out of his head, arched his back, grease-farted like a blast from Gabriel's trumpet, and checked his tired old soul out of the Mud Creek Shady Rest Convalescence Home; flushed it on out and across the great shitty beyond.

Later that day, Elvis lay sleeping, his lips fluttering the bad taste of lunch—steamed zucchini and boiled peas—out of his belly. He awoke to a noise, rolled over to see a young attractive woman cleaning out Bull's dresser drawer. The curtains over the window next to Bull's bed were pulled wide open, and the sunlight was cutting through it and showing her to great advantage. She was blonde and nordic-featured and her long hair was tied back with a big red bow and she wore big, gold, hoop earrings that shimmered in the sunlight. She was dressed in a white blouse and a short black skirt and dark hose and high heels. The heels made her ass ride up beneath her skirt like soft bald baby heads under a thin blanket.

She had a big, yellow, plastic trashcan and she had one of Bull's dresser drawers pulled out, and she was picking through it, like a magpie looking for bright things. She found a few— coins, a pocket knife, a cheap watch. These were plucked free and laid on the dresser top, then the remaining contents of the drawer—Bull's photographs of himself when young, a rotten pack of rubbers (wishful thinking never deserted Bull), a bronze star and a purple heart from his performance in the Vietnam War—were dumped into the trashcan with a bang and a flutter.

Elvis got hold of his bed lift button and raised himself for a better look. The woman had her back to him now, and didn't notice. She was replacing the dresser drawer and pulling out another. It was full of clothes. She took out the few shirts and pants and socks and underwear, and laid them on Bull's bed— remade now, and minus Bull, who had been toted off to be taxidermied, embalmed, burned up, whatever.

"You're gonna toss that stuff," Elvis said. "Could I have one of them pictures of Bull? Maybe that purple heart? He was proud of it."

The young woman turned and looked at him. "I suppose," she said. She went to the trashcan and bent over it and showed her black panties to Elvis as she rummaged. He knew the revealing of her panties was neither intentional or unintentional. She just didn't give a damn. She saw him as so physically and

84

sexually non-threatening, she didn't mind if he got a birds-eye view of her; it was the same to her as a house cat sneaking a peek.

Elvis observed the thin panties straining and slipping into the caverns of her ass cheeks and felt his pecker flutter once, like a bird having a heart attack, then it laid down and remained limp and still.

Well, these days, even a flutter was kind of reassuring.

The woman surfaced from the trashcan with a photo and the purple heart, went over to Elvis's bed and handed them to him.

Elvis dangled the ribbon that held the purple heart between his fingers, said, "Bull your kin?"

"My daddy," she said.

"I haven't seen you here before."

"Only been here once before," she said. "When I checked him in."

"Oh," Elvis said. "That was three years ago, wasn't it?"

"Yeah. Were you and him friends?"

Elvis considered the question. He didn't know the real answer. All he knew was Bull listened to him when he said he was Elvis Presley and seemed to believe him. If he didn't believe him, he at least had the courtesy not to patronize. Bull always called him Elvis, and before Bull grew too ill, he always played cards and checkers with him.

"Just roommates," Elvis said. "He didn't feel good enough to say much. I just sort of hated to see what was left of him go away so easy. He was an all right guy. He mentioned you a lot. You're Callie, right?"

"Yeah," she said. "Well, he was all right."

"Not enough you came and saw him though."

"Don't try to put some guilt trip on me, Mister. I did what I could. Hadn't been for Medicaid, Medicare, whatever that stuff was, he'd have been in a ditch somewhere. I didn't have the money to take care of him."

Elvis thought of his own daughter, lost long ago to him. If she knew he lived, would she come to see him? Would she care? He feared knowing the answer.

"You could have come and seen him," Elvis said.

"I was busy. Mind your own business. Hear?"

The chocolate skin nurse with the grapefruit tits came in. Her white uniform crackled like cards being shuffled. Her little, white, nurse hat was tilted on her head in a way that said she loved mankind and made good money and was getting regular dick. She smiled at Callie and then at Elvis. "How are you this morning, Mr. Haff?"

"All right," Elvis said. "But I prefer Mr. Presley. Or Elvis. I keep telling you that. I don't go by Sebastian Haff anymore. I don't try to hide anymore."

"Why, of course," said the pretty nurse. "I knew that. I forgot. Good morning, Elvis."

Her voice dripped with sorghum syrup. Elvis wanted to hit her with his bed pan.

The nurse said to Callie: "Did you know we have a celebrity here, Miss Jones? Elvis Presley. You know, the rock and roll singer?"

"I've heard of him," Callie said. "I thought he was dead."

Callie went back to the dresser and squatted and set to work on the bottom drawer. The nurse looked at Elvis and smiled again, only she spoke to Callie. "Well, actually, Elvis is dead, and Mr. Haff knows that, don't you, Mr. Haff?"

"Hell no," said Elvis. "I'm right here. I ain't dead, yet."

"Now, Mr. Haff, I don't mind calling you Elvis, but you're a little confused, or like to play sometimes. You were an Elvis impersonator. Remember? You fell off a stage and broke your hip. What was it . . . Twenty years ago? It got infected and you went into a coma for a few years. You came out with a few problems."

"I was impersonating myself," Elvis said. "I couldn't do nothing else. I haven't got any problems. You're trying to say my brain is messed up, aren't you?"

Callie quit cleaning out the bottom drawer of the dresser. She was interested now, and though it was no use, Elvis couldn't help but try and explain who he was, just one more time. The explaining had become a habit, like wanting to smoke a cigar long after the enjoyment of it was gone.

"I got tired of it all," he said. "I got on drugs, you know. I wanted out. Fella named Sebastian Haff, an Elvis imitator, the best of them. He took my place. He had a bad heart and he liked drugs too. It was him died, not me. I took his place."

"Why would you want to leave all that fame," Callie said, "all that money?" and she looked at the nurse, like "Let's humor the old fart for a lark."

"Cause it got old. Woman I loved, Priscilla, she was gone. Rest of the women . . . were just women. The music wasn't mine anymore. *I* wasn't even me anymore. I was this thing they made up. Friends were sucking me dry. I got away and liked it, left all the money with Sebastian, except for enough to sustain me if things got bad. We had a deal, me and Sebastian. When I wanted to come back, he'd let me. It was all written up in a contract in case he wanted to give me a hard time, got to liking my life too good. Thing was, copy of the contract I had got lost in a trailer fire. I was living simple. Way Haff had been. Going from town to town doing the Elvis act. Only I felt like I was really me again. Can you dig that?"

"We're digging it, Mr. Haff . . . . Mr. Presley," said the pretty nurse.

"I was singing the old way. Doing some new songs. Stuff I wrote. I was getting attention on a small but good scale. Women throwing themselves at me, cause they could imagine I was Elvis, only I was Elvis, playing Sebastian Haff Playing Elvis . . . . It was all pretty good. I didn't mind the contract being burned up. I didn't even try to go back and convince anybody. Then I had the accident. Like I was saying, I'd laid up a little money in case of illness, stuff like that. That's what's paying for here. These nice facilities. Ha!"

"Now, Elvis," the nurse said. "Don't carry it too far. You may just get way out there and not come back."

"Oh fuck you," Elvis said.

The nurse giggled.

Shit, Elvis thought. *Get old, you can't even cuss somebody and have it bother them. Everything you do is either worthless or sadly amusing.*

"You know, Elvis," said the pretty nurse, "we have a Mr. Dillinger here too. And a President Kennedy. He says the bullet only wounded him and his brain is in a fruit jar at the White House, hooked up to some wires and a battery, and as long as the battery works, he can walk around without it. His brain, that is. You know, he says everyone was in on trying to assassinate him. Even Elvis Presley."

"You're an asshole," Elvis said.

"I'm not trying to hurt your feelings, Mr. Haff," the nurse said. "I'm merely trying to give you a reality check."

"You can shove that reality check right up your pretty black ass," Elvis said.

The nurse made a sad little snicking sound. "Mr. Haff, Mr. Haff. Such language."

"What happened to get you here?" said Callie. "Say you fell off a stage?"

"I was gyrating," Elvis said. "Doing *Blue Moon,* but my hip went out. I'd been having trouble with it." Which was quite true. He'd sprained it making love to a blue haired old lady with ELVIS

88

tattooed on her fat ass. He couldn't help himself from wanting to fuck her. She looked like his mother, Gladys.

"You swiveled right off the stage?" Callie said. "Now that's sexy."

Elvis looked at her. She was smiling. This was great fun for her, listening to some nut tell a tale. She hadn't had this much fun since she put her old man in the rest home.

"Oh, leave me the hell alone," Elvis said.

The women smiled at one another, passing a private joke. Callie said to the nurse: "I've got what I want." She scraped the bright things off the top of Bull's dresser into her purse. "The clothes can go to Goodwill or the Salvation Army."

The pretty nurse nodded to Callie. "Very well. And I'm very sorry about your father. He was a nice man."

"Yeah," said Callie, and she started out of there. She paused at the foot of Elvis's bed. "Nice to meet you, Mr. Presley."

"Get the hell out," Elvis said.

"Now, now," said the pretty nurse, patting his foot through the covers, as if it were a little cantankerous dog. "I'll be back later to do that . . . little thing that has to be done. You know?"

"I know," Elvis said, not liking the words "little thing."

Callie and the nurse started away then, punishing him with the clean lines of their faces and the sheen of their hair, the jiggle of their asses and tits. When they were out of sight, Elvis heard them laugh about something in the hall, then they were gone, and Elvis felt as if he were on the far side of Pluto without a jacket. He picked up the ribbon with the purple heart and looked at it.

Poor Bull. In the end, did anything really matter?

Meanwhile . . .

The Earth swirled around the sun like a spinning turd in the toilet bowl (to keep up with Elvis's metaphors) and the good old abused Earth clicked about on its axis and the hole in the ozone spread slightly wider, like a shy lady fingering open her vagina, and the South American trees that had stood for centuries, were visited by the dozer the chainsaw and the match, and they rose up in burned black puffs that expanded and dissipated into miniscule wisps, and while the puffs of smoke dissolved, there were IRA bombings in London, and there was more war in the Mid-East. Blacks died in Africa of famine, the HIV virus infected a million more, the Dallas Cowboys lost again, and that Ole Blue Moon that Elvis and Patsy Cline sang so well about, swung around the Earth and came in close and rose over the Shady Grove Convalescent Home, shone its bittersweet, silver-blue rays down on the joint like a flashlight beam shining through a blue-haired lady's do, and inside the rest home, evil waddled about like a duck looking for a spot to squat, and Elvis rolled over in his sleep and awoke with the intense desire to pee.

All right, thought Elvis. *This time I make it.* No more piss or crap in the bed. (Famous last words.)

Elvis sat up and hung his feet over the side of the bed and the bed swung far to the left and around the ceiling and back, and then it wasn't moving at all. The dizziness passed.

Elvis looked at his walker and sighed, leaned forward, took hold of the grips and eased himself off the bed and clumped the rubber padded tips forward, made for the toilet.

He was in the process of milking his bump-swollen weasel, when he heard something in the hallway. A kind of scrambling, like a big spider scuttling about in a box of gravel.

There was always some sound in the hallway, people coming and going, yelling in pain or confusion, but this time of night, three A.M., was normally quite dead.

It shouldn't have concerned him, but the truth of the matter was, now that he was up and had successfully pissed in the pot, he was no longer sleepy; he was still thinking about that bimbo, Callie, and the nurse (what the hell was her name?) with the tits like grapefruits, and all they had said.

Elvis stumped his walker backwards out of the bathroom, turned it, made his way forward into the hall. The hall was semi-dark, with every other light cut, and the lights that were on were dimmed to a watery egg yoke yellow. The black and white tile floor looked like a great chessboard, waxed and buffed for the next game of life, and here he was, a semi-crippled pawn, ready to go.

Off in the far wing of the home, Old Lady McGee, better known in the home as The Blue Yodeler, broke into one of her famous yodels (she claimed to have sung with a Country and Western band in her youth) then ceased abruptly. Elvis swung the walker forward and moved on. He hadn't been out of his room in ages, and he hadn't been out of his bed much either. Tonight, he felt invigorated because he hadn't pissed his bed, and he'd heard the sound again, the spider in the box of gravel. (Big spider. Big box. Lots of gravel.) And following the sound gave him something to do.

Elvis rounded the corner, beads of sweat popping out on his forehead like heat blisters. Jesus. He wasn't invigorated now. Thinking about how invigorated he was had bushed him. Still, going back to his room to lie on his bed and wait for morning so he could wait for noon, then afternoon and night, didn't appeal to him.

He went by Jack McLaughlin's room, the fellow who was convinced he was John F. Kennedy, and that his brain was in the White House running on batteries. The door to Jack's room was open. Elvis peeked in as he moved by, knowing full well that Jack might not want to see him. Sometimes he accepted Elvis as the real Elvis, and when he did, he got scared, saying it was Elvis who had been behind the assassination.

Actually, Elvis hoped he felt that way tonight. It would at least be some acknowledgement that he was who he was, even if the acknowledgement was a fearful shriek from a nut.

'Course, Elvis thought, *maybe I'm nuts too. Maybe I am Sebastian Haff and I fell off the stage and broke more than my hip, cracked some part of my brain that lost my old self and made me think I'm Elvis.*

No. He couldn't believe that. That's the way they wanted him to think. They wanted him to believe he was nuts and he wasn't Elvis, just some sad old fart who had once lived out part of another man's life because he had none of his own.

He wouldn't accept that. He wasn't Sebastian Haff. He was Elvis Goddamn Aaron Fucking Presley with a boil on his dick.

'Course, he believed that, maybe he ought to believe Jack was John F. Kennedy, and Mums Delay, another patient here at Shady Rest, was Dillinger. Then again, maybe not. They were kind of scanty on evidence. He at least looked like Elvis gone old and sick. Jack was black—he claimed The Powers That Be had dyed him that color to keep him hidden—and Mums was a woman who claimed she'd had a sex change operation.

Jesus, was this a rest home or a nut house?

Jack's room was one of the special kind. He didn't have to share. He had money from somewhere. The room was packed with books and little luxuries. And though Jack could walk well, he even had a fancy electric wheelchair that he rode about in sometimes. Once, Elvis had seen him riding it around the outside circular drive, popping wheelies and spinning doughnuts.

When Elvis looked into Jack's room, he saw him lying on the floor. Jack's gown was pulled up around his neck, and his bony black ass appeared to be made of licorice in the dim light. Elvis figured Jack had been on his way to the shitter, or was coming back from it, and had collapsed. His heart, maybe.

"Jack," Elvis said.

Elvis clumped into the room, positioned his walker next to Jack, took a deep breath and stepped out of it, supporting himself with one side of it. He got down on his knees beside Jack, hoping he'd be able to get up again. God, but his knees and back hurt.

Jack was breathing hard. Elvis noted the scar at Jack's hairline, a long scar that made Jack's skin lighter there, almost grey. ("That's where they took the brain out," Jack always explained, "put it in that fucking jar. I got a little bag of sand up there now.")

Elvis touched the old man's shoulder. "Jack. Man, you okay?"

No response.

Elvis tried again. "Mr. Kennedy."

"Uh," said Jack (Mr. Kennedy).

"Hey, man. You're on the floor," Elvis said.

"No shit? Who are you?"

Elvis hesitated. This wasn't the time to get Jack worked up. "Sebastian," he said. "Sebastian Haff."

Elvis took hold of Jack's shoulder and rolled him over. It was about as difficult as rolling a jelly roll. Jack lay on his back now. He strayed an eyeball at Elvis. He started to speak, hesitated. Elvis took hold of Jack's nightgown and managed to work it down around Jack's knees, trying to give the old fart some dignity.

Jack finally got his breath. "Did you see him go by in the hall? He scuttled like."

"Who?"

"Someone they sent."

"Who's they?"

"You know. Lyndon Johnson. Castro. They've sent someone to finish me. I think maybe it was Johnson himself. Real ugly. Real goddamn ugly."

"Johnson's dead," Elvis said.

"That won't stop him," Jack said.

Later that morning, sunlight shooting into Elvis's room through venetian blinds, Elvis put his hands behind his head and considered the night before while the pretty black nurse with the grapefruit tits salved his dick. He had reported Jack's fall and the aides had come to help Jack back in bed, and him back on his walker. He had clumped back to his room (after being scolded for being out there that time of night) feeling that an air of strangeness had blown into the rest home, an air that wasn't there as short as the day before. It was at low ebb now, but certainly still present, humming in the background like some kind of generator ready to buzz up to a higher notch at a moment's notice.

And he was certain it wasn't just his imagination. The scuttling sound he'd heard last night, Jack had heard it too. What was that all about? It wasn't the sound of a walker, or a crip dragging their foot, or a wheelchair creeping along, it was something else, and now that he thought about it, It wasn't exactly spider legs in gravel, more like a roll of barbed wire tumbling across tile.

Elvis was so wrapped up in these considerations, he lost awareness of the nurse until she said, "Mr. Haff!"

"What . . . " and he saw that she was smiling and looking down at her hands. He looked too. There, nestled in one of her gloved palms was a massive, blue-veined hooter with a pus-filled bump on it the size of a pecan. It was *his* hooter and *his* pus-filled bump.

"You ole rascal," she said, and gently lowered his dick between his legs. "I think you better take a cold shower, Mr. Haff."

Elvis was amazed. That was the first time in years he'd had a boner like that. What gave here?

Then he realized what gave. He wasn't thinking about not being able to do it. He was thinking about something that interested him, and now, with something clicking around inside his head besides old memories and confusions, concerns about his next meal and going to the crapper, he had been given a dose of life again. He grinned his gums and what teeth were in them at the nurse.

"You get in there with me," he said, "and I'll take that shower."

"You silly thing," she said, and pulled his night gown down and stood and removed her plastic gloves and dropped them in the trash can beside his bed.

"Why don't you pull on it a little," Elvis said.

"You ought to be ashamed," the nurse said, but she smiled when she said it.

She left the room door open after she left. This concerned Elvis a little, but he felt his bed was at such an angle no one could look in, and if they did, tough luck. He wasn't going to look a gift hard-on in the pee-hole. He pulled the sheet over him and pushed his hands beneath the sheets and got his gown pulled up over his belly. He took hold of his snake and began to choke it with one hand, running his thumb over the pus-filled bump. With his other hand, he fondled his balls. He thought of Priscilla and the pretty black nurse and Bull's daughter and even the blue-haired fat lady with ELVIS tattooed on her butt, and he stroked harder and faster, and goddamn but he got stiffer and stiffer, and the bump on his cock gave up its load first, exploded hot pus down his thighs, and then his balls, which he thought forever empty, filled up with juice and electricity, and finally he threw the switch. The dam broke and the juice flew. He heard himself scream happily and felt hot wetness jetting down his legs, splattering as far as his big toes.

"Oh God," he said softly. "I like that. I like that."

He closed his eyes and slept. And for the first time in a long time, not fitfully.

Lunchtime. The Shady Grove lunch room.

Elvis sat with a plate of steamed carrots and broccoli and flaky roast beef in front of him. A dry roll, a pat of butter and a short glass of milk soldiered on the side. It was not inspiring.

Next to him, The Blue Yodeler was stuffing a carrot up her nose while she expounded on the sins of God, The Heavenly Father, for knocking up that nice Mary in her sleep, slipping up her ungreased poontang while she snored, and—bless her little heart—not even knowing it, or getting a clit throb from it, but waking up with a belly full of baby and no memory of action.

Elvis had heard it all before. It used to offend him, this talk of God as rapist, but he'd heard it so much now he didn't care. She rattled on.

Across the way, an old man who wore a black mask and sometimes a white stetson, known to residents and staff alike as Kemosabe, snapped one of his two capless cap pistols at the floor and called for an invisible Tonto to bend over so he could drive him home.

At the far end of the table, Dillinger was talking about how much whisky he used to drink, and how many cigars he used to smoke before he got his dick cut off at the stump and split so he could become a she and hide out as a woman. Now she said she no longer thought of banks and machine guns, women and fine cigars. She now thought about spots on dishes, the colors of curtains and drapes as coordinated with carpets and walls.

Even as the depression of his surroundings settled over him again, Elvis deliberated last night, and glanced down the length of the table at Jack (Mr. Kennedy) who headed it's far end. He saw the old man was looking at him, as if they shared a secret.

Elvis's ill mood dropped a notch; a real mystery was at work here, and come nightfall, he was going to investigate.

Swing the Shady Grove Rest Home's side of the Earth away from the sun again, and swing the moon in close and blue again. Blow some gauzy clouds across the nasty, black sky. Now ease on into 3 A.M.

Elvis awoke with a start and turned his head toward the intrusion. Jack stood next to the bed looking down at him. Jack was wearing a suit coat over his nightgown and he had on thick glasses. He said, "Sebastian. It's loose."

Elvis collected his thoughts, pasted them together into a not too scattered collage. "What's loose?"

"It," said Sebastian. "Listen."

Elvis listened. Out in the hall he heard the scuttling sound of the night before. Tonight, it reminded him of great locust-wings beating frantically inside a small cardboard box, the tips of them scratching at the cardboard, cutting it, ripping it apart.

"Jesus Christ, what is it?" Elvis said.

"I thought it was Lyndon Johnson, but it isn't. I've come across new evidence that suggests another assassin."

"Assassin?"

Jack cocked an ear. The sound had gone away, moved distant, then ceased.

"It's got another target tonight," said Jack. "Come on. I want to show you something. I don't think it's safe if you go back to sleep."

"For Christ sake," Elvis said. "Tell the administrators."

"The suits and the white starches," Jack said. "No thanks. I trusted them back when I was in Dallas, and look where that got my brain and me. I'm thinking with sand here, maybe picking up a few waves from my brain. Someday, who's to say they won't just disconnect the battery at the White House?"

"That's something to worry about, all right," Elvis said.

"Listen here," Jack said. "I know you're Elvis, and there were rumors, you know . . . about how you hated me, but I've thought it over. You hated me, you could have finished me the other night. All I want from you is to look me in the eye and assure me you had nothing to do with that day in Dallas, and that you never knew Lee Harvey Oswald or Jack Ruby."

Elvis stared at him as sincerely as possible. "I had nothing to do with Dallas, and I knew neither Lee Harvey Oswald or Jack Ruby."

"Good," said Jack. "May I call you Elvis instead of Sebastian?"

"You may."

"Excellent. You wear glasses to read?"

"I wear glasses when I really want to see," Elvis said.

"Get 'em and come on."

Elvis swung his walker along easily, not feeling as if he needed it too much tonight. He was excited. Jack was a nut, and maybe he himself was nuts, but there was an adventure going on.

They came to the hall restroom. The one reserved for male visitors. "In here," Jack said.

"Now wait a minute," Elvis said. "You're not going to get me in there and try and play with my pecker, are you?"

Jack stared at him. "Man, I made love to Jackie and Marilyn and a ton of others, and you think I want to play with your nasty ole dick?"

"Good point," said Elvis.

They went into the restroom. It was large, with several stalls and urinals.

"Over here," said Jack. He went over to one of the stalls and pushed open the door and stood back by the commode to make room for Elvis's walker. Elvis eased inside and looked at what Jack was now pointing to.

Graffiti.

"That's it?" Elvis said. "We're investigating a scuttling in the hall, trying to discover who attacked you last night, and you bring me in here to show me stick pictures on the shit house wall?"

"Look close," Jack said.

Elvis leaned forward. His eyes weren't what they used to be, and his glasses probably needed to be upgraded, but he could see that instead of writing, the graffiti was a series of simple pictorials.

A thrill, like a shot of good booze, ran through Elvis. He had once been a fanatic reader of ancient and esoteric lore, like *The Egyptian Book of the Dead* and *The Complete Works of H.P. Lovecraft,* and straight away he recognized what he was staring at. "Egyptian hieroglyphics," he said.

"Right-a-reen-O," Jack said. "Hey, you're not as stupid as some folks made you out."

"Thanks," Elvis said.

Jack reached into his suit coat pocket and took out a folded piece of paper and unfolded it. He pressed it to the wall. Elvis saw that it was covered with the same sort of figures that were on the wall of the stall.

"I copied this down yesterday. I came in here to shit because they hadn't cleaned up my bathroom. I saw this on the wall, went back to my room and looked it up in my books and wrote it all down. The top line translates something like: *Pharaoh gobbles donkey goober.* And the bottom line is: *Cleopatra does the dirty.*"

"What?"

"Well, pretty much," Jack said.

Elvis was mystified. "All right," he said. "One of the nuts here, present company excluded, thinks he's Tutankhamun or something, and he writes on the wall in hieroglyphics. So what? I mean, what's the connection? Why are we hanging out in a toilet?"

"I don't know how they connect exactly," Jack said. "Not yet. But this . . . thing, it caught me asleep last night, and I came awake just in time to . . . well, he had me on the floor and had his mouth over my asshole."

"A shit eater?" Elvis said.

"I don't think so," Jack said. "He was after my soul. You can get that out of any of the major orifices in a person's body. I've read about it."

"Where?" Elvis asked. *"Hustler?"*

"The Everyday Man or Woman's Book of the Soul" by David Webb. It has some pretty good movie reviews about stolen soul movies in the back too."

"Oh, that sounds trustworthy," Elvis said.

They went back to Jack's room and sat on his bed and looked through his many books on astrology, the Kennedy assassination, and a number of esoteric tomes, including the philosophy book, *The Everyday Man or Woman's Book of the Soul.*

Elvis found that book fascinating in particular; it indicated that not only did humans have a soul, but that the soul could be stolen, and there was a section concerning vampires and ghouls and incubi and succubi, as well as related soul suckers. Bottom line was, one of those dudes was around, you had to watch your holes. Mouth hole. Nose hole. Asshole. If you were a woman, you needed to watch a different hole. Dick pee holes and ear holes—male or female—didn't matter. The soul didn't hang out there. They weren't considered major orifices for some reason.

In the back of the book was a list of items, related and not related to the book, that you could buy. Little plastic pyramids. Hats you could wear while channeling. Subliminal tapes that would help you learn Arabic. Postage was paid.

"Every kind of soul eater is in that book except politicians and science fiction fans," Jack said. "And I think that's what we got here in Shady Rest. A soul eater. Turn to the Egyptian section."

Elvis did. The chapter was prefaced by a movie still from *The Ten Commandments* with Yul Brynner playing Pharaoh. He was standing up in his chariot looking serious, which seemed a fair enough expression, considering the red sea, which had been parted by Moses, was about to come back together and drown him and his army.

Elvis read the article slowly while Jack heated hot water with his plug-in heater and made cups of instant coffee. "I get my niece to smuggle this stuff in," said Jack. "Or she claims to be my niece. She's a black woman. I never saw her before I was shot that day in Dallas and they took my brain out. She's part of the new identity they've given me. She's got a great ass."

"Damn," said Elvis. "What it says here, is that you can bury some dude, and if he gets the right tanna leaves and spells said over him and such bullshit, he can come back to life some thousands of years later, and to stay alive, he has to suck on the souls of the living, and that if the souls are small, his life force doesn't last long. Small. What's that mean?"

"Read on . . . . No, never mind, I'll tell you." Jack handed Elvis his cup of coffee and sat down on the bed next to him. "Before I do, want a Ding-Dong? Not mine. The chocolate kind. Well, I guess mine is chocolate, now that I've been dyed."

"You got Ding-Dongs?" Elvis asked.

"Couple of Pay Days and Baby Ruth too," Jack said. "Which will it be? Let's get decadent."

Elvis licked his lips. "I'll have a Ding-Dong."

While Elvis savored the Ding-Dong, gumming it sloppily, sipping his coffee between bites, Jack, coffee cup balanced on his knee, a Baby Ruth in one mitt, expounded.

"Small souls means those without much fire for life," Jack said. "You know a place like that?"

"If souls were fires," Elvis said, "they couldn't burn much lower without being out than here. Only thing we got going in this joint is the pilot light."

"Exactamundo," Jack said. "What we got here in Shady Rest is an Egyptian soul sucker of some sort. A mummy hiding out, coming in here to feed on the slooping. It's perfect, you see. The souls are little, and don't provide him with much. If this thing comes back two or three times in a row to wrap his lips around some elder's asshole, that elder is going to die pretty soon, and who's the wiser? Our mummy may not be getting much energy out of this, way he would with big souls, but the prey is easy. A mummy couldn't be too strong, really. Mostly just husk. But we're pretty much that way ourselves. We're not too far off being mummies."

"And with new people coming in all the time," Elvis said, "he can keep this up forever, this soul robbing."

"That's right. Because that's what we're brought here for. To get us out of the way until we die. And the ones don't die first of disease, or just plain old age, he gets."

Elvis considered all that. "That's why he doesn't bother the nurses and aides and administrators? He can go unsuspected."

"That, and they're not asleep. He has to get you when you're sleeping or unconscious."

"All right, but the thing throws me, Jack, is how does an ancient Egyptian end up in an East Texas rest home, and why is he writing on shit house walls?"

"He went to take a crap, got bored, and wrote on the wall. He probably wrote on pyramid walls, centuries ago."

"What would he crap?" Elvis said. "It's not like he'd eat, is it?"

"He eats souls," Jack said, "so I assume, he craps soul residue. And what that means to me is, you die by his mouth, you don't go to the otherside, or wherever souls go. He digests the souls till they don't exist anymore—"

"And you're just so much toilet water decoration," Elvis said.

"That's the way I've got it worked out," Jack said. "He's just like anyone else when he wants to take a dump. He likes a nice clean place with a flush. They didn't have that in his time, and I'm sure he finds it handy. The writing on the walls is just habit. Maybe, to him, Pharaoh and Cleopatra were just yesterday."

Elvis finished off the Ding-Dong and sipped his coffee. He felt a rush from the sugar and he loved it. He wanted to ask Jack for the Pay Day he had mentioned, but restrained himself. Sweets, fried foods, late nights and drugs, had been the beginning of his original down-hill spiral. He had to keep himself collected this time. He had to be ready to battle the Egyptian soul sucking menace.

Soul sucking menace?

God. He *was* really bored. It was time for him to go back to his room and to bed so he could shit on himself, get back to normal.

But Jesus and Ra, this was different from what had been going on up until now! It might all be bullshit, but considering what was going on in his life right now, it was absorbing bullshit. It might be worth playing the game to the hilt, even if he was playing it with a black guy who thought he was John F. Kennedy and believed an Egyptian mummy was stalking the corridors of Shady Rest Convalescent Home, writing graffiti on toilet stalls, sucking people's souls out through their assholes, digesting them, and crapping them down the visitor's toilet.

Suddenly Elvis was pulled out of his considerations. There came from the hall the noise again. The sound that each time he heard it reminded him of something different. This time it was dried corn husks being rattled in a high wind. He felt goose bumps travel up his spine and the hairs on the back of his neck and arms stood up. He leaned forward and put his hands on his walker and pulled himself upright.

"Don't go in the hall," Jack said.

"I'm not asleep."

"That doesn't mean *it* won't hurt you."

"*It*, my ass, there isn't any mummy from Egypt."

"Nice knowing you, Elvis."

Elvis inched the walker forward. He was halfway to the open door when he spied the figure in the hallway.

As the thing came even with the doorway, the hall lights went dim and sputtered. Twisting about the apparition, like pet crows, were flutters of shadows. The thing walked and stumbled, shuffled and flowed. It's legs moved like Elvis's own, meaning not too good, and yet, there was something about it's locomotion that was impossible to identify. Stiff, but ghostly smooth. It was dressed in nasty looking jeans, a black shirt, a black cowboy hat that came down so low it covered where the thing's eyebrows should be. It wore large cowboy boots with the toes curled up, and there came from the thing a kind of mixed-stench: a compost pile of mud, rotting leaves, resin, spoiled fruit, dry dust, and gassy sewage.

Elvis found that he couldn't scoot ahead another inch. He froze. The thing stopped and cautiously turned its head on its apple stem neck and looked at Elvis with empty eye sockets, revealing that it was, in fact, uglier than Lyndon Johnson.

Surprisingly, Elvis found he was surging forward as if on a zooming camera dolly, and that he was plunging into the thing's right eye socket, which swelled speedily to the dimensions of a vast canyon bottomed by blackness.

Down Elvis went, spinning and spinning, and out of the emptiness rushed resin-scented memories of pyramids and boats on a river, hot, blue skies, and a great silver bus lashed hard by black rain, a crumbling bridge and a charge of dusky water and a gleam of silver. Then there was a darkness so caliginous it was beyond being called dark, and Elvis could feel and taste mud in his mouth and a sensation of claustrophobia beyond expression. And he could perceive the thing's hunger, a hunger that prodded him like hot pins, and then—

—there came a *popping* sound in rapid succession, and Elvis felt himself whirling even faster, spinning backwards out of that deep memory canyon of the dusty head, and now he stood once again within the framework of his walker, and the mummy—for Elvis no longer denied to himself that it was such—turned its head away and began to move again, to shuffle, to flow, to stumble, to glide, down the hall, its pet shadows screeching with rusty throats around its head. *Pop! Pop! Pop!*

As the thing moved on Elvis compelled himself to lift his walker and advance into the hall. Jack slipped up beside him, and they saw the mummy in cowboy clothes traveling toward the exit door at the back of the home. When it came to the locked door, it leaned against where the door met the jam and twisted and writhed, squeezed through the invisible crack where the two connected. Its shadows pursued it, as if sucked through by a vacuum cleaner.

The popping sound went on, and Elvis turned his head in that direction, and there, in his mask, his double concho-studded holster belted around his waist, was Kemosabe, a silver Fanner Fifty in either hand. He was popping caps rapidly at where the mummy had departed, the black spotted red rolls flowing out from behind the hammers of his revolvers in smoky relay.

"Asshole!" Kemosabe said. "Asshole!"

And then Kemosabe quivered, dropped both hands, popped a cap from each gun toward the ground, stiffened, collapsed.

Elvis knew he was dead of a ruptured heart before he hit the black and white tile; gone down and out with both guns blazing, soul intact.

The hall lights trembled back to normal.

The administrators, the nurses and the aides came then. They rolled Kemosabe over and drove their palms against his chest, but he didn't breathe again. No more Hi-Yo-Silver. They sighed over him and clucked their tongues, and finally an aide reached over and lifted Kemosabe's mask, pulled it off his head and dropped it on the floor, nonchalantly, and without respect, revealed his identity.

It was no one anyone really knew.

Once again, Elvis got scolded, and this time he got quizzed about what had happened to Kemosabe, and so did Jack, but neither told the truth. Who was going to believe a couple of nuts? Elvis and Jack Kennedy explaining that Kemosabe was gunning for a mummy in cowboy duds, a Bubba Ho-Tep with a flock of shadows roiling about his cowboy hatted head?

So, what they did was lie.

"He came snapping caps and then he fell," Elvis said, and Jack corroborated his story, and when Kemosabe had been carried off, Elvis, with some difficulty, using his walker for support, got down on his knee and picked up the discarded mask and carried it away with him. He had wanted the guns, but an aide had taken those for her four-year-old son.

Later, he and Jack learned through the grapevine that Kemosabe's roommate, an eighty-year-old man who had been in a semi-comatose condition for several years, had been found dead on the floor of his room. It was assumed Kemosabe had lost it and dragged him off his bed and onto the floor and the eighty-year-old man had kicked the bucket during the fall. As for Kemosabe, they figured he had then gone nuts when he realized what he had done, and had wandered out in the hall firing, and had a heart attack.

Elvis knew different. The mummy had come and Kemosabe had tried to protect his roommate in the only way he knew how. But instead of silver bullets, his gun smoked sulphur. Elvis felt a rush of pride in the old fart.

He and Jack got together later, talked about what they had seen, and then there was nothing left to say.

Night went away and the sun came up, and Elvis who had slept not a wink, came up with it and put on khaki pants and a khaki shirt and used his walker to go outside. It had been ages since he had been out, and it seemed strange out there, all that sunlight and the smells of flowers and the Texas sky so high and the clouds so white.

It was hard to believe he had spent so much time in his bed. Just the use of his legs with the walker these last few days had tightened the muscles, and he found he could get around better.

The pretty nurse with the grapefruit tits came outside and said: "Mr. Presley, you look so much stronger. But you shouldn't stay out too long. It's almost time for a nap and for us, to, you know . . . ."

"Fuck off, you patronizing bitch," said Elvis. "I'm tired of your shit. I'll lube my own transmission. You treat me like a baby again, I'll wrap this goddamn walker around your head."

The pretty nurse stood stunned, then went away quietly.

Elvis inched his way with the walker around the great circular drive that surrounded the home. It was a half hour later when he reached the back of the home and the door through which the mummy had departed. It was still locked, and he stood and looked at it amazed. How in hell had the mummy done that, slipping through an indiscernible chink between door and frame?

Elvis looked down at the concrete that lay at the back of the door. No clues there. He used the walker to travel toward the growth of trees out back, a growth of pin-oaks and sweet gums and hickory nut trees that shouldered on either side of the large creek that flowed behind the home.

The ground tipped sharply there, and for a moment he hesitated, then reconsidered *Well, what the fuck?* he thought.

He planted the walker and started going forward, the ground sloping ever more dramatically. By the time he reached the bank of the creek and came to a gap in the trees, he was exhausted. He had the urge to start yelling for help, but didn't want to belittle himself, not after his performance with the nurse. He knew that he had regained some of his former confidence. His cursing and abuse had not seemed cute to her that time. The words had bitten her, if only slightly. Truth was, he was going to miss her greasing his pecker.

He looked over the bank of the creek. It was quite a drop there. The creek itself was narrow, and on either side of it was a gravel-littered six-feet of shore. To his left, where the creek ran beneath a bridge, he could see where a mass of weeds and mud had gathered over time, and he could see something shiny in their midst.

Elvis eased to the ground inside his walker and sat there and looked at the water churning along. A huge woodpecker laughed in a tree nearby and a jay yelled at a smaller bird to leave his territory.

Where had ole Bubba Ho-Tep gone? Where did he come from? How in hell did he get here?

He recalled what he had seen inside the mummy's mind. The silver bus, the rain, the shattered bridge, the wash of water and mud.

Well, now wait a minute, he thought. Here we have water and mud and a bridge, though it's not broken, and there's something shiny in the midst of all those leaves and limbs and collected debris. All these items were elements of what he had seen in Bubba Ho-Tep's head. Obviously there was a connection.

But what was it?

When he got his strength back, Elvis pulled himself up and got the walker turned, and worked his way back to the home. He was covered in sweat and stiff as wire by the time he reached his room and tugged himself into bed. The blister on his dick throbbed and he unfastened his pants and eased down his underwear. The blister had refilled with pus, and it looked nastier than usual.

It's a cancer, he determined. He made the conclusion in a certain final rush. They're keeping it from me because I'm old and to them it doesn't matter. They think age will kill me first, and they are probably right.

Well, fuck them. I know what it is, and if it isn't, it might as well be.

He got the salve and doctored the pus-filled lesion, and put the salve away, and pulled up his underwear and pants, and fastened his belt.

Elvis got his TV remote off the dresser and clicked it on while he waited for lunch. As he ran the channels, he hit upon an advertisement for Elvis Presley week. It startled him. It wasn't the first time it had happened, but at the moment it struck him hard. It showed clips from his movies, *Clambake, Roustabout,* several others. All shit movies. Here he was complaining about loss of pride and how life had treated him, and now he realized he'd never had any pride and much of how life had treated him had been quite good, and the bulk of the bad had been his own fault. He wished now he'd fired his manager, Colonel Parker, about the time he got into films. The old fart had been a fool, and he had been a bigger fool for following him. He wished too he had treated Priscilla right. He wished he could tell his daughter he loved her.

Always the questions. Never the answers. Always the hopes. Never the fulfillments.

Elvis clicked off the set and dropped the remote on the dresser just as Jack came into the room. He had a folder under his arm. He looked like he was ready for a briefing at the White House.

"I had the woman who calls herself my niece come get me," he said. "She took me downtown to the newspaper morgue. She's been helping me do some research."

"On what?" Elvis said.

"On our mummy."

"You know something about him?" Elvis asked.

"I know plenty."

Jack pulled a chair up next to the bed, and Elvis used the bed's lift button to raise his back and head so he could see what was in Jack's folder.

Jack opened the folder, took out some clippings, and laid them on the bed. Elvis looked at them as Jack talked.

"One of the lesser mummies, on loan from the Egyptian government, was being circulated across the United States. You know, museums, that kind of stuff. It wasn't a major exhibit, like the King Tut exhibit some years back, but it was of interest. The mummy was flown or carried by train from state to state. When it got to Texas, it was stolen.

"Evidence points to the fact that it was stolen at night by a couple of guys in a silver bus. There was a witness. Some guy walking his dog or something. Anyway, the thieves broke in the museum and stole it, hoping to get a ransom probably. But in came the worst storm in East Texas history. Tornadoes. Rain. Hail. You name it. Creeks and rivers overflowed. Mobile homes were washed away. Livestock drowned. Maybe you remember it . . . . No matter. It was one hell of a flood.

"These guys got away, and nothing was ever heard from them. After you told me what you saw inside the mummy's head—the silver bus, the storm, the bridge, all that—I came up with a more interesting, and I believe, considerably more accurate scenario."

"Let me guess. The bus got washed away. I think I saw it today. Right out back in the creek. It must have washed up there years ago."

"That confirms it. The bridge you saw breaking, that's how the bus got in the water, which would have been as deep then as a raging river. The bus was carried downstream. It lodged somewhere nearby, and the mummy was imprisoned by debris, and recently it worked its way loose."

"But how did it come alive?" Elvis asked. "And how did I end up inside its memories?"

"The speculation is broader here, but from what I've read, sometimes mummies were buried without their names, a curse put on their sarcophagus, or coffin, if you will. My guess is our guy was one of those. While he was in the coffin, he was a drying corpse. But when the bus was washed off the road, the coffin was overturned, or broken open, and our boy was freed of coffin and curse. Or more likely, it rotted open in time, and the holding spell was broken. And think about him down there all that time, waiting for freedom, alive, but not alive. Hungry, and no way to feed. I said he was free of his curse, but that's not entirely true. He's free of his imprisonment, but he still needs souls.

"And now, he's free to have them, and he'll keep feeding unless he's finally destroyed . . . . You know, I think there's a part of him, oddly enough, that wants to fit in. To be human again. He doesn't entirely know what he's become. He responds to some old desires and the new desires of his condition. That's why he's taken on the illusion of clothes, probably copying the dress of one of his victims.

"The souls give him strength. Increase his spectral powers, One of which was to hypnotize you, kinda, draw you inside his head. He couldn't steal your soul that way, you have to be unconscious to have that done to you, but he could weaken you, distract you."

"And those shadows around him?"

"His guardians. They warn him. They have some limited powers of their own. I've read about them in the *Every Man or Woman's Book of Souls.*"

"What do we do?" Elvis said.

"I think changing rest homes would be a good idea," Jack said. "I can't think of much else. I will say this. Our mummy is a nighttime kind of guy. 3 A.M. actually. So, I'm going to sleep now, and again after lunch. Set my alarm for before dark so I can fix myself a couple cups of coffee. He comes tonight, I don't want him slapping his lips over my asshole again. I think he heard you coming down the hall about the time he got started on me the other night, and he ran. Not because he was scared, but because he didn't want anyone to find out he's around. Consider it. He has the proverbial bird's nest on the ground here."

After Jack left, Elvis decided he should follow Jack's lead and nap. Of course, at his age, he napped a lot anyway, and could fall asleep at any time, or toss restlessly for hours. There was no rhyme or reason to it.

He nestled his head into his pillow and tried to sleep, but sleep wouldn't come. Instead, he thought about things. Like, what did he really have left in life but this place? It wasn't much of a home, but it was all he had, and he'd be damned if he'd let a foreign, graffiti-writing, soul-sucking sonofabitch in an oversized hat and cowboy boots (with elf toes) take away his family member's souls and shit them down the visitors toilet.

In the movies he had always played heroic types. But when the stage lights went out, it was time for drugs and stupidity and the coveting of women. Now it was time to be a little of what he had always fantasized being.

A hero.

Elvis leaned over and got hold of his telephone and dialed Jack's room. "Mr. Kennedy," Elvis said when Jack answered. "Ask not what your rest home can do for you. Ask what you can do for your rest home."

"Hey, you're copping my best lines," Jack said.

"Well then, to paraphrase one of my own, 'Let's take care of business.'"

"What are you getting at?"

"You know what I'm getting at. We're gonna kill a mummy."

The sun, like a boil on the bright blue ass of day, rolled gradually forward and spread its legs wide to reveal the pubic thatch of night, a hairy darkness in which stars crawled like lice, and the moon crabbed slowly upward like an albino dog tick thriving for the anal gulch.

During this slow rolling transition, Elvis and Jack discussed their plans, then they slept a little, ate their lunch of boiled cabbage and meat loaf, slept some more, ate a supper of white bread and asparagus and a helping of shit on a shingle without the shingle, slept again, awoke about the time the pubic thatch appeared and those starry lice began to crawl.

And even then, with night about them, they had to wait until midnight to do what they had to do.

Jack squinted through his glasses and examined his list. "Two bottles of rubbing alcohol?" Jack said.

"Check," said Elvis. "And we won't have to toss it. Look here." Elvis held up a paint sprayer. "I found this in the storage room."

"I thought they kept it locked," Jack said.

"They do. But I stole a hair pin from Dillinger and picked the lock."

"Great!" Jack said. "Matches?"

"Check. I also scrounged a cigarette lighter."

"Good. Uniforms?"

Elvis held up his white suit, slightly greyed in spots with a chili stain on the front. A white, silk scarf, and the big gold and silver and ruby studded belt that went with the outfit lay on the bed. There were zippered boots from K-Mart. "Check."

Jack held up a grey business suit on a hanger. "I've got some nice shoes and a tie to go with it in my room."

"Check," Elvis said.

"Scissors?"

"Check."

"I've got my motorized wheelchair oiled and ready to roll," Jack said, "and I've looked up a few words of power in one of my magic books. I don't know if they'll stop a mummy, but they're supposed to ward off evil. I wrote them down on a piece of paper."

"We use what we got," Elvis said. "Well then. Two forty-five out back of the place."

"Considering our rate of travel, better start moving about two-thirty," Jack said.

"Jack," Elvis asked. "Do we know what we're doing?"

"No, but they say fire cleanses evil. Let's hope they, whoever they are, is right."

"Check on that too," said Elvis. "Synchronize watches."

They did, and Elvis added: "Remember. The key words for tonight are Caution and Flammable. And Watch Your Ass."

The front door had an alarm system, but it was easily manipulated from the inside. Once Elvis had the wires cut with the scissors, they pushed the compression lever on the door, and Jack shoved his wheelchair outside, and held the door while Elvis worked his walker through. Elvis tossed the scissors into the shrubbery, and Jack jammed a paperback book between the doors to allow them re-entry, should re-entry be an option at a later date.

Elvis was wearing a large pair of glasses with multi-colored gem-studded chocolate frames and his stained white jump suit with scarf and belt and zippered boots. The suit was open at the front and hung loose on him, except at the belly. To make it even tighter there, Elvis had made up a medicine bag of sorts, and stuffed it inside his jumpsuit. The bag contained Kemosabe's mask, Bull's purple heart, and the newspaper clipping where he had first read of his alleged death.

Jack had on his grey business suit with a black and red striped tie knotted carefully at the throat, sensible black shoes, and black nylon socks. The suit fit him well. He looked like a former president.

In the seat of the wheelchair was the paint-sprayer, filled with rubbing alcohol, and beside it, a cigarette lighter and a paper folder of matches. Jack handed Elvis the paint sprayer. A strap made of a strip of torn sheet had been added to the device. Elvis hung the sprayer over his shoulder, reached inside his belt and got out a flattened, half-smoked stogie he had been saving for a special occasion. An occasion he had begun to think would never arrive. He clenched the cigar between his teeth, picked the matches from the seat of the wheelchair, and lit his cigar. It tasted like a dog turd, but he puffed it anyway. He tossed the folder of matches back on the chair and looked at Jack, said, "Let's do it, amigo."

Jack put the matches and the lighter in his suit pocket. He sat down in the wheelchair, kicked the foot stanchions into place and rested his feet on them. He leaned back slightly and flicked a switch on the arm rest. The electric motor hummed, the chair eased forward.

"Meet you there," said Jack. He rolled down the concrete ramp, on out to the circular drive, and disappeared around the edge of the building.

Elvis looked at his watch. It was nearly two forty-five. He had to hump it. He clenched both hands on the walker and started truckin'.

Fifteen exhaustive minutes later, out back, Elvis settled in against the door, the place where Bubba Ho-Tep had been entering and exiting. The shadows fell over him like an umbrella. He propped the paint gun across the walker and used his scarf to wipe the sweat off his forehead.

In the old days, after a performance, he'd wipe his face with it and toss it to some woman in the crowd, watch as she creamed on herself. Panties and hotel keys would fly onto the stage at that point, bouquets of roses.

Tonight, he hoped Bubba Ho-Tep didn't use the scarf to wipe his ass after shitting him down the crapper.

Elvis looked where the circular concrete drive rose up slightly to the right, and there, seated in the wheelchair, very patient and still, was Jack. The moonlight spread over Jack and made him look like a concrete yard gnome.

Apprehension spread over Elvis like a dose of the measles. He thought: *Bubba Ho-Tep comes out of that creek bed, he's going to come out hungry and pissed, and when I try to stop him, he's going to jam this paint gun up my ass, then jam me and that wheelchair up Jack's ass.*

He puffed his cigar so fast it made him dizzy. He looked out at the creek bank, and where the trees gaped wide, a figure rose up like a cloud of termites, scrabbled like a crab, flowed like water, chunked and chinked like a mass of oil field tools tumbling downhill.

Its eyeless sockets trapped the moonlight and held it momentarily before permitting it to pass through and out the back of its head in irregular gold beams. The figure that simultaneously gave the impression of shambling and gliding, appeared one moment as nothing more than a shadow surrounded by more active shadows, then it was a heap of twisted brown sticks and dried mud molded into the shape of a human being, and in another moment, it was a cowboy-hatted, booted thing taking each step as if it were its last.

Halfway to the rest home it spotted Elvis, standing in the dark framework of the door. Elvis felt his bowels go loose, but he determined not to shit his only good stage suit. His knees clacked together like stalks of ribbon cane rattling in a high wind. The dog turd cigar fell from his lips.

He picked up the paint gun and made sure it was ready to spray. He pushed the butt of it into his hip and waited.

Bubba Ho-Tep didn't move. He had ceased to come forward. Elvis began to sweat more than before. His face and chest and balls were soaked. If Bubba Ho-Tep didn't come forward, their plan was fucked. They had to get him in range of the paint sprayer. The idea was he'd soak him with the alcohol, and Jack would come wheeling down from behind, flipping matches or the lighter at Bubba, catching him on fire.

Elvis said softly, "Come and get it, you dead piece of shit."

Jack had nodded off for a moment, but now he came awake. His flesh was tingling. It felt as if tiny ball bearings were being rolled beneath his skin. He looked up and saw Bubba Ho-Tep paused between the creek bank, himself, and Elvis at the door.

Jack took a deep breath. This was not the way they had planned it. The mummy was supposed to go for Elvis because he was blocking the door. But, no soap.

Jack got the matches and the cigarette lighter out of his coat pocket and put them between his legs on the seat of the chair. He put his hand on the gear box of the wheelchair, gunned it forward. He had to make things happen; had to get Bubba Ho-Tep to follow him, come within range of Elvis's spray gun.

Bubba Ho-Tep stuck out his arm and clotheslined Jack Kennedy. There was a sound like a rifle crack (no question Warren Commission, this blow was from the front), and over went the chair, and out went Jack, flipping and sliding across the driveway, the cement tearing his suit knees open, gnawing into his hide. The chair, minus its rider, tumbled over and came upright, and still rolling, veered downhill toward Elvis in the doorway, leaning on his walker, spray gun in hand.

The wheelchair hit Elvis's walker. Elvis bounced against the door, popped forward, grabbed the walker just in time, but dropped his spray gun.

He glanced up to see Bubba Ho-Tep leaning over the unconscious Jack. Bubba Ho-Tep's mouth went wide, and wider yet, and became a black toothless vacuum that throbbed pink as a raw wound in the moonlight; then Bubba Ho-Tep turned his head and the pink was not visible. Bubba Ho-Tep's mouth went down over Jack's face, and as Bubba Ho-Tep sucked, the shadows about it thrashed and gobbled like turkeys.

Elvis used the walker to allow him to bend down and get hold of the paint gun. When he came up with it, he tossed the walker aside, eased himself around, and into the wheelchair. He found the matches and the lighter there. Jack had done what he had done to distract Bubba Ho-Tep, to try and bring him down closer to the door. But he had failed. Yet by accident, he had provided Elvis with the instruments of mummy destruction, and now it was up to him to do what he and Jack had hoped to do together. Elvis put the matches inside his open chested outfit, pushed the lighter tight under his ass.

Elvis let his hand play over the wheelchair switches, as nimbly as he had once played with studio keyboards. He roared the wheelchair up the incline toward Bubba Ho-Tep, terrified, but determined, and as he rolled, in a voice cracking, but certainly reminiscent of him at his best, he began to sing "Don't Be Cruel," and within instants, he was on Bubba Ho-Tep and his busy shadows.

Bubba Ho-Tep looked up as Elvis roared into range, singing. Bubba Ho-Tep's open mouth irised to normal size, and teeth, formerly non-existent, rose up in his gums like little, black stumps. Electric locusts crackled and hopped in his empty sockets. He yelled something in Egyptian. Elvis saw the words jump out of Bubba Ho-Tep's mouth in visible hieroglyphics like dark beetles and sticks.

Elvis bore down on Bubba Ho-Tep. When he was in range, he ceased singing, and gave the paint sprayer trigger a squeeze. Rubbing alcohol squirted from the sprayer and struck Bubba Ho-Tep in the face.

Elvis swerved, screeched around Bubba Ho-Tep in a sweeping circle, came back, the lighter in his hand. As he neared Bubba, the shadows swarming around the mummy's head separated and flew high up above him like startled bats.

The black hat Bubba wore wobbled and sprouted wings and flapped away from his head, becoming what it had always been, a living shadow. The shadows came down in a rush, screeching like harpies. They swarmed over Elvis's face, giving him the sensation of skinned animal pelts—blood-side in—being dragged over his flesh.

Bubba bent forward at the waist like a collapsed puppet, bopped his head against the cement drive. His black bat hat came down out of the dark in a swoop, expanding rapidly and falling over Bubba's body, splattering it like spilled ink. Bubba blob-flowed rapidly under the wheels of Elvis's mount and rose up in a dark swell beneath the chair and through the spokes of the wheels and billowed over the front of the chair and loomed upwards, jabbing his ravaged, ever-changing face through the flittering shadows, poking it right at Elvis.

Elvis, through gaps in the shadows, saw a face like an old jack-o-lantern gone black and to rot, with jagged eyes, nose and mouth. And that mouth spread tunnel wide, and down that

* *"By the unwinking red eye of Ra!"*

tunnel-mouth Elvis could see the dark and awful forever that was Bubba's lot, and Elvis clicked the lighter to flame, and the flame jumped, and the alcohol lit Bubba's face, and Bubba's head turned baby-eye blue, flowed jet-quick away, splashed upward like a black wave carrying a blazing oil slick. Then Bubba came down in a shuffle of blazing sticks and dark mud, a tar baby on fire, fleeing across the concrete drive toward the creek. The guardian shadows flapped after it, fearful of being abandoned.

Elvis wheeled over to Jack, leaned forward and whispered: "Mr. Kennedy."

Jack's eyelids fluttered. He could barely move his head, and something grated in his neck when he did. "The President is soon dead," he said, and his clenched fist throbbed and opened, and out fell a wad of paper. "You got to get him."

Jack's body went loose and his head rolled back on his damaged neck and the moon showed double in his eyes. Elvis swallowed and saluted Jack. "Mr. President," he said.

Well, at least he had kept Bubba Ho-Tep from taking Jack's soul. Elvis leaned forward, picked up the paper Jack had dropped. He read it aloud to himself in the moonlight: "You nasty thing from beyond the dead. No matter what you think and do, good things will never come to you. If evil is your black design, you can bet the goodness of the Light Ones will kick your bad behind."

That's it? thought Elvis. That's the chant against evil from the *Book of Souls?* Yeah, right, boss. And what kind of decoder ring does that come with? Shit, it doesn't even rhyme well.

Elvis looked up. Bubba Ho-Tep had fallen down in a blue blaze, but he was rising up again, preparing to go over the lip of the creek, down to wherever his sanctuary was.

Elvis pulled around Jack and gave the wheelchair full throttle. He gave out with a rebel cry. His white scarf fluttered in the wind as he thundered forward.

Bubba Ho-Tep's flames had gone out. He was on his feet. His head was hissing grey smoke into the crisp night air. He turned completely to face Elvis, stood defiant, raised an arm and shook a fist. He yelled, and once again Elvis saw the hieroglyphics leap out of his mouth. The characters danced in a row, briefly—

—and vanished.

Elvis let go of the protective paper. It was dog shit. What was needed here was action.

When Bubba Ho-Tep saw Elvis was coming, chair geared to high, holding the paint sprayer in one hand, he turned to bolt, but Elvis was on him.

Elvis stuck out a foot and hit Bubba Ho-Tep in the back, and his foot went right through Bubba. The mummy squirmed, spitted on Elvis's leg. Elvis fired the paint sprayer, as Bubba Ho-Tep, himself, and chair, went over the creek bank in a flash of moonlight and a tumble of shadows.

Elvis screamed as the hard ground and sharp stones snapped his body like a pinata. He made the trip with Bubba

---

* *"Eat the dog dick of Anubis, you ass wipe!"*

Ho-Tep still on his leg, and when he quit sliding, he ended up close to the creek.

Bubba Ho-Tep, as if made of rubber, twisted around on Elvis's leg, and looked at him.

Elvis still had the paint sprayer. He had clung to it as if it were a life preserver. He gave Bubba another dose. Bubba's right arm flopped way out and ran along the ground and found a hunk of wood that had washed up on the edge of the creek, gripped it, and swung the long arm back. The arm came around and hit Elvis on the side of the head with the wood.

Elvis fell backwards. The paint sprayer flew from his hands. Bubba Ho-Tep was leaning over him. He hit Elvis again with the wood. Elvis felt himself going out. He knew if he did, not only was he a dead sonofabitch, but so was his soul. He would be just so much crap; no after-life for him; no reincarnation; no angels with harps. Whatever lay beyond would not be known to him. It would all end right here for Elvis Presley. Nothing left but a quick flush.

Bubba Ho-Tep's mouth loomed over Elvis's face. It looked like an open manhole. Sewage fumes came out of it.

Elvis reached inside his open jumpsuit and got hold of the folder of matches. Laying back, pretending to nod out so as to bring Bubba Ho-Tep's ripe mouth closer, he thumbed back the flap on the matches, thumbed down one of the paper sticks, and pushed the sulphurous head of the match across the black strip.

Just as Elvis felt the cloying mouth of Bubba Ho-Tep falling down on his kisser like a Venus Flytrap, the entire folder of matches ignited in Elvis's hand, burned him and made him yell.

The alcohol on Bubba's body called the flames to it, and Bubba burst into a stalk of blue flame, singeing the hair off Elvis's head, scorching his eyebrows down to nubs, blinding him until he could see nothing more than a scalding white light.

Elvis realized that Bubba Ho-Tep was no longer on or over him, and the white light became a stained white light, then a grey light, and eventually, the world, like a Polaroid negative developing, came into view, greenish at first, then full of the night's colors.

Elvis rolled on his side and saw the moon floating in the water. He saw too a scarecrow floating in the water, the straw separating from it, the current carrying it away.

No, not a scarecrow. Bubba Ho-tep. For all his dark magic and ability to shift, or to appear to shift, fire had done him in, or had it been the stupid words from Jack's book on souls? Or both?

It didn't matter. Elvis got up on one elbow and looked at the corpse. The water was dissolving it more rapidly and the current was carrying it away.

Elvis fell over on his back. He felt something inside him grate against something soft. He felt like a water balloon with a hole poked in it.

He was going down for the last count, and he knew it.

But I've still got my soul, he thought. Still mine. All mine. And the folks in Shady Rest, Dillinger, the Blue Yodeler, all of them, they have theirs, and they'll keep 'em.

Elvis stared up at the stars between the forked and twisted boughs of an oak. He could see a lot of those beautiful stars, and he realized now that the constellations looked a little like the outlines of great hieroglyphics. He turned away from where he was looking, and to his right, seeming to sit on the edge of the bank, were more stars, more hieroglyphics.

He rolled his head back to the figures above him, rolled to the right and looked at those. Put them together in his mind.

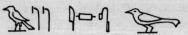

He smiled. Suddenly, he thought he could read hieroglyphics after all, and what they spelled out against the dark beautiful night was simple, and yet profound.

ALL IS WELL.

Elvis closed his eyes and did not open them again.

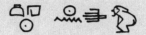

THE END

Thanks to

(Mark Nelson) for translating East Texas "Egyptian" Hieroglyphics.

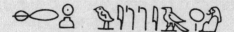

For Chet Williamson

MAN WITH TWO LIVES

It was July the Fourth and Nacogdoches, the oldest town in Texas, was hung with banners declaring the holiday. The old man read them and continued walking. He was not in a festive mood at all. It was too hot and he was too old. He continued around the square toward the general store.

Yes, too hot and too old, but he kept going full steam ahead, for this was how he had always lived, and he knew no other way.

Sometimes, especially when it was hot he had noticed, he thought perhaps it would have been better had he really died in that saloon facedown on the card table; really been buried in a good hard box in that dark, rocky ground.

Certainly it would have been better than this. Less painful than this; wasting away of old age, being a man out of place and time, a nobody. Considering the fact that in his first life he had been very important made this all the worse.

Once he had carried a brace of revolvers, but now it was all he could do to carry himself down the street.

Once his calm voice was enough to quiet violent men in a Wild West saloon, but now he did well to talk above the screams of his grandchildren.

Sometimes he considered telling family and friends who he really was. But who would believe him? They would think he had finally gone over the lip.

No. They would not believe him and there was no way for him to prove otherwise. Even digging up the grave wouldn't help. Inside they would find a rotted corpse, and though not his, how would he prove to the contrary? There just wasn't any way he could convince people he was that famous man about whom stories were told and books were written.

John Spradley, sheriff of Nacogdoches, strolled by and nodded at him. "How're you doing, Jim?"

"Fine, fine," he said, but wanted to yell, "Miserable, that's how I'm doing. I was a famous man in my time and now no one even knows who I am."

But he said nothing beyond his false reply. Just walked on, toting his memories like a peddler toting his sack.

God, but it was hard to believe he had begun a new life thirty-eight years ago. Here it was 1914 and he remembered that day as if it were yesterday. He should. He had had the rare honor of attending his own funeral and walking away.

In those days he had been a famous gunhand, a man known far and wide as a great pistoleer. But his hand was slowing and his eyes were dimming. Not so unusual for a man in his late thirties, but very disconcerting for a man whose life depended on the speed of his draw, the accuracy of his aim.

He was in Dakota Territory in those days, and as always, his reputation had proceeded him. It was a newly formed mining town where he stopped, and immediately his arrival set some concerned parties to buzzing. In the past he had had a reputation as a town tamer, and that just wouldn't do. Not when a handful of folks had it going good for them with illicit gambling and vice. They feared he'd clean up the town, institute law and order.

Rumor of that got around to him and he chuckled. No, he was through cleaning up towns, he'd had his fill of town marshaling. But he decided to use that to his advantage.

There was a guy named Varnes who probably had the biggest bite in the town, and more to lose than anyone should law and order be established and enforced. He went directly to Varnes and did not mince words.

"Varnes," he had said, "I'll tell you this, and tell you straight. I'm thinking about cleaning up this rathole and making it decent. But I can make a deal with you. I'm a bit tired of all this, and to tell you the truth, I fear this just might be my last camp. So, before one of your hired guns kills me, I'm going to arrange it so you can get it done proper."

He could still remember the way Varnes looked at him, mouth open, eyes startled.

"No," he told Varnes, "I'm not about to commit suicide. I won't make it that easy for you, but I do have a plan. A plan that'll leave the town to you and free me of my reputation."

The plan was simple: Varnes was to help him fake his death. For insurance, in case Varnes decided to make it for real, Varnes was to sign out a statement of his involvement beforehand and leave it with Charlie Utter, a friend of Jim's. Once the deal was pulled off, Charlie was to return the paper to Varnes to do as he chose.

If Charlie did not return the paper, and should Varnes appear to be in hot water, he could always have the body exhumed to prove that the man in question was not there, and had not actually been murdered.

To do the deed, and to keep his hands out of it, Varnes had hired a cross-eyed drunk to do the shooting; gave him a snootful of whiskey and a gun full of defective cartridges, though the one that would fall under the hammer was designed to go pop. That would make the assassination appear real to any witnesses in the saloon.

The old man laughed thinking back on it. He remembered how he had sat with his back to the door for the first time ever, and how right on schedule the drunk had entered and walked up behind him. "Take that," the drunk had said pulling and firing his pistol, and he, the great gunman, who had some acting experience from a Wild West show, fell forward on the table with a moan.

So he lay there on his side until the doctor came in—a man on Varnes's payroll. The doctor quickly pronounced him dead, and with the aid of Charlie, carried him away.

A few days later, after hiding out in Charlie's tent, playing hand after hand of poker, he had to perform an even greater acting job—be the corpse at his own funeral.

Charlie, the doctor and Varnes helped him into a coffin and carried him out to be put on display. It was an odd feeling to have all those people passing by, and him trying to concentrate on shallow breathing and not moving a muscle, but Charlie had holped by not allowing viewers to linger, kept saying, "Move on, please, there are a lot of folks that want to pay their respects." He could still hear some of the talking as they passed.

"Isn't he lifelike?"

"He has a smile on his lips."

"Oh, did you see that? Didn't he breathe?"

"Hell no, he didn't breathe. He's dead and he looks it."

"Prettiest corpse I've ever seen."

And then they placed the lid on him and put him six feet down, with Charlie and Varnes supervising.

It was no mean trick to relax in the darkness, breathe easily and calmly while dirt clods sounded on the lid of the box, while it grew warm and sweaty within. He still remembered that moment, remembered wanting to kick and yell, scream out, "The deal is off!"

But he had remained calm, and shortly thereafter he heard the sound of spades, then hands on the box, and up he came.

Once out of the coffin, he had Charlie return Varnes's affidavit, and made Charlie promise to let him, "stay dead."

"You've got it, old pard," Charlie told him. "You're a corpse from here out."

And Charlie had lived by his word. For that matter, so had Varnes. And why not? He had gotten what he wanted most, control of Deadwood, and to reveal that the great gunman was still alive would have made him a fool.

A few years later Jim had read a newspaper account of "his" body having been dug up—due to the expansion of Deadwood—and reburied. The body had been examined for some ghoulish reason, and good old Charlie had been on hand to state that "The body still maintained its features, and even the pleatings in the dress shirt were intact."

Since there were a number of witnesses present, Jim wondered just whose body Charlie had put in that coffin to substitute for him. He sort of hoped it was Varnes.

Yes, Charlie had been a true friend to the end. And perhaps that was what he missed most, friends like Charlie. He had never seen him again after that day at the grave site, for he had left Deadwood, shaved his mustache, cut his long hair, and ventured down South to eventually end up in Nacogdoches, Texas.

If anyone had told him that someday he'd give up his guns and meet up with some Texas farm girl and become a farmer, he'd have shot them on the spot. But that was exactly what had happened. He and Mattie had married, raised a beautiful daughter who married in turn and was raising his two lovely grandchildren, a boy and a girl.

Sometimes he wished he'd told Mattie who he really was instead of making up a past for her. She would have believed him.

But he hadn't told her, and now she was gone.

God, but he missed her.

He strolled into the general store and bought a bag of hard rock candy and a few peppermints.

"Thank you, Mr. Butler," the storekeeper said.

"You're welcome," Jim said, and he strolled out, thinking in my prime folks used to stand and stare when I walked in. Not only because of my reputation as a gunman, but because I was a fine figure of a man, tall and clear-eyed. Now I'm bent and half blind and do good to get a nod and a smile.

Sometimes he wished he'd really died that day in Deadwood, gone out at the top of his form.

He walked around the square and headed north down the treelined streets, toward his daughter's house.

After a while he stepped into her yard and started for the door, sighing heavily as he went.

"Grandpa!" came a voice from the side of the house. Turning, he saw nine-year-old Jimmy darting toward him, and not far behind came his five-year-old granddaughter Lottie, who was now saying, "Gwanpa, Gwanpa," fast as revolver fire.

Stooping, his old bones creaking as he did, he took them in his arms, hugged them close.

"What you got in the sack, Grandpa?" Jimmy asked. "What you got?"

"Sack?" the old man said, as though he had not noticed it before. "What sack?"

"Oh, Grandpa," Jimmy said.

"Oh, Gwanpa," Lottie echoed.

Jim laughed and stood, opened his bag and poured candy into the two sets of hands that greedily reached up.

132

"You'll spoil them," came a voice, and he turned to see his daughter standing in the doorway. My, but she was the spitting image of her mother, a beautiful woman. Especially with her hands on her hips like that, and that half-concerned look on her face.

"I certainly hope so," Jim said. "What grandbabies are for."

She smiled. "Children, put the candy up until after supper. Come into this house, all three of you. Let's eat. Right now! Time for supper."

The children ran ahead of him, and he watched them with pride. Following them inside, he went to the dinner table, hung his hat on the back of a chair as he sat. His son-in-law, Bob, was already at the table and he said, "Hi, Dad. Got your favorite today, mashed potatoes."

"Bring 'em on," the old man said with a grin.

After dinner, while June washed the dishes and Bob fed the chickens out back, he seated himself on the front porch swing and lit his pipe.

The evening had brought a bit of a cool spell with it, and it was a comfortable contrast to the muggy heat of the earlier day.

The grandchildren came out on the porch to bathe in the aroma of his pipe smoke. Little Lottie, making quite a chore of it, climbed up on his knee and hugged him. Jimmy sat beside him on the swing.

"Going to stay the night, Grandpa?" Jimmy asked.

"I think so."

Somewhere, not far away, a horde of firecrackers went off in celebration of the Fourth of July. They sounded like gunfire, and for a moment the old man's thoughts went back to the old days; back to when he had pulled his revolvers and heard them sing.

Yes, sometimes he wished he had died that day in the Ten Spot saloon.

"I wuv you Gwanpa," Lottie said.

And sometimes not, he thought smiling at the pretty little girl.

"Grandpa," Jimmy said, "tell us a story."

The old man smiled, and said in a conspiratorial whisper, "I'll tell you a story, a secret one. Did you know that I'm really Wild Bill Hickok?"

"Oh Grandpa," Jimmy said. "He's dead."

The old man laughed again. "Yes," he said taking Lottie under one arm and Jimmy under the other. "I suppose he is."

"I wuv you Gwanpa," Lottie repeated.

"And I love you too," the old man said, and he told them a story. But it had nothing to do with Wild Bill Hickok.

PILOTS

JOE R. LANSDALE AND
DAN LOWRY

Micky was at it again. His screams echoed up the fuse-
lage, blended with the wind roaring past the top gunner port.
The Pilot released Sparks from his radio duty long enough to
send him back to take care of and comfort Micky.

The day had passed slowly and they had passed it in the
hanger, listening to the radio, taking turns at watch from the
tower, making battle plans. Just after sundown they got into
their gear and took off, waited high up in cover over the
well-traveled trade lanes. Waited for prey.

Tonight they intended to go after a big convoy. Get as
many kills as they could, then hit the smaller trade lanes later
on, search and destroy. With luck their craft would be covered
with a horde of red kill marks before daybreak. At the thought
of that, the Pilot formed the thing he used as a mouth into a
smile. He was the one who painted the red slashes on the sides

of their machine (war paint), and it was a joy to see them grow. It was his hope that someday they would turn the craft from black to red.

Finally the Pilot saw the convoy. He called to Sparks.

In the rear, Micky was settled down to sobs and moans, had pushed the pain in the stumps of his legs aside, tightened his will to the mission at hand.

As Sparks came forward at a stoop, he reached down and patted Ted, the turret gunner, on the flight jacket, then settled back in with the radio.

"It's going to be a good night for hunting," Sparks said to the Pilot. "I've been intercepting enemy communiques. There must be a hundred in our operational area. There are twelve in the present enemy convoy, sir. Most of the state escorts are to the north, around the scene of last night's sortie."

The Pilot nodded, painfully formed the words that came out of his fire-gutted throat. "It'll be a good night, Sparks. I can feel it."

"Death to the enemy," Sparks said. And the words were repeated as one by the crew.

So they sat high up, on the overpass, waiting for the convoy of trucks to pass below.

"This is the Tulsa Tramp. You got the Tulsa Tramp. Have I got a copy there? Come back."

"That's a big 10-4, Tramp. You got the L.A. Flash here."

"What's your 20, L.A.?"

"East bound and pounded down on this I-20, coming up on that 450 marker. How 'bout yourself, Tramp?"

"West bound for Dallas town with a truck load of cakes. What's the Smokey situation? Come back?"

"Got one at the Garland exit. Big ole bear. How's it look over your shoulder?"

"Got it clear, L.A., clear back to that Hailsville town. You got a couple County Mounties up there at the Owentown exit."

"Where's all the super troopers?"

"Haven't you heard, Tramp?"

"Heard what, L.A.? Come back."

"Up around I-30, that Mount Pleasant town. Didn't you know about Banana Peel?"

"Don't know Banana Peel. Come back with it."

"Black Bird got him."

"Black Bird?"

"You have been out of it."

"Been up New York way for a while, just pulled down and loaded up at Birmingham, heading out to the West Coast."

"Some psycho's knocking off truckers. Banana Peel was the last one. Someone's been nailing us right and left. Banana Peel's cab was shot to pieces, just like the rest. Someone claims he saw the car that got Banana Peel. A black Thunderbird, all cut down and rigged special. Over-long looking. Truckers have got to calling it the Black Bird. There's even rumor it's a ghost. Watch out for it."

"Ghosts don't chop down and rerig Thunderbirds. But I'll sure watch for it."

"10-4 on that. All we need is some nut case messing with us. Business is hard enough as it is."

"A big 10-4 there. Starting to fade, catch you on the flip-flop."

"10-4."

"10-4. Puttin' the pedal to the metal and gone."

The Tramp, driving a White Freight Liner equipped with shrunken head dangling from the cigarette-lighter knob and a men's magazine foldout taped to the cab ceiling, popped a Ronny Milsap tape into the deck, sang along with three songs, and drowned Milsap out.

It was dead out there on the highway. Not a truck or car in sight. No stars above. Just a thick black cloud cover with a moon hidden behind it.

Milsap wasn't cutting it. Tramp pulled out the tape and turned on the stereo, found a snappy little tune he could whistle along with. For some reason he felt like whistling, like making noise. He wondered if it had something to do with the business L.A. had told him about. The Black Bird.

Or perhaps it was just the night. Certainly was unusual for the Interstate to be this desolate, this dead. It was as if his were the only vehicle left in the world . . . .

He saw something. It seemed to have appeared out of nowhere, had flicked beneath the orangish glow of the upcoming underpass lights. It looked like a car running fast without lights.

Tramp blinked. Had he imagined it? It had been so quick. Certainly only a madman would be crazy enough to drive that fast on the Interstate without lights.

A feeling washed over him that was akin to pulling out of a dive; like when he was in Nam and he flew down close to the foliage to deliver flaming death, then at the last moment he would lift his chopper skyward and leave the earth behind him in a burst of red-yellow flame. Then, cruising the Vietnamese skies, he could only feel relief that his hands had responded and he had not been peppered and salted all over Nam.

Tramp turned off the stereo and considered. A bead of sweat balled on his upper lip. *Perhaps he had just seen the Black Bird.*

" . . . ought to be safe in a convoy this size . . . " the words filtered out of Tramp's CB. He had been so lost in thought, he had missed the first part of the transmission. He turned it up. The chatter was furious. It was a convoy and its members were exchanging thoughts, stories, and good time rattle like a bunch of kids swapping baseball cards.

The twangy, scratchy voices were suddenly very comfortable; forced memories of Nam back deep in his head, kept that black memory-bat from fluttering.

He thought again of what he might have seen. But now he had passed beneath the underpass and there was nothing. No car. No shape in the night. Nothing.

Imagination, he told himself. He drove on, listening to the CB.

The bead of sweat rolled cold across his lips and down his chin.

Tramp wasn't the only one who had seen something in the shadows, something like a car without lights. Sloppy Joe, the convoy's back door, had glimpsed an odd shape in his sideview mirror, something coming out of the glare of the overpass lights, something as sleek and deadly-looking as a hungry barracuda.

"Breaker 1-9, this is Sloppy Joe, your back door."

"Ah, come ahead, back door, this is Pistol Pete, your front door. Join the conversation."

"Think I might have something here. Not sure. Thought I saw something in the sideview, passing under those overpass lights."

Moments of silence.

"You say, think you saw? Come back."

"Not sure. If I did, it was running without lights."

"Smokey?" another trucker asked.

"Don't think so . . . Now wait a minute. I see something now. A pair of dim, red lights."

"Uh oh, cop cherries," a new trucker's voice added.

"No. Not like that."

Another moment of silence.

Sloppy Joe again: "Looks a little like a truck using nothing but its running lights . . . but they're hung too far down
for that . . . and they're shaped like eyes."

"Eyes! This is Pistol Pete, come back."

"Infrared lights, Pistol Pete, that's what I'm seeing."

"Have . . . have we got the Black Bird here?"

Tramp, listening to the CB, felt that pulling out of a div
sensation again. He started to reach for his mike, tell them
he was their back door, but he clenched the wheel harder
instead. No. He was going to stay clear of this. What could
a lone car—if in fact it was a car—do to a convoy of big trucks
anyway?

The CB chattered.

"This is Sloppy Joe. Those lights are moving up fast."

"The Black Bird?" asked Pistol Pete.

"Believe we got a big positive on that."

"What can he do to a convoy of trucks anyway," said
another trucker.

My sentiments exactly, thought Tramp.

"*Pick you off one by one,*" came a voice made of smoke and
hot gravel.

"What, back door?"

"Not me, Pistol Pete."

"Who? Bear Britches? Slipped Disk? Merry—"

"*None of them. It's me, the Black Bird.*"

"This is Sloppy Joe. It's the Black Bird, all right. Closing
on my tail, pulling alongside."

"Watchyerself!"

"I can see it now . . . running alongside . . . I can make out
some slash marks—"

"*Confirmed kills,*" said the Pilot. "*If I were an artist, I'd
paint little trucks.*"

"Back door, back door! This is Pistol Pete. Come in."

"Sloppy Joe here . . . . There's a man with a gun in the sunroof."

"Run him off the road, Sloppy Joe! Ram him!"

Tramp, his window down, cool breeze blowing against his face, heard three quick, flat snaps. Over the whine of the wind and the roar of the engine, they sounded not unlike the rifle fire he had heard over the wind and the rotor blades of his copter in Nam. And he thought he had seen the muzzle blast of at least one of those shots. Certainly he had seen something light up the night.

"I'm hit! Hit!" Sloppy Joe said.

"What's happening? Come back, Sloppy Joe. This is Pistol Pete. What's happening?"

"Hit . . . can't keep on the road."

"Shut down!"

Tramp saw an arc of flame fly high and wide from the dark T-bird—which looked like little more than an elongated shadow racing along the highway—and strike Sloppy Joe's truck. The fire boomed suddenly, licked the length of the truck, blossomed in the wind. A molotov, thought Tramp.

Tramp pulled over, tried to gear down. Cold sweat popped on his face like measles, his hands shook on the wheel.

Sloppy Joe's Mack had become a quivering, red flower of flame. It whipped its tail, jackknifed, and flipped, rolled like a toy truck across the concrete highway divider. When it stopped rolling, it was wrapped in fire and black smoke, had transformed from glass and metal to heat and wreckage.

The Bird moved on, slicing through the smoke, avoiding debris, blending with the night like a dark ghost.

As Tramp passed the wrecked truck he glimpsed something moving in the cab, a blackened, writhing thing that had once been human. But it moved only for an instant and was still.

Almost in a whisper, came: "This is Bear Britches. I'm the back door now. Sloppy Joe's in flames . . . . Gone . . . ."

Those flames, that burnt-to-a-crisp body, sent Tramp back in time, back to Davy Cluey and that hot-as-hell afternoon in Nam. Back to when God gave Tramp his personal demon.

They had been returning from a routine support mission, staying high enough to avoid small arms fire. Their rockets and most of their M-60 ammo were used up. The two choppers were scurrying back to base when they picked up the urgent call. The battered remains of a platoon were pinned down on a small hill off Highway One. If the stragglers didn't get a dust-off in a hurry, the Cong were going to dust them off for good.

He and Davy had turned back to aid the platoon, and soon they were twisting and turning in the air like great dragonflies performing a sky ballet. The Cong's fire buzzed around them.

Davy sat down first and the stranded Marines rushed the copter. That's when the Cong hit.

Why they hadn't waited until he too was on the ground he'd never know. Perhaps the sight of all those Marines—far too many to cram into the already heavily manned copter—was just too tempting for patience. The Cong sent a stream of liquid fire rolling lazily out of the jungle, and it had entered Davy's whirling rotors. When it hit the blades it suddenly transformed into a spinning parasol of flames.

That was his last sight of the copter and Davy. He had lifted upward and flown away. To this day, the image of that machine being showered by flames came back to him in vivid detail. Sometimes it seemed he was no longer driving on the highway, but flying in Nam. The rhythmic beat of the tires rolling over tar strips in the highway would pick up tempo until they became the twisting chopper blades, and soon, out beyond the windshield, the highway would fade and the cement would become the lush jungles of Nam.

Sometimes, the feeling was so intense he'd have to pull over until it passed.

A CB voice tossed Nam out of Tramp's head.

"This is Bear Britches. The Bird is moving in on me."

"Pistol Pete here. Get away, get away."

"He's alongside me now. Can't shake him. Something sticking out of a hole in the trunk—a rifle barrel!"

A shot could be heard clearly over the open airways, then the communications button was released and there was silence. Ahead of him Tramp could see the convoy and he could see the eighteen-wheeler that was its back door. The truck suddenly swerved, as if to ram the Black Bird, but Tramp saw a red burst leap from the Bird's trunk, and instantly the eighteen-wheeler was swerving back, losing control. It crossed the meridian, whipping its rear end like a crocodile's tail, plowed through a barbed-wire fence, and smacked a row of pine trees with a sound like a thunderclap. The cab smashed up flat as a pancake. Tramp knew no one could have lived through that.

And now ahead of him, Tramp saw another molotov flipping through the air, and in an instant, another truck was out of commission, wearing flames and flipping in a frenzy along the side of the road. Tramp's last memory of the blazing truck was its tires, burning brightly, spinning wildly around and around like little inflamed ferris wheels.

"Closing on me," came a trucker's voice. "The sonofabitch is closing on me. Help me! God, someone help me here."

Tramp remembered a similar communication from Davy that day in Nam; the day he had lifted up to the sky and flown his bird away and left Davy there beneath that parasol of fire.

Excited chatter sounded over the air waves as the truckers tried to summon up the highway boys, tried to call for help.

Tramp saw a sign for a farmroad exit, half a mile away. The stones settled in his gut again, his hands filmed with sweat. It was like that day in Nam, when he had the choice to turn back and help or run like hell.

No trucks took the exit. Perhaps their speed was up too much to attempt it. But he was well back of them and the Bird. What reason did he have to close in on the Bird? What could he do? As it was, the Bird could see his lights now and they might pop a shot at him any second.

Tramp swallowed. It was him or them.

He slowed, took the exit at fifty, which was almost too fast, and the relief that first washed over him turned sour less than a second later. He felt just like he had that day in Nam when he had lifted up and away, saved himself from Death at the expense of Davy.

"Report!" said the Pilot.

Through the headphones came Micky's guttural whine. "Tail gunner reporting, sir. Three of the enemy rubbed out, sir."

"Confirmed," came the voice of the turret gunner. "I have visual confirmation on rear gunners report. Enemy formation affecting evasive maneuvers. Have sighted two more sets of enemy lights approaching on the port quarter. Request permission to break off engagement with forward enemy formation and execute strafing attack on approaching formation."

"Permission granted," said the Pilot. "Sparks! Report State Escort wherebouts."

"Catching signals of approaching State Escorts, sir. ETA three minutes."

"Number of Escorts?"

"Large squadron, sir."

"Pilot to flight crew. Change in orders. Strafe forward formation, to prepare to peel off at next exit."

The Bird swooped down on the forward truck, the turret gun slamming blast after blast into the semi's tires. The truck was suddenly riding on the rims. Steel hit concrete and sparks popped skyward like overheated fireflys.

The Bird moved around the truck just as it lost control and went through a low guardrail fence and down into a deep ditch.

Black smoke boiled up from the Black Bird's tires, mixed with the night. A moment later the sleek car was running alongside another truck. The turret gunner's weapon barked like a nervous dog, kept barking as it sped past the trucks and made its way to the lead semi. The turret gunner barked a few more shots as they whipped in front of the truck, and the tail gunner put twenty fast rounds through the windshield. Even as the driver slumped over the semi's wheel and the truck went barreling driverless down the highway, the Bird lost sight of it and took a right exit, and like a missile, was gone.

Black against black, the Bird soared, and inside the death machine the Pilot, with the internal vision of his brain, turned the concrete before him into a memory:

Once he had been whole, a tall young man with a firm body and a head full of technicolor dreams. The same had been true of his comrades. There had been a time when these dreams had been guiding lights. They had wanted to fly, had been like birds in the nest longing for the time when they would try their wings; thinking of that time, living for that time when they would soar in silver arrows against a fine blue sky, or climb high up to the face of the moon.

Each of them had been in the Civil Air Patrol. Each of them had hours of air time, and each of them had plans for the Air Force. And these plans had carried them through many a day and through many a hard exam and they had talked these plans until they felt they were merely reciting facts from a future they had visited.

But then there was the semi and that very dark night.

The four of them had been returning from Barksdale Air Force Base. They had made a deal with the recruiter to keep them together throughout training, and their spirits were high.

And the driver who came out of the darkness, away from the honky-tonk row known as Hell's Half Mile, had been full of spirits too.

There had been no lights, just a sudden looming darkness that turned into a White Freight Liner crossing the middle of the highway; a stupid, metallic whale slapdash in the center of their path.

The night screamed with an explosion of flesh, metal, glass, and chrome. Black tire smoke boiled to the heavens and down from the heavens came a rain of sharp, hot things that engulfed the four; and he, the one now called the Pilot, awoke to whiteness. White everywhere, and it did not remind him of cleanliness, this whiteness. No. It was empty, this whiteness, empty like the ever-hungry belly of time; people floated by him in white, not angel-white, but wraith-white; and the pain came to live with him and it called his body home.

When enough of the pain had passed and he was fully aware, he found a monster one morning in the mirror. A one-legged thing with a face and body like melted plastic. But the eyes. Those sharp hawk eyes that had anticipated seeing the world from the clouds, were as fine as ever; little green gems that gleamed from an overcooked meat rind.

And the others:

Sparks had lost his left arm and half his head was metal. He had been castrated by jagged steel. Made sad jokes about being the only man who could keep his balls in a plastic bag beside his bed.

Ted had metal clamps on his legs and a metal jaw. His scalp had been peeled back like an orange. Skin grafts hadn't worked. Too burned. From now on, across his head—like some sort of toothless mouth—would be a constantly open wound behind which a smooth, white skull would gleam.

Micky was the worst. Legs fried off. One eye cooked to boiled egg consistency—a six-minute egg. Face like an exploding sore. Throat and vocal cords nearly gone. His best sound was a high, piercing whine.

Alone they were fragments of humanity. Puzzle parts of a horrid whole.

Out of this vengeance grew.

They took an old abandoned silo on Spark's farm—inherited years back when his father had died—fixed it up to suit their needs; had the work done and used Spark's money.

They also pooled their accounts, and with the proper help, they had elevators built into the old gutted silo. Had telescopes installed. Radios. And later they bought maps and guns. Lots of guns. They bought explosives and made super molotovs of fuel and plastic explosives. Bad business.

And the peculiar talents that had been theirs individually, became a singular thing that built gadgets and got things done. So before long, the Pilot, stomping around on his metallic leg, looking like a run-through-the-wringer Ahab, became their boss. They cut Micky's T-bird down and rerigged it, rebuilt it as a war machine. And they began to kill. Trucks died on the highway, became skeletons, black charred frames. And the marks on the sides of the Black Bird grew and grew as they went about their stalks . . . .

Highway now. Thoughts tucked away. Cruising easily along the concrete sky. Pilot and crew.

Tramp felt safe, but he also felt low, real low. He kept wondering about Nam, about the trucks, about that turnoff he'd taken a few miles and long minutes back, but his considerations were cut short when fate took a hand.

To his left he saw eyes, red eyes, wheeling out of a dark connecting road, and the eyes went from dim to sudden-bright (fuck this sneaking around), and as Tramp passed that road, the eyes followed, and in the next instant they were looking up his tailpipe, and Tramp knew damn good and well whose eyes they were, and he was scared.

Cursing providence, Tramp put the pedal to the metal and glanced into his sideview mirror and saw the eyes were very close. Then he looked forward and saw that the grade was climbing. He could feel the truck losing momentum. The Bird was winging around on the left side.

The hill was in front of him now, and though he had the gas pedal to the floor, things were Slow-City, and the truck was chugging, and behind him, coming ass-over-tires, was the Black Bird.

Tramp trembled, thought: This is redemption. The thought hung in his head like a shoe on a peg. It was another chance for him to deal the cards and deal them right.

Time started up for Tramp again, and he glanced into the sideview mirror at the Bird, whipped his truck hard left in a wild move that nearly sent the White Freight Liner side-over-side. He hit the Bird a solid bump and drove it off the road, almost into a line of trees. The Bird's tires spat dirt and grass in dark gouts. The Bird slowed, fell back.

Tramp cheered, tooted his horn like a madman, and made that hill; two toots at the top and he dipped over the rise and gave two toots at the bottom.

The Black Bird made the road again and the Pilot gave the car full throttle. In a moment the Bird found its spot on Tramp's ass.

Tramp's moment of triumph passed. That old Boogy Man sat down on his soul again. Sweat dripped down his face and hung on his nose like a dingleberry on an ass hair, finally fell with a plop on the plastic seat cover between Tramp's legs, and in the fearful silence of the cab the sound was like a boulder dropping on hard ground.

Tramp's left side window popped and became a close-weave net of cracks and clusters. A lead wasp jumped around the cab and died somewhere along the floorboard. It was a full five seconds before Tramp realized he'd been grazed across the neck, just under his right ear. The glass from the window began to fall out like slow, heavy rain.

Tramp glanced left and saw the Bird was on him again, and he tried to whip in that direction, tried to nail the bastard again. But the Bird wasn't having any. It moved forward and away, surged around in front of Tramp.

The Bird, now directly in front of him, farted a red burst from its trunk. The front window of the truck became a spiraling web and the collar of Tramp's shirt lifted as if plucked by an unseen hand. The bullet slammed into the seat and finally into the back wall of the truck.

The glass was impossible to see out of. Tramp bent forward and tried to look out of a small area of undamaged windshield. The Bird's gun farted again, and Tramp nearly lost control as fragments flew in on him like shattered moonlight. Something hot and sharp went to live in his right shoulder, down deep next to the bone. Tramp let out a scream and went momentarily black, nearly lost the truck.

Carving knives of wind cut through the windshield and woke him, watered his eyes, and made the wound ache like a bad tooth. He thought: The next pop that comes I won't hear, because that will be the one that takes my skull apart, and they say the one that gets you is the one you don't hear.

But suddenly the two asslights of the Bird fell away and dipped out of sight.

The road fell down suddenly into a dip, and though it was not enormous, he had not expected it and his speed was up full tilt. The truck cab lifted into the air and shot forward and dragged the whipping cargo trailer behind it. As the cab came down, Tramp fully expected the trailer to keep whipping and jackknife him off the road, but instead it came down and fell in line behind the cab and Tramp kept going.

Ahead a narrow bridge appeared, its suicide rails painted phosphorescent white. The bridge appeared just wide enough to keep the guardrail post from slicing the door handles off a big truck.

Tramp's hand flew to the gear shift. He shifted and gassed and thought: This is it, the moment of truth, the big casino, die dog or eat the hatchet; my big shot to repay the big fuckup. Tramp shifted again and gave the White Freight Liner all it had.

The White Freight Liner was breathing up the tailpipe of the Black Bird and the Pilot was amazed at how much speed the driver was getting out of that rig; a part of him appreciated the skill involved in that. No denying, that sonofabitch could drive.

Then the Pilot caught a scream in his ruptured throat. They were coming up on the bridge, and there were no lefts or rights to take them away from that. The bridge was narrow. Tight. Room for one, and the Pilot knew what the truck driver had in mind. The truck was hauling ass, pushing to pass, trying to run alongside the Bird, planning to push it through the rails and down twenty feet into a wet finale of fast-racing creek. The senseless bastard was going to try and get the Bird if he had to go with it.

The Pilot smiled. He could understand that. He smelled death, and it had the odor of gasoline fumes, burning rubber, and flying shit.

Behind the Bird, like a leviathan of the concrete seas, came the White Freight Liner. It bumped the Bird's rear and knocked the car to the right, and in that moment, the big truck, moving as easily as if it were a compact car, came around on the Bird's left.

The semi began to bear right, pushing at the Bird. The Pilot knew his machine was fated to kiss the guardrail post.

"Take the wheel!" the Pilot screamed to Sparks, and he rose up to poke his head through the sunroof, pull on through, and crawl along top. He grabbed the semi's left sideview mirror and allowed the truck's momentum to pull him away from the car, keeping his good and his ruined leg high to keep from being pinched in half between the two machines.

Sparks leaped for the steering wheel, got a precious grip on it even as the Pilot was dangling on top of the car, reaching for the truck's mirror frame. But Sparks saw immediately that his grabbing the wheel meant nothing. He and the others were goners; he couldn't get the Bird ahead of the truck and there just wasn't room for two, they were scraping the guardrail post as it was, and now he felt the Bird going to the right and it hit the first post with a *kaplodata* sound, then the car gathered in three more posts, and just for an instant, Sparks thought he might be able to keep the Bird on the bridge, get ahead of the semi. But it was a fleeting fancy. The Bird's right wheels were out in the air with nothing to grab; it smashed two more posts, then hurtled off the bridge. In dim chorus the crew of the Bird screamed all the way down to where the car struck the water and went nose first into the creek bed. Then the car's rear end came down and, except for a long strip of roof, the car settled underwater.

No one swam out.

The Pilot saw the car go over out of the corner of his eye, heard the screams, but so be it. He had tasted doom before. It was his job to kill trucks.

Tramp jerked his head to the right, saw the maimed face of the Pilot, and for one brief moment, he felt as if he were looking not at a face but into the cold, dark depths of his very own soul.

The Pilot smashed the window with the hilt of a knife he pulled from a scabbard on his metal leg, and started scuttling through the window.

Tramp lifted his foot off the gas, kicked out at the door handle, and the door swung open and carried the Pilot with it. The Pilot and the door hit a guardrail post and sparks flew up from the Pilot's metal leg as it touched concrete.

The door swung back in, the Pilot still holding on, and Tramp kicked again, and out went the door, and another post hit the Pilot and carried him and the door away, down into the water below.

And in the same moment, having stretched too far to kick the door, and having pulled the wheel too far right, the White Freight Liner went over the bridge and smashed half in the water and half out.

Crawling through the glassless front of the truck, Tramp rolled out onto the hood and off, landed on the wet ground next to the creek.

Rising up on his knees and elbows, Tramp looked out at the creek and saw the Pilot shoot up like a porpoise, splash back down, and thrash wildly in the water, thrashing in a way that let Tramp know that the Pilot's body was little more than shattered bones and ruptured muscles held together by skin and clothes.

The Pilot looked at him, and Tramp thought he saw the Pilot nod, though he could not be sure. And just before the Pilot went under as if diving, the tip of his metal leg winking up and then falling beneath the water, Tramp lifted his hand and shot the Pilot the finger.

"Jump up on that and spin around," Tramp said.

The Pilot did not come back up.

Tramp eased onto his back and felt the throbbing of the bullet wound and thought about the night and what he had done. In the distance, but distinct, he could hear the highway whine of truck tires on the Interstate.

Tramp smiled at that. Somehow it struck him as amusing. He closed his eyes, and just before he drifted into an exhausted sleep, he said aloud, "How about that, Davy? How about that?"

THE PHONE WOMAN

Journal Entries

A week to remember . . .

After this, my little white page friend, you shall have greater security, kept under not only lock and key, but you will have a hiding place. If I were truly as smart as I sometimes think I am, I wouldn't write this down. I know better. But, I am compelled.

Compulsion. It comes out of nowhere and owns us all. We put a suit and tie and hat on the primitive part of our brain and call it manners and civilization, but ultimately, it's just a suit and tie and a hat. The primitive brain is still primitive, and it compels, pulses to the same dark beat that made our less civilized ancestors and the primordial ooze before them throb to simple, savage rhythms of sex, death and destruction.

Our nerves call out to us to touch and taste life, and without our suits of civilization, we can do that immediately. Take what we need if we've muscle enough. Will enough. But all dressed up in the trappings of civilization, we're forced to find our thrills vicariously. And eventually, that is not enough. Controlling our impulses that way is like having someone eat your food for you. No taste. No texture. No nourishment. Pitiful business.

Without catering to the needs of our primitive brains, without feeding impulses, trying instead to get what we need through books and films and the lives of the more adventurous, we cease to live. We wither. We bore ourselves and others. We die. And are glad of it.

Whatcha gonna do, huh?

✦   ✦

Saturday morning, June 10th through Saturday 17th:

I haven't written in a while, so I'll cover a few days, beginning with a week ago today.

It was one of those mornings when I woke up on the wrong side of the bed, feeling a little out of sorts, mad at the wife over something I've forgotten and she probably hasn't forgotten, and we grumbled down the hall, into the kitchen, and there's our dog, a Siberian Husky—my wife always refers to him as a Suburban Husky because of his pampered lifestyle, though any resemblance to where we live and suburbia requires a great deal of faith—and he's smiling at us, and then we see why he's smiling. Two reasons: (1) He's happy to see us. (2) He feels a little guilty.

He has reason to feel guilty. Not far behind him, next to the kitchen table, was a pile of shit. I'm not talking your casual little whoopsie-doo, and I'm not talking your inconvenient pile, and I'm not talking six to eight turds the size of large bananas. I'm talking a certified, pure-dee, goddamn prize-winning SHIT. There were enough dog turds there to shovel out in a pickup truck and dump on the lawn and let dry so you could use them to build an adobe hut big enough to keep your tools in and have room to house your cat in the winter.

And, right beside this sterling deposit, was a lake of piss wide enough and deep enough to go rowing on.

I had visions of a Siberian Husky hat and slippers, or possibly a nice throw rug for the bedroom, a necklace of dog claws and teeth; maybe cut that smile right out of his face and frame it.

But the dog-lover in me took over, and I put him outside in his pen where he cooled his dewclaws for a while. Then I spent about a half-hour cleaning up dog shit while my wife spent the same amount of time keeping our two-year-old son, Kevin, known to me as Fruit of My Loins, out of the shit.

Yep, Oh Great White Page of a Diary, he was up now. It always works that way. In times of greatest stress, in times of greatest need for contemplation or privacy, like when you're trying to get that morning piece off the Old Lady, the kid shows up, and suddenly it's as if you've been deposited inside an ant farm and the ants are crawling and stinging. By the time I finished cleaning up the mess, it was time for breakfast, and I got to tell you, I didn't want anything that looked like link sausage that morning.

So Janet and I ate, hoping that what we smelled while eating was the aroma of disinfectant and not the stench of shit wearing a coat of disinfectant, and we watched the kid spill his milk eighty-lebben times and throw food and drop stuff on the floor, and me and the wife we're fussing at each other more and more, about whatever it was we were mad about that morning—a little item intensified by our dog's deposits—and by the time we're through eating our meal, and Janet leaves me with Fruit of My Loins and his View Master and goes out to the laundry room to do what the room is named for—probably went out there to beat the laundry clean with rocks or bricks, pretending shirts and pants were my head—I'm beginning to think things couldn't get worse. About that time the earth passes through the tail of a comet or something, some kind of dimensional gate is opened, and the world goes weird.

There's a knock at the door.

At first I thought it was a bird pecking on the glass, it was that soft. Then it came again and I went to the front door and opened it, and there stood a woman about five feet tall wearing a long, wool coat, and untied, flared-at-the-ankles shoes, and a ski cap decorated with a silver pin. The wool ski cap was pulled down so tight over her ears her face was pale. Keep in mind that it was probably eighty degrees that morning, and the temperature was rising steadily, and she was dressed like she was on her way to plant the flag at the summit of Everest. Her age was hard to guess. Had that kind of face. She could have been twenty-two or forty-two.

She said, "Can I use your phone, mister? I got an important call to make."

Well, I didn't see any ready-to-leap companions hiding in the shrubbery, and I figured if she got out of line I could handle her, so I said, "Yeah, sure. Be my guest," and let her in.

The phone was in the kitchen, on the wall, and I pointed it out to her, and me and Fruit of My Loins went back to doing what we were doing, which was looking at the View Master. We switched from Goofy to Winnie the Pooh, the one about Tigger in the tree, and it was my turn to look at it, and I couldn't help but hear my guest's conversation with her mother was becoming stressful—I knew it was her mother because she addressed her by that title—and suddenly Fruit of My Loins yelled, "Wook, Daddy wook."

I turned and "wooked," and what do I see but what appears to be some rare tribal dance, possibly something having originated in higher altitudes where the lack of oxygen to the brain causes wilder abandon with the dance steps. This gal was all over the place. Fred Astaire with a hot coat hanger up his ass couldn't have been any brisker. I've never seen anything like it. Then, in mid-dossey-do, she did a leap like cheerleaders do, one of those things where they kick their legs out to the side, open up like a nutcracker and kick the palms of their hands, then she hit the floor on her ass, spun, and wheeled as if on a swivel into the hallway and went out of sight. Then there came a sound from in there like someone on speed beating the bongos. She hadn't dropped the phone either. The wire was stretched tight around the corner and was vibrating like a big fish was on the line.

I dashed over there and saw she was lying crosswise in the hallway, bamming her head against the wall, clutching at the phone with one hand and pulling her dress up over her waist with the other, and she was making horrible sounds and rolling her eyes, and I immediately thought: this is it, she's gonna die. Then I saw she wasn't dying, just thrashing, and I decided it was an epileptic fit.

I got down and took the phone away from her, took hold of her jaw, got her tongue straight without getting bit, stretched her out on the floor away from the wall, picked up the phone and told her mama, who was still fussing about something or another, that things weren't so good, hung up on her in mid-sentence and called the ambulance.

I ran out to the laundry room, told Janet a strange woman was in our hallway pulling her dress over her head and that an ambulance was coming. Janet, bless her heart, has become quite accustomed to weird events following me around, and she went outside to direct the ambulance, like one of those people at the airport with light sticks.

I went back to the woman and watched her thrash a while, trying to make sure she didn't choke to death, or injure herself, and Fruit of My Loins kept clutching my leg and asking me what was wrong. I didn't know what to tell him.

After what seemed a couple of months and a long holiday, the ambulance showed up with a whoop of siren, and I finally decided the lady was doing as good as she was going to do, so I went outside. On either side of my walk were all these people. It's like Bradbury's story "The Crowd." The one where when there's an accident all these strange people show up out of nowhere and stand around and watch.

I'd never seen but two of these people before in my life, and I've been living in this neighborhood for years.

One lady immediately wanted to go inside and pray for the woman, who she somehow knew, but Janet whispered to me there wasn't enough room for our guest in there, let alone this other woman and her buddy, God, so I didn't let her in.

All the other folks are just a jabbering, and about all sorts of things. One woman said to another, "Mildred, how you been?"

"I been good. They took my kids away from me this morning, though. I hate that. How you been?"

"Them hogs breeding yet?" one man says to another, and the other goes into not only that they're breeding, but he tells how much fun they're having at it.

Then here comes the ambulance boys with a stretcher. One of the guys knew me somehow, and he stopped and said, "You're that writer, aren't you?"

I admitted it.

"I always wanted to write. I got some ideas that'd make a good book and a movie. I'll tell you about 'em. I got good ideas, I just can't write them down. I could tell them to you and you could write them up and we could split the money."

"Could we talk about this later?" I said. "There's a lady in there thrashing in my hallway."

So they went in with the stretcher, and after a few minutes the guy I talked to came out and said, "We can't get her out of there and turned through the door. We may have to take your back door out."

That made no sense to me at all. They brought the stretcher through and now they were telling me they couldn't carry it out. But I was too addled to argue and told them to do what they had to do.

Well, they managed her out the back door without having to remodel our home after all, and when they came around the edge of the house I heard the guy I'd talked to go, "Ahhh, damn, I'd known it was her I wouldn't have come."

I thought they were going to set her and the stretcher down right there, but they went on out to the ambulance and jerked open the door and tossed her and the stretcher inside like they were tossing a dead body over a cliff. You could hear the stretcher strike the back of the ambulance and bounce forward and slide back again.

I had to ask: "You know her?"

"Dark enough in the house there, I couldn't tell at first. But when we got outside, I seen who it was. She does this all the time, but not over on this side of town in a while. She don't take her medicine on purpose so she'll have fits when she gets stressed, or she fakes them, like this time. Way she gets attention. Sometimes she hangs herself, cuts off her air. Likes the way it feels. Sexual or something. She's damn near died half-dozen times. Between you and me, wish she'd go on and do it and save me some trips."

And the ambulance driver and his assistant were out of there. No lights. No siren.

Well, the two people standing in the yard that we knew were still there when I turned around, but the others, like mythical creatures, were gone, turned to smoke, dissolved, become one with the universe, whatever. The two people we knew, elderly neighbors, said they knew the woman, who by this time, I had come to think of as the Phone Woman.

"She goes around doing that," the old man said. "She stays with her mamma who lives on the other side of town, but they get in fights on account of the girl likes to hang herself sometimes for entertainment. Never quite makes it over the ridge, you know, but gets her mother worked up. They say her mother used to do that too, hang herself, when she was a little girl. She outgrowed it. I guess the girl there . . . you know I don't even know her name . . . must have seen her mamma do that when she was little, and it kind of caught on. She has that 'lepsy stuff too, you know, thrashing around and all, biting on her tongue?"

I said I knew and had seen a demonstration of it this morning.

"Anyway," he continued, "they get in fights and she comes over here and tries to stay with some relatives that live up the street there, but they don't cotton much to her hanging herself to things. She broke down their clothesline post last year. Good thing it was old, or she'd been dead. Wasn't nobody home that time. I hear tell they sometimes go off and leave her there and leave rope and wire and stuff laying around, sort of hoping, you know. But except for that time with the clothesline, she usually does her hanging when someone's around. Or she goes in to use the phone at houses and does what she did here."

"She's nutty as a fruitcake," said the old woman. "She goes back on behind here to where that little trailer park is, knocks on doors where the wetbacks live, about twenty to a can, and they ain't got no phone, and she knows it. She's gotten raped couple times doing that, and it ain't just them Mex's that have got to her. White folks, niggers. She tries to pick who she thinks will do what she wants. She wants to be raped. It's like the hanging. She gets some kind of attention out of it, some kind of loving. Course, I ain't saying she chose you cause you're that kind of person."

I assured her I understood.

The old couple went home then, and another lady came up, and sure enough, I hadn't seen her before either, and she said, "Did that crazy ole girl come over here and ask to use the phone, then fall down on you and flop?"

"Yes, m'am."

"Does that all the time."

Then this woman went around the corner of the house and was gone, and I never saw her again. In fact, with the exception of the elderly neighbors and the Phone Woman, I never saw any of those people again and never knew where they came from. Next day there was a soft knock on the door. It was the Phone Woman again. She asked to use the phone.

I told her we'd had it taken out.

She went away and I saw her several times that day. She'd come up our street about once every half hour, wearing that same coat and hat and those sad shoes, and I guess it must have been a hundred and ten out there. I watched her from the window. In fact I couldn't get any writing done because I was watching for her. Thinking about her lying there on the floor, pulling her dress up, flopping. I thought too of her hanging herself now and then, like she was some kind of suit on a hanger.

Anyway, the day passed and I tried to forget about her, then the other night, Monday probably, I went out on the porch to smoke one of my rare cigars (about four to six a year), and I saw someone coming down the dark street, and from the way that someone walked, I knew it was her, the Phone Woman.

She went on by the house and stopped down the road a piece and looked up and I looked where she was looking, and through the trees I could see what she saw. The moon.

We both looked at it a while, and she finally walked on, slow, with her head down, and I put my cigar out well before it was finished and went inside and brushed my teeth and took off my clothes, and tried to go to sleep. Instead, I lay there for a long time and thought about her, walking those dark streets, maybe thinking about her mom, or a lost love, or a phone, or sex in the form of rape because it was some kind of human connection, about hanging herself because it was attention and it gave her a sexual high . . . and then again, maybe I'm full of shit and she wasn't thinking about any of these things.

Then it struck me suddenly, as I lay there in bed beside my wife, in my quiet house, my son sleeping with his teddy bear in the room across the way, that maybe she was the one in touch with the world, with life, and that I was the one gone stale from civilization. Perhaps life had been civilized right out of me.

The times I had truly felt alive, in touch with my nerve centers, were in times of violence or extreme stress.

Where I had grown up, in Mud Creek, violence simmered underneath everyday life like lava cooking beneath a thin crust of earth, ready at any time to explode and spew. I had been in fights, been cut by knives. I once had a job bouncing drunks. I had been a bodyguard in my earlier years, had illegally carried a .38. On one occasion, due to a dispute the day before while protecting my employer, who sometimes dealt with a bad crowd, a man I had insulted and hit with my fists pulled a gun on me, and I had been forced to pull mine. The both of us ended up with guns in our faces, looking into each other's eyes, knowing full well our lives hung by a thread and the snap of a trigger.

I had killed no one, and had avoided being shot. The Mexican stand-off ended with us both backing away and running off, but there had been that moment when I knew it could all be over in a flash. Out of the picture in a blaze of glory. No old folks home for me. No drool running down my chin and some young nurse wiping my ass, thinking how repulsive and old I was, wishing for quitting time so she could roll up with some young stud some place sweet and cozy, open her legs to him with a smile and a sigh, and later a passionate scream, while in the meantime, back at the old folks ranch, I lay in the bed with a dead dick and an oxygen mask strapped to my face.

Something about the Phone Woman had clicked with me. I understood her suddenly. I understood then that the lava that had boiled beneath the civilized facade of my brain was no longer boiling. It might be bubbling way down low, but it wasn't boiling, and the realization of that went all over me and I felt sad, very, very sad. I had dug a grave and crawled into it and was slowly pulling the dirt in after me. I had a home. I had a wife. I had a son. Dirt clods all. Dirt clods filling in my grave while life simmered somewhere down deep and useless within me.

I lay there for a long time with tears on my cheeks before exhaustion took over and I slept in a dark world of dormant passion.

Couple days went by, and one night after Fruit of My Loins and Janet were in bed, I went out on the front porch to sit and look at the stars and think about what I'm working on—a novella that isn't going well—and what do I see but the Phone Woman, coming down the road again, walking past the house, stopping once more to look at the moon. .

I didn't go in this time, but sat there waiting, and she went on up the street and turned right and went out of sight. I walked across the yard and went out to the center of the street and watched her back going away from me, mixing into the shadows of the trees and houses along the street, and I followed.

I don't know what I wanted to see, but I wanted to see something, and I found for some reason that I was thinking of her lying there on the floor in my hallway, her dress up, the mound of her sex, as they say in porno novels, pushing up at me. The thought gave me an erection, and I was conscious of how silly this was, how unattractive this woman was to me, how odd she looked, and then another thought came to me: I was a snob. I didn't want to feel sexual towards anyone ugly or smelly in a winter coat in the dead of summer.

But the night was cool and the shadows were thick, and they made me feel all right, romantic maybe, or so I told myself.

I moved through a neighbor's backyard where a dog barked at me a couple of times and shut up. I reached the street across the way and looked for the Phone Woman, but didn't see her.

I took a flyer, and walked on down the street toward the trailer park where those poor illegal aliens were stuffed in like sardines by their unscrupulous employers, and I saw a shadow move among shadows, and then there was a split in the trees that provided the shadows, and I saw her, the Phone Woman. She was standing in a yard under a great oak, and not far from her was a trailer. A pathetic air conditioner hummed in one of its windows.

She stopped and looked up through that split in the trees above, and I knew she was trying to find the moon again, that she had staked out spots that she traveled to at night; spots where she stood and looked at the moon or the stars or the pure and sweet black eternity between them.

Like the time before, I looked up too, took in the moon, and it was beautiful, as gold as if it were a great glob of honey. The wind moved my hair, and it seemed solid and purposeful, like a lover's soft touch, like the beginning of foreplay. I breathed deep and tasted the fragrance of the night, and my lungs felt full and strong and young.

I looked back at the woman and saw she was reaching out her hand to the moon. No, a low limb. She touched it with her fingertips. She raised her other hand, and in it was a short, thick rope. She tossed the rope over the limb and made a loop and pulled it taut to the limb. Then she tied a loop to the other end, quickly expertly, and put that around her neck.

Of course, I knew what she was going to do. But I didn't move. I could have stopped her, I knew, but what was the point? Death was the siren she had called on many a time, and finally, she had heard it sing.

She jumped and pulled her legs under her and the limb took her jump and held her. Her head twisted to the left and she spun about on the rope and the moonlight caught the silver pin on her ski cap and it threw out a cool beacon of silver light, and as she spun, it hit me once, twice, three times.

On the third spin her mouth went wide and her tongue went out and her legs dropped down and hit the ground and she dangled there, unconscious.

I unrooted my feet and walked over there, looking about as I went.

I didn't see anyone. No lights went on in the trailer.

I moved up close to her. Her eyes were open. Her tongue was out. She was swinging a little, her knees were bent and the toes and tops of her silly shoes dragged the ground. I walked around and around her, an erection pushing at my pants. I observed her closely, trying to see what death looked like.

She coughed. A little choking cough. Her eyes shifted toward me. Her chest heaved. She was beginning to breathe. She made a feeble effort to get her feet under her, to raise her hands to the rope around her neck.

She was back from the dead.

I went to her. I took her hands, gently pulled them from her throat, let them go. I looked into her eyes. I saw the moon there. She shifted so that her legs held her weight better. Her hands went to her dress. She pulled it up to her waist. She wore no panties. Her bush was like a nest built between the boughs of a snow-white elm.

I remembered the day she came into the house. Everything since then, leading up to this moment, seemed like a kind of perverse mating ritual. I put my hand to her throat. I took hold of the rope with my other hand and jerked it so that her knees straightened, then I eased behind her, put my forearm against the rope around her throat, and I began to tighten my hold until she made a soft noise, like a virgin taking a man for the first time. She didn't lift her hands. She continued to tug her dress up. She was trembling from lack of oxygen. I pressed myself against her buttocks, moved my hips rhythmically, my hard-on bound by my underwear and pants. I tightened the pressure on her throat.

And choked her.

And choked her.

She gave up what was left of her life with a shiver and a thrusting of her pelvis, and finally she jammed her buttocks back into me and I felt myself ejaculate, thick and hot and rich as shaving foam.

Her hands fell to her side. I loosened the pressure on her throat but clung to her for a while, getting my breath and my strength back. When I felt strong enough, I let her go. She swung out and around on the rope and her knees bent and her head cocked up to stare blindly at the gap in the trees above, at the honey-golden moon.

I left her there and went back to the house and slipped into the bedroom and took off my clothes. I removed my wet underwear carefully and wiped them out with toilet paper and flushed the paper down the toilet. I put the underwear in the clothes hamper. I put on fresh and climbed into bed and rubbed my hands over my wife's buttocks until she moaned and woke up. I rolled her on her stomach and mounted her and made love to her. Hard, violent love, my forearm around her throat, not squeezing, but thinking about the Phone Woman, the sound she had made when I choked her from behind, the way her buttocks had thrust back into me at the end. I closed my eyes until the sound that Janet made was the sound the Phone Woman made and I could visualize her there in the moonlight, swinging by the rope.

When it was over, I held Janet and she kissed me and joked about my arm around her throat, about how it seemed I had wanted to choke her. We laughed a little. She went to sleep. I let go of her and moved to my side of the bed and looked at the ceiling and thought about the Phone Woman. I tried to feel guilt. I could not. She had wanted it. She had tried for it many times. I had helped her do what she had never been able to manage. And I had felt alive again. Doing something on the edge. Taking a risk.

Well, journal, here's the question: Am I a sociopath?

No. I love my wife. I love my child. I even love my Suburban Husky. I have never hunted and fished, because I thought I didn't like to kill. But there are those who want to die. It is their one moment of life; to totter on the brink between light and darkness, to take the final, dark rush down a corridor of black, hot pain.

So, Oh Great White Pages, should I feel guilt, some inner torment, a fear that I am at heart a cold-blooded murderer?

I think not.

I gave the sweet gift of truly being alive to a woman who wanted someone to participate in her moment of joy. Death ended that, but without the threat of it, her moment would have been nothing. A stage rehearsal for a high-school play in street clothes.

Nor do I feel fear. The law will never suspect me. There's no reason to. The Phone Woman had a record of near suicides.

It would never occur to anyone to think she had died by anyone's hand other than her own.

I felt content, in touch again with the lava beneath the primal crust. I have allowed it to boil up and burst through and flow, and now it has gone down once more. But it's no longer a distant memory. It throbs and rolls and laps just below, ready to jump and give me life. Are there others out there like me? Or better yet, others for me, like the Phone Woman?

Most certainly.

And now I will recognize them. The Phone Woman has taught me that. She came into my life on a silly morning and brought me adventure, took me away from the grind, and then she brought me more, much, much more. She helped me recognize the fine but perfect line between desire and murder; let me know that there are happy victims and loving executioners.

I will know the happy victims now when I see them, know who needs to be satisfied. I will give them their desire, while they give me mine.

This last part with the Phone Woman happened last night and I am recording it now, while it is fresh, as Janet sleeps. I think of Janet in there and I have a hard time imagining her face. I want her, but I want her to be the Phone Woman, or someone like her.

I can feel the urge rising up in me again. The urge to give someone that tremendous double-edged surge of life and death.

It's like they say about sex. Once you get it, you got to have it on a regular basis. But it isn't sex I want. It's something like it, only sweeter.

I'll wrap this up. I'm tired. Thinking that I'll have to wake Janet and take the edge off my need, imagine that she and I are going to do more than fornicate; that she wants to take that special plunge and that she wants me to shove her.

But she doesn't want that. I'd know. I have to find that in my dreams, when I nestle down into the happy depths of the primitive brain.

At least until I find someone like the Phone Woman, again, that is. Someone with whom I can commit the finest of adultery.

And until that search proves fruitful and I have something special to report, dear diary, I say, goodnight.

For Ed Gorman

THE DIAPER

OR

THE ADVENTURE OF THE LITTLE ROUNDER

Googoo, teevee, teevee. Baby turn on—

Waaaaaaaaaaaaa. Potty. Doodoo. Peepee! Shock baby, shock . . . Wow! Shit, like Daddy say. Got smart shock there. Feel different. IQ climb the ladder. Gonna get some twisty thoughts lined out here through the googoos, uhhuh. Baby done peepeed his Pampers.

Whoa! Feeling much smarter now. What this? Pampers going nutty. Wriggling. Pampers alive. Gotta rip em off sweet Little Rounder's ass. Oh potty, goddamnit, as Daddy say before Mommy say, Don't talk like that in front of Little

Lenny, and Daddy say, Oh, Little Rounder (he call me Little Rounder) don't know from dick. One word's like another to him, ain't that so Little Rounder, and Mommy say, Don't do it anyhow and—

Whoa! Rip these dudes off, as Daddy say when changing Little Rounder. They move too much. Scary business.

Got them dudes off and me crawling like hell, as Daddy say. Pampers done crawling behind me. Don't under—

Whoa! $$A = \frac{\partial^2 s}{\partial t^2} + \frac{1}{P}\left(\frac{\partial s}{\partial t}\right)^2_N \tag{1}$$

Numbers fall into Baby's head like teddy bear in toilet that time, and me understand, then it go away, and by God, as Daddy say, that some goddamn serious thinking I'm doing there.

What the living hell, as Daddy say, is wrong with Pampers and what with numbers jumping around in my head, and here come Pampers still hot on trail like posse with a noose, as cowboy say on teevee, goddamnit. Mommy hear me talk like Daddy she say what she say to him, Such language, but Mommy hanging clothes on the line, so me talk like Daddy, by God, by damned and go to hell.

Down the hall crawl like hell, as Daddy say, crawl till nearly burn holes in precious little knees, as Mommy call them . . . and whoa, what this?

$$\theta_{ind} = \frac{N_2\varnothing}{2t} \tag{2}$$

---

[1] Formula for acceleration as the second derivative of displacement. Suggests speed of Pampers.

[2] Formula for induced voltage. Suggests electrical shock.

Understanding some business here now. Diaper done got electric type charge from old boob tube and little fella live in other dimension get zipped on through like owl shit through a funnel, as Daddy say, hit ammonia in diaper and that cause some serious chemical diddly-do, and that goddamn shock, as Daddy would say, make me one smart sonofabitch of a baby.

Lookee back, baby does, and what do him see (not band of angels like song Mommy sing) but goddamn diaper, as Daddy say, diaper comin' after my ultra-young ass, and whoa, that mother, as Daddy say when not even talking about Mommy, done nearly got on my precious posterior.

Round that corner, baby dear. Ahboo, ahboo, as me say when not quite so smart but pretty excited.

What this? Diaper done gainin' on baby still, and me scuttlin' fast as little, tired, pink knees will done be takin' me.

Gettin' a little more snap in the old punkin' as time go on here—Whoa! Them smart thoughts be running through baby's head like dogs with their tails on fire, as Daddy say.

Diaper still gainin'. Time to get tough. Think tough: By God, like Daddy say, I tell you now, diaper, look out, cause baby gonna knock the shit out of you, as Daddy say to guy at door with little suitcase one time.

Me goin' under bed where it's dark and there me can bushwhack this damn diaper like cowboy do in movie me and Daddy see. Cowboy go in cave and jump this rustler and whup on him, and . . . Oooooohhhhhh, dark as inside of a Tennessee Walker's ass, as Daddy say, dark like room at night when lights go out and me scared and cry and Mommy and Daddy come in and hold me and bounce me around and say things and Daddy finally laughs and says, Doesn't this cute little turd ever get sleepy (that me, the cute little turd, better known as Little Rounder or Little Lenny)? Look at them hooty owl eyes. He's wide awake.

But that then and this now and me braver and smarter. Dark not bother baby now, by God.

Me hope.

Whoa! What this? Diaper done got me. Why the sneaky, backshootin' sonofabitch, as Daddy say when watch cowboy movie and see good cowboy get shot from behind, diaper done got on my face and it be smellin' like serious peepee, and me, Little Rounder, be grabbin' at that motherfucker, as Daddy say one time when cut his hand on can opener, and now me say, Take that, you sonofabitch, as Daddy say when him watch men in ring throwing arms at one another.

Whoa! Him take that pretty goddamn good, as Daddy say. Me not think ambush/bushwhack rustler/diaper such a good idea after all, by God, by damn.

Me done lose three out of three falls, as say on show where big fat men jump together, roll around and grunt and pull on each other's underwear and scream inside of ropes.

Try crawl out from under bed, diaper pull me back, try again, pull me back again, all over my face like before and stink so bad baby see little pictures run around in front of eyes.

On back and got hind feet under diaper and pushin'. Rustler pop off my face and me crawl like hell, as Daddy say, and behind me comes diaper just a humpin'—

$$y = y_m{}^{\sin\frac{2\pi}{\lambda}(x-ut)} \tag{3}$$

—hop in baby's head and along with come all these little pictures, and diaper still coming, lickitysplit, and me still crawling like big old snake me see from car seat while it go across the road in front of car and Daddy hit on brakes and

---

[3]*Formula for a wave of elastic media. Suggests snakish movement.*

yells, Look at the size of that sonofabitch, will you? and Mommy say, Not in front of Little Lenny.

But now me getting smarter as go along and close bedroom door on diaper-sucker by pull at bottom where crack big enough for hand. Don't mash baby, door! Good, not mash. Baby's hand small, and door make me think of Mommy when she say to Daddy, When you going to get that door fixed, Leonard; why it's too short and hung two inches too high, and Daddy say, Sounds like me, and Mommy throw pillow and Daddy laugh, say, I'll fix it soon, both me and the door.

But what the living hell is this, as Daddy say when find in Mommy's underwear drawer big white pickle that shake when wire in wall. Diaper done crawl under goddamn door, and me thinking me smart Little Rounder, cowpoke with a plan, but damn diaper smart as, maybe smarter than, electric shock-smart baby.

Slap that little booger upside head (front must be head, me think) with palm of precious little hand and it jump back. How about that diaper! Ha! Poke little nose under and me wham shit out of you, as Daddy say.

What this. Whoa! Him a whimperin' like baby's puppy Popo when Mommy not see and step on. Diaper stick its head under door again and me jump on sucker with butt and it cry loud now, and me feel bad about it, it not seem like me doing what Daddy say cowboys ought to do when he tell me about them and he say, Little Rounder, you got to treat people and things right and do right because it's right and for no other reason, and that's the goddamned Code of the West.

What this now, somethin' in my head done gone smart enough to pick up diaper's thoughts (telepathy what it called, but how me know that?) What this? Diaper want to go home, it say in baby's head. Diaper must want to get back into Pamper's box.

Whoa! Back off. That dumb baby thought. Have goo-goo relapse there for a moment. Diaper mean back in teevee and shock hell across space/time/dimensional continuum, which sort of translate get on back to the old hacienda and chow down and sing trail songs or some such thing. Whoa! Baby just love shit out of this smart stuff.

Baby feel sorry for old stinky diaper and get butt off and stroke little booger's . . . whatever up front, and it mew like baby's cat Frisky (me call it Friky when not so big IQ) and now diaper cuddle close, ain't him cute little turd like me, my ownself, the Little Rounder. Friendly diaper, but it stink like nasty ol' baby whiz. Wheee, not make good friend on account of me be sick to goddamn stomach, as Daddy say, all the time.

Okay diaper, buddy. Me help—

$$x = \frac{F_m}{G} \sin(w'' + a), \text{ where} \tag{4}$$

$$G = \sqrt{m^2 (w''^2 - w'')^2} + b^2 w''^2 , \ \alpha = \cos^{-1} \frac{bw}{G}$$

Ahha, so it you make baby smart all along so he can help. Smart diaper. Smart baby. What?

$$\upsilon\left(x = \infty\right) - \upsilon\left(x = \sqrt[6]{\frac{2a}{b}} = \alpha\right)\left(\frac{a}{4a^2/b^2} - \frac{b}{2a/b}\right) = \frac{b^2}{4a} \tag{5}$$

---

[4] *Formula for forced oscillation (i.e., why soldiers do not march in step across bridges). Suggests forced intelligence enhancement.*
[5] *Formula for dissassociation energy of a particle from an atom. Suggests freedom. Or, in Western terms, "getting out of Dodge."*

So, that how baby help stinky diaper. But whoa, this gonna hurt baby some, ain't it? Me thought so, goddamnit, as Daddy say, but what the Code of the West if you don't help your friends, just so many goddamn words is what.

Diaper ride on back while me crawl to teevee. Got to hurry before Mommy come.

Diaper get off and get on floor and me sit down on it—whoa! Peepee turned cold as witch's tit in brass bra, as Daddy say when he go outside to get newspaper when it come ice.

All righty, here come time to do what a man's got to do cause it's what a man's got to do and all that Code of the West stuff. Diaper send thoughts through head and me feel smart stuff moving through me and get some ideas and great notions and wish teddy bear or Popo or Frisky were here to stand by me, but me all alone 'cept for diaper, but sometimes you got to do what you got to do alone, and all that stuff me remember from teevee cowboy movies that I not normally remember, and take em to Missouri and smile when you say that and stuff.

Diaper, he say put finger on teevee right here and—

Waaaaaaaaaaaaaaaaaaaaaaaaaaa Holy Moses! Goddamn hell and flying dogshit with purple wings, as Daddy say, that hurt like the proverbial sonofabitch, by God, by cornholing damn. Sparks jump like windup frogs through me and into television set and set goes on and off and plays soap operas and cowboy movie and Sesame Street pieces faster than bunny fucks, as Daddy say, whatever bunny and fucks is . . . and now me feel funny, like something crawling out of head, like numbers and ideas and new colors and shapes are going down a hole like dirt off baby in bath . . . . goo-goo relapse inevitable . . . visitor from dimension gone, diaper just diaper, goo-goo, and me am wet . . . goo-goo . . . Peepee, peepee, Mommy, Mommy, waaaaaaaaaa . . .

Thanks to Edd Vick for the formulas.

EVERYBODY
PLAYS THE FOOL

The day of his ride on the big tornado in the brand new pink and white double-wide, Jerry Freeman began to view the world differently. Considering his luck with all things weather wise, and his constant concern with the workings of the heavens, this was quite a change for him, because it wasn't the weather he thought about now when the subject of tornados came up. Someone mentioned a tornado, he read about one in the papers, saw one on the TV news, first thing that came to his mind wasn't the storm and the fact he'd been in one, but what he'd *found* in that storm.

He'd actually been in two tornados. That's why he was so weather wise. The first tornado didn't bear the same merit in his book though. It had come about when he was ten, had jumped over his house not hurting anyone, only shaking them up a bit and filling their nostrils with the smell of rain and ozone.

It had jerked away his family's TV antenna, and had stolen a Holstein cow from the pasture at the back of their house.

Jerry had seen the cow go. He'd been standing on the back porch looking across the yard, out through Old Man Winston's barbed wire fence and into the pasture at the cow, when the storm, moaning like a locomotive, came over the house in a bad goddamn mood and in the shape of a giant asphalt-colored snowcone container. It jumped down on the cow, wadded the antenna around her before whirling her up into the blackness of the storm, and carrying her off without so much as time for the cow to look up or say "moo."

Neither cow, antenna, or that particular tornado, to the best of Jerry's knowledge, were ever seen again. As a kid, Jerry liked to think that the cow was over in Oz somewhere, watching TV with Dorothy, the Wizard, the Lion, the Scarecrow and the Tin Man. Watching TV using his Mama and Daddy's antenna, which had somehow gotten all straightened out.

If so, he figured they were getting better reception than his family ever had. Back then, come nine or ten o'clock at night, you had to go out and turn the antenna some to keep Shreveport coming in if you wanted to watch a late movie or whatever showed after the news. And it hadn't gotten any better when they got the new antenna either. You had to start jacking with that one an hour earlier, trying to twist it just right so the TV waves, or whatever the hell carried the picture through the air, would float in from Shreveport and leap into that aluminum sucker and run down it and through the main wire and into the Sylvania television set with the white dolly on top supporting a batch of dust-covered plastic roses and a sprig of green plastic leaves, species unidentifiable.

One time, Jerry's Old Man, geared up for a John Wayne movie that was coming on after the news, had been out there twisting the antenna around and yelling, "How's things now? Can you see somethin'? Is that too far? How's that? Is that sonofabitch clear?" when a bolt of lightning with a fork in it came out of the clear, moonlit sky, hit the antenna and knocked Old Man Freeman on his fat ass.

After that, Old Man Freeman got him a better growth of hair than he'd had before—so good in fact, it almost covered up his bald spot—and a cautious view of the weather that he passed on to his offspring. He became suspicious of clear sky forecasts and had bad things to say about people who worked at the weather bureau.

From then, Old Man Freeman was cautious when there was something he wanted to see. He sent Jerry or one of the other boys out to turn the antenna, saying, "Now watch the skies, hear. You got to be careful with that weather."

Incidents like this caused Jerry and his three brothers to grow up kind of nervous; they lived with the certainty that the Freemans had to be damn careful when it came to bad weather. Its presence always seemed to lead to disaster.

But this other storm, the second tornado Jerry was in, that was a booger. It had revealed to him a horror, and had cleared up a fact long considered and hotly contested before by him. A double-wide mobile home, with or without pink trim, was not that well built and it was undoubtedly a tornado magnet.

Tornado got a brewing in the heavens, first thing that good buddy wanted was a mobile home. It's like a drunk has to have a drink, and a tornado has to have a mobile home, or maybe a whole fleet of them. Cows and antennas were just make-do material. A mobile home was the ticket. Especially one of those finer mobile homes, the double-wide. And if that mobile home belonged to a Freeman, that was just icing on the fucking cake.

The time of the second tornado, Jerry had been sitting in a lawn chair in the front yard of his boy Daryl's place out near the satellite dish, watching Daryl barbecue chicken.

Daryl had just split up with Carol, his wife of two years, a Sunday school teacher and a rodeo barrel racer, and he was still mopey about it. He said she got up one morning and went out to feed the birds sunflower seeds, like she did every morning, and had gotten into a car with a strange man and driven off without so much as a "kiss my ass." He hadn't heard from her since. Daryl said he figured she'd had the whole escape planned for a month. She'd gotten out of there fast and clever, hadn't even bothered with her clothes, or belongings, except, Daryl said, for a black velvet orange day glow painting of Jesus crying a purple tear. Daryl took care of the rest of her clothes and goods by donating them to Goodwill.

Jerry thought it was good riddance. She liked too much gospel music for his taste, and she'd done what she called "primitive paintings" and he called ugly. His granddaughter by his lawyer son Henry did about the same level work, and she didn't expect to get paid for it. Just hung it on the refrigerator with a Snoopy Magnet.

And Carol, she had fat thighs. Jerry couldn't stand fat thighs. His wife had fat thighs and he went to bed at night with it on his mind. It made him kind of sick to his stomach, those fat thighs. When his wife walked they shook the way his belly shook when he laughed hard, which wasn't all that often, since Jerry wasn't finding too much funny these days.

But he wasn't going to let that get to him. Fat thighs would not depress him. Not today. In spite of Daryl's mood, Jerry felt good. It was a bright and sunny day, but it wasn't really hot yet. Just warm, and there was a little wind carrying the smell of pines with it.

Jerry liked it out here in the country, even though Daryl's idea of landscaping was a bit on the stupid side. Daryl bought two acres in the center of some fine pine woods, then hired a bulldozer to come in and scrape his two acres down to the red clay, then he had bought a pink and white double-wide mobile home and moved it in, had a septic tank dug and electricity hooked up.

You came down the dirt road that led to Daryl's property, first thing you saw on a summer day was a kind of tomato red sheen as the sun hit the clay and bounced back the earth's colors ten fold. Next thing you saw after rounding the corner was the pink and white double-wide. There was an electricity pole on one side of it, the satellite dish on the other, and a blue plastic bird feeder out front. There were four anemic bushes planted on either side of six chunky flagstones that were laid out slightly crooked in front of the mobile home door, making up the walk. From there, it was a small leap up to the metal steps that led into the trailer. You could get a hernia making that first step.

Driving up on the place, it was a sight best seen through cheap sunglasses. None the less, Jerry liked coming out to see his son and getting away from his second wife, who didn't really like him or the boy. Jerry thought that maybe she didn't really like anyone, for that matter. A kind word never left her lips. About once a month, consumed by a sense of duty, she let him fuck her, prefacing the event with either: "Well, all right, but hurry" or "I guess so." It wasn't the sort of foreplay that made a man hard as steel. Jerry thought maybe he ought to buy her a little night light, some magazines or something, so she could read about clothes and makeup while he pounded away, trying to drop anchor in her sea of flesh, her thighs foaming up over his legs and ass as if he were driving into a tub of silly putty. It had gotten so the idea of asking her for sex was so demeaning, he spent more time in the bathroom than usual these days, looking at the lingerie section in the

Sears catalogue and exercising the hand, wrist and forearm muscles in his right arm.

But to hell with all that. He was relaxed on this day. He sat in a lawn lounger, his hat tipped back and his feet stretched out so he could see the toes of his ostrich skin boots just beyond the rise of his T-shirt covered belly. A cold long neck, Lone Star beer cooled one fist and a cigar dangled from the other. He hadn't lit the cigar yet. He was enjoying the wait.

From time to time, if he felt the need of it, Jerry turned his head a little so he could see the blue, plastic bird feeder. There were a couple of scruffy blue jays sitting on the edge of it, quarreling. It seemed that blue jays always quarreled about something.

Missing his wife had made Daryl buy the feeder, as he said that she loved nature. But the feeder had some huge chunks out of it where Daryl, late at night and drunk out of his mind, had taken some pot shots at it with his .22 pistol. Mention that bird feeder now, Daryl got livid. He'd start ranting about how he was gonna use it as a place to shit, and pretend that it was his wife's face. There was no reasoning with him.

If Jerry turned his head in the opposite direction, he could see Daryl, wearing a big white apron with *Lets Eat* stitched in red across it. He had on a *John Deere* gimme cap and held a long handled fork, as he watched a chunk of chicken blacken and smoke on a barbecue grill. Daryl's mouth was open and his bottom lip drooped as if it were melting wax. He had a flat bumpy nose that reminded Jerry of an albino pickle mashed flat by a truck tire. It disturbed Jerry to think that people said the boy looked just like him. Secretly, he thought his son was terribly on the homely side, and he'd always thought of himself as on the left hand side of handsome.

Jerry was just about to light his cigar, when the sky turned a kind of green color in the west. Then he heard the signature roar.

A tornado.

A goddamn tornado come out of nowhere. Fat thighs and tornadoes. They were his lot in life.

"Tornado," Jerry yelled, and Daryl, a chicken breast on his cooking fork, turned to say "What," but saw the pine trees two acres away heaving up and launching themselves into the rolling, black sky as if they had secretly been missiles disguised as trees. They twisted and cracked and became part of the tornado's huge flexible funnel.

Daryl bolted for the double-wide, still holding his chicken on the fork, making good time for a man in a knee length apron. He reached the high step just ahead of his Daddy and dropped the chicken and fork to jerk open the door. He then stepped inside, wheeled, and stuck out a hand for his Daddy. Jerry took it, then the tornado took them.

It jumped down on that mobile home with a whoop and a howl, crumpling it as if it were nothing more than a Saltine Cracker box. A second later, they were airborne.

Later, Jerry and Daryl couldn't remember much after that, at least not until the find, that is. Jerry said that all he knew was that he was standing in the doorway one moment, and the next thing he knew, the mobile home was wrapped around him like a Christmas present, and somehow he had been blown across the trailer backwards until his ass had been forced through a half open window. Only thing that held the rest of him inside the flying double-wide were his arms spread crucifixion style on either side of the trailer wall, which he could feel vibrating like a hula girl's ass.

All Daryl remembered was lying on the floor on his stomach, wearing a velvet Elvis painting around his face, a heavy day bed couch on his back. The trailer trip was too brief for any real memories. Course, he remembered the afterwards of the storm, as he had to admit to some things down at the police station later.

After the storm got through beating up the countryside and wadding up the mobile home, Jerry was the first to wake from the ordeal. First thing he saw was a large fragment of the bird feeder lodged in the branches of some trees. The sky was as blue as the background on Old Glory beyond that.

He raised up on one elbow, looked for Daryl.

The storm had carried them across Daryl's land into the woods beyond, and had plowed a path through an acre or so of the woods before letting them go as it bounced on its merry way or dissipated in that mysterious manner tornados practice.

All that remained of the mobile home was collected in the trees and scattered about on the ground.

Daryl was no where to be seen.

Jerry raised up and discovered he was wearing the aluminum trim of the window he'd been lodged in. He slipped the trim off, stood, tried his legs and arms and found that everything worked. He started to call for Daryl, but saw the boy's feet, one shoe on, one shoe off, sticking out from behind a mangled fragment of the satellite dish.

Jerry felt as if a ball of razor wire were in his gut. "Daryl," he croaked through a mouth as dry as cotton.

He eased over to Daryl and saw him lying face down, the velvet Elvis painting wrapped around his head, his arms pushed out before him, his wrists and hands buried in the oak leaves, pine needles, and rich forest soil.

Jerry dropped to his knees, calling Daryl's name again and Daryl moaned a little, giving Jerry a smidgen of relief. The boy was alive at least. Jerry reached out to get the velvet painting off Daryl's head, but paused. A hand stuck up between Daryl's outspread arms. It was poking out of the dirt, palm toward him, and the fingers were loosely together, as if the hand was raised to wave.

"Oh, God, Daryl," Jerry said. "Your hand!"

But at that moment, Daryl pulled his arms aback and under him and lifted himself to his knees and started unwrapping the Elvis painting from his head. He used both hands.

Relief rushed through Jerry, but then another sensation instantly took its place. He looked at the hand again. It was a small left hand, and the wedding ring finger wore a wedding ring. Jerry could see the thumbnail where the thumb was curled toward the palm. The nail was painted red.

It was a woman's hand. The storm had uncovered it, and there was more. Beneath where the tornado had plowed the dirt, Jerry could see the rest of the body. It was wrapped in a black velvet cloth sporting an orange day glow painting, the dead hand escaping from a rip in it. Jerry crawled over and looked directly into the eye of Jesus crying a purple tear. He peeled the cloth back, revealing a face that looked like it was made of wet paper mache. He could still recognize her as Daryl's wife, though, and knew that the black wound across her forehead certainly wasn't natural.

Daryl sat on the ground folding the Elvis painting absently, looking up at his Daddy, then over at the body. "I was gonna turn myself in anyhow," Daryl said. "I was gonna tell you about it after we had chicken. I know how you hate bad news on an empty stomach. I was gonna say all about it to you cause I couldn't live with it no longer. I dreamed last night I could hear her out here calling."

Jerry wasn't looking at him. He was looking at the hand and the painting. "You did hear her," Jerry said. "She wasn't dead when you buried her. She dug her way out this far then called to you for a while before she finally died."

Jerry peeled the cloth open and looked at the body, which was naked. The girl had fat thighs.

Figured.
A shadow moved overhead.
Jerry looked up at the sky.
Rain clouds.
Typical.

A HARD-ON FOR HORROR: LOW-BUDGET EXCITEMENT

It's difficult to know precisely where it all began, this love for that third world of films, the low-budget horror movie (and I prefer "movie" to "film" and will use that term from here on out), but I suppose for me it began in my own living room, most likely when I was ten or eleven years old and not reading comic books or playing with my pecker, two favorite boy pastimes just above cussing when your parents aren't around, and poking at something dead you've found with a stick .

I had been exposed to horror before that time, but only in oblique ways, a moment in a fairy tale, ghostly anecdotes told by relatives, an animated corpse in the aforementioned comic book, the odor of a neighbor's outhouse, the Sunday-school terrors of the Bible.

Thinking on it now, I'd have to say the Bible is probably the strongest influence on my attraction to horror. God was always brutally bullying somebody in the Old Testament, showing far less patience and mercy than his minions. Truth to tell, you read the Old Testament, and especially if you're one of those who believe this stuff literally, you're bound to get scared. God comes across in the Old Testament as someone whose caffeine level should be strictly monitored.

In fact, Mr. All-Powerful-Know-It-All is, most of the time, just short of rabid. The old boy (and I suppose a case might be made for God as female or as an It, but I think it's pretty clear the celestial force in the Old Testament is presented as male) is always putting folks, who'd rather be left alone to herd their sheep, up to tests, seeing if they'll stab their young'ns if he asks, getting mad when someone like Onan uses the jerk-back method during sexual relations and splatters his seed on the ground. An event that put God in one of his worst humors. God, the old voyeur, wanted that seed in the vagina where it belonged, so he slew Onan for practicing birth control. Maybe sent a thunderbolt up his ass, I don't remember.

Think about it. Guy shits in the woods where you can step on it, it's all right, but if he decides to practice a little birth control, squirts a load of sperm in the dirt, he's out of here. Get out the shovels and put him in the dirt.

The New Testament is only a little less horrifying, what with its reformed approach in the person of a country-boy carpenter named Jesus.

On the surface, Jesus looks like a stand-up kind of guy. But you look at his life head-on, you begin to notice he had some defects. He didn't think things through. Maybe it's a parable, I don't know, but one example of his simple-headedness is displayed in the New Testament. Here we have a story about Jesus coming to this burg where there's a fellow full of devils living there. I mean, full of them dudes. He's popping to the eyeballs with them. Slobbering around, short on manners. Being Southern, this last part about manners deeply disturbs me. Nobody likes to have someone around that can't be invited for dinner and be expected to behave, though come to think of it, I don't know a Southerner who hasn't got at least one story about someone dying at the table with a chicken bone or some such lodged in their throat.

Anyway, Jesus got on the job in an instant. He pulled those devils out of that poor infested soul and freed him. 'Course, then he had the devils to get rid of. You can't keep something like that under your hat, so J.C. spotted some innocent pigs wandering nearby, doing pig things, I reckon, and he stuffed those devils into the pigs.

Think on that. You're some piglet cruising along, just eating what you can find, thinking a few minor pig thoughts, and the next thing you know, you need an exorcist. But Jesus had a simpler answer, and any pig hearing of this biblical event for the first time is bound to lose the curl in his or her tail. It's that drastic.

What Jesus did is, he compelled the pigs *he*, his own merciful self, had infested with those devils, to run into a pond. Lickity-split, right there into the water.

This is not part of normal pig activity, brethren. This was achieved by Jesus putting the hex on the pigs, the evil eye, something like that. Anyway, the pigs ran into the pond, and the Bible says something like "and they were choked," drowned being a bit less descriptive. It's always important in the Bible that the right words for suffering are chosen, and this precision is something I admire, and this sort of descriptive writing puts God and his biographers clearly and cleanly in the literary arena sometimes described as splatterpunk. It gives the pigs a less welcome title. Deceased.

I used to wake up at night after Sunday school and consider on those pigs. A cruel way to go, that, and pork chops wasted besides. Even the dumbest son of a bitch amongst us, short of a sociopath, would have put those devils in a rock and thrown it in the pond, but not Jesus. As is the general case with the Bible, someone or something innocent needs to suffer, and if you think this doesn't bring us to films, you're wrong.

Scary mythology—Greek, Roman, and those of the afore-mentioned Testaments—fairy tales, the like, led to horrific pictures in my head, and later they attracted me to the more pleasant horrors of the movies, and the movies in turn sent me to the books, which were the source for many of the films I saw. *Invasion of the Body Snatchers, Day of the Triffids, The Pit and the Pendulum* among them.

My first solid memory of low-budget horror and horror/sci-ence-fiction movies were presented to me by a long-haired, good-looking witch named Evilyn who came to me out of Shreveport, Louisiana, every Friday night, courtesy of the boob tube and a program called *Terror!*

Evilyn would come out wearing a slinky black dress with her black hair parted in the middle, say a few words about the movie of the night, then spring it on us.

Those movies ran the gamut, from the classic Universal stuff, *The Wolf Man* (a personal favorite), *Dracula, Franken-stein,* etc., to humbler non-Universal efforts such as *I Married a Monster from Outer Space* and *Invaders from Mars,* to William Castle extravaganzas like *Thirteen Ghosts* and *The Tingler,* to Roger Corman's *Attack of the Crab Monsters* and *Little Shop of Horrors.* In other words, a smorgasbord of stuff ranging from the good low-budgets to the indisputable ass wipes of the genre.

And brothers and sisters, I'm here today to witness to you today and say without hesitation, I loved them all.

Let me hear one from the amen corner.

Hallelujah!

Loved every goddamn one of them, from the classy Val Lewton stuff like *The Cat People* and *I Walked with a Zombie*, on down to the slightly off-center ones like *The Beast with Five Fingers* and *The Crawling Eye*, on lower into the sewerish ranks of picture-show produce wherein trees from hell and rocks from outer space threatened innocent civilians who only wanted to marry and raise three kids in a little house next to another house and have a good lawn mower and a barbecue grill in their garage, along with a new Chevy, of course.

And if Evilyn gave me my first dose of cinematic horror, the Cozy Theater gave me my second dose. Come Saturdays, I practically lived in that sticky-floored, roach-infested theater.

The Cozy showed all kinds of movies, but the kiddie matinee, and the main feature, were quite often men-in-monster-suit movies, apes on the loose, and good stuff like those Corman gems *Diary of a Madman*, based on Guy de Maupassant's "The Horla," and countless other films loosely—quite loosely—based on Edgar Allan Poe stories like "The Pit and the Pendulum" and "The Masque of the Red Death."

Drive-ins gave me my third dose of horror movies, and this one, dear hearts, was as intense as a dose of the clap. Oh man, I loved drive-ins, still do, but now they're as scarce as intellectuals in the political system.

Admittedly, my first drive-in experiences were courtesy of my parents and older brother and his family, and what I saw then was more in the way of Disney films, westerns, that sort of thing, and I loved them, too. But when I was in my teens, I began to go to the drive-in on my own, and that's when the real brain damage took place.

Most of the stuff I saw, and it was not all horror, was just downright bad. But thing was, this way, I was getting to see something I wasn't supposed to see in my living room, something my parents wouldn't want me to see, and finally, there was a certain mystique about the low-budget horror movies, because most likely, one of those dudes passed through town and I missed it, unless it came to a town nearby. I was shit out of luck, 'cause there wasn't any video, and the networks damn sure weren't going to show that crap on television on account of these movies weren't made for art, they were made exclusively as drive-in cannon fodder, produced for one reason only—to separate me, the moviegoer, from his buck.

To some drive-in goers, and I have to speak from a male point of view here, these movies were something to kill time with while pausing between necking with dates, a little breather while putting the clothes back on. Or if you couldn't get a date, you could sit with buddies and watch this crap while you lied about getting a look up Debra Jane's skirt in social studies.

(Let me pause for a historical point of importance. This optical event of boy-eyeball-on-girl-panty was referred to in Gladewater High School as "shooting squirrel."

Write that down, you might need it on a Trivial Pursuit question or something.)

Another thing about the drive-in was it was sort of like a teenage guy itself. It liked dark private places, and it bragged, downright lied actually, about how well it could perform. Compare the lies some guys tell about all the tail they've banged to drive-in advertisements, and you'll begin to see what I mean.

Example: We'd drive on over to the Riverroad in Longview, Texas, and the coming attractions we'd see before the movies would turn out to be more stimulating than the movie we ended up watching, which, of course, we'd come to see because last week's previews had turned out to be better than the movies we watched then.

In my novel *The Drive-In*, I talked about these kinds of movies and the drive-in experience, and I said this of my mythical drive-in, the Orbit:

Now you're ready. The movies begin. B-string and basement budget pictures. A lot of them made with little more than a Kodak, some spit and a prayer. And if you've watched enough of this stuff, you develop a taste for it, sort of like learning to like sauerkraut.

Drooping mikes, bad acting and the rutting of rubber-suited monsters who want women, not for food, but to mate with, become a genuine pleasure. You can simultaneously hoot and cringe when a monster attacks a screaming female on the beach or in the woods and you see the zipper on the back of the monster suit winking at you like the quick, drunk smile of a Cheshire cat.

Yes sir, there was something special about the Orbit all right. It was romantic. It was outlaw. It was crazy.

For all practical purposes, the drive-in is gone, replaced by cable channels and video. Both are nice, but I still miss being out under that Texas sky, the party or picnic atmosphere drive-ins had, and dammit, I even miss that foul mosquito coil you bought at the concession to ward off the little bloodsuckers. You were supposed to light it and in theory the smoke from it had something in it mosquitoes hated, and they wouldn't come around. This bit of advertisement was in line with the drive-in previews. It lied.

You lit that thing and put it on your dash, and about the only way it stopped a mosquito was if the ignorant sonofabitch sat on the coil and caught on fire.

But, drive-in or no drive-in, the low-budget movie is still with us, and though I'm a bit more selective these days, the same attraction remains for me as before.

Other than nostalgia, why is this?

Hell, I don't know, not really, but, let me venture a smidgen of academic analysis—just a little, I don't want to throw up in my trash can here—and toss in a whole bean pot full of opinion.

The low-budget horror film is, on one hand, one of the most maligned forms of entertainment, and on the other hand, is often given a significance far beyond its worth.

As a sometimes writer of stories and novels of questionable taste, meaning fiction that is the equivalent of a dinner guest enthusiastically burping and farting at their host's table between asking why a better beer wasn't stocked for dinner and complaining about the lumps in the gravy, and yet being able to discuss Hemingway and Faulkner and Flannery O'Connor and the Doc Savage book where ol' Doc goes to hell, films of John Huston and John Ford and innovative crapmaker Roger Corman, I am quite aware of these extremes.

Seems many people, knowing my love for low-budget horror movies, think I can't wait to see the next evisceration extravaganza, some exploitation flick that shows in detail how to gut a human being and preserve the body parts, and I must admit I always feel, to put it mildly, distressed. To these folks, any low-budget horror movie with blood and grue is the same as the next, but in my eyes, there is quite a distinction between *Re-Animator* and *Friday the 13th Part Six Million*, or some of its more brain-damaged cousins that were once the fodder of second-feature drive-in bills and are now consigned to Made for Video, their packaging commonly appearing to have been designed by malicious children with crayons made of blood and soot and shit and smoke.

Some video packages, however, show a delightful lack of class. Take for instance *The Dead Pit*. This baby has a zombie and a button on the cover. You press the button and the zombie's eyes light up. My wife and I, while eating popcorn and watching this baby, would take turns pressing the button on the box when the theatric excitement slowed up or the backlighting in the movie made you think of a disco-zombie-jamboree. Needless to say, time we turned that little buddy back into the video store, the battery-powered green light behind the zombie's eyes had grown a mite faint.

But this confusion is understandable. The difference between a bad low-budget horror movie and a good one is, at times, difficult to discern. The problem being, a bad one and a good one share the same elements, and at a glance, the distinction between *The Texas Chainsaw Massacre* and *Attack of the Radioactive Testicles from Mars* may seem slight.

The low-budget horror movie stands on the line of good taste and bad taste, and like a scarecrow in a high wind, flaps its arms and leans first in one direction, then the other. What gives the good film its power is its bravery, its willingness to let the wind blow it across the line of good taste, into that part of the field that is less mannerly and sometimes downright rude.

Possibly that wind will blow off our symbolic scarecrow's hat and sail it into oblivion, tear out some stuffing as well, but the good movie is unwilling to let its support pole topple completely before the wind shifts and redirects it in the direction we call art, and when referring to these movies, or, if you must, films, the word "art" more often than not will be spoken softly and with a cough.

And if we refuse to call bad acting and sloppy effects and stupid plotting art, we can at least say some of these movies, the ones that lost their hat and some of their stuffing, are at their best trying hard to be more than what they appear to be on the surface.

An example being *Street Trash*. You won't get me up on a soapbox expounding on how this little buddy is art. It's kind of a mess really. It rapidly loses its hat to the wind, as well as a large portion of its stuffing, and goes blowing hell-bent for leather over into the field of bad taste and just plain sloppy filmmaking. Still, at its core, I believe it has (cough) artistic intent.

You can feel it. It's clever. *Street Trash* has a sense of irony and satire, a desire to be more than a scarecrow in a high wind. But, like the Oz scarecrow, it needs a brain, but unlike the Oz scarecrow, it never quite gets one.

This aside, it never allows its base pole to come undone, though it does lean precariously far at times, and when the film's over, *Street Trash*'s symbolic scarecrow, minus hat and two-thirds of its stuffing, still has an arm and a leg and a head to nod toward the (cough) artistic side. It's a crippled creature, admittedly, but it's still standing.

It should be obvious by now that my feelings concerning the difference between bad and good is the ability, or inability, to negotiate the wind. Our movie scarecrows often lose their foundation and go flying off too far in one direction or the other, satisfying neither on an exploitation level nor an artistic one.

What the good low-budget horror movie does is attract through exploitation, then, with imagination, cleverness, and greater intent than to appeal to the lowest common denominator, or through a desire to manipulate that low denominator with irony or satire or archetypal imagery, it becomes artistic or shows artistic bents, which is not necessarily the same as becoming art, though at its very best, it can be that, too.

Fact is, any low-budget movie, even the good ones, should make the viewer wonder which camp it wants to be in. That of art or exploitation. That's part of its appeal, and part of the reason these movies are often underestimated, or at times, overestimated.

Big-budget films generally announce which camp they're in early on. They want there to be no mistake. They either see themselves as art, or as a roller-coaster ride—one of those overworked advertising terms used to describe a host of "slick" movies that have less brains than our aforementioned *Street Trash* scarecrow—and they damn well want you to know which one they are before you view the first frame. It's a subliminal way of telling you not to expect much for your dollars.

Enjoying a good low-budget horror movie should be akin to being in love with a good-looking woman with a mysterious past, a past that might possibly include something nefarious. Like murder or voting for Richard Nixon. A little scrambling of intent is what makes the good low-budget movie interesting and thought-provoking.

I'm not trying to say that *Night of the Living Dead* and *The Texas Chainsaw Massacre* kept me awake at night pondering the meaning of it all. I've seen far too much attention given to the existentialist nature of these movies, and all I have to say to that is: Bullshit, pilgrim!

But these movies did address some rather primal fears for me far better than most of their filmatic relatives, some sporting fancier credentials.

Saw, like only a handful of other movies, tapped a nerve with me that is more often than not better accomplished with fiction and nonfiction. It touched that part of my brain, the primitive part, that made me realize that at some point the difference between the loving husband and doting father and a fellow with a chainsaw and evil intent, can be uncomfortably close. It accomplished this by simply making its villains a loving and loyal, if quarrelsome, family, and making their victims, if not murderous, less than loving. It takes skill to make a wheelchair-bound victim unsympathetic, but this is managed early on, and quite soon the audience is eager to see a helpless cripple get his, even if his only crime is assholism.

Night of the Living Dead's message is simple as well, but once again, primal. It shows that even the dead get no respect. It makes them a spectacle. Shows that once you're laid to rest in good old Mother Earth, you're going to rot and be full of worms. Not tidy. Once again, good manners have been breached. The director, George Romero, has put his finger on an often unspoken fear that many of us have. Your body is about as much a temple as a sagging, clapboard shithouse. Worse than that, the hero bites the big one in the end, pointing out an even worse horror: It doesn't matter how you live, who you are, there just ain't no such thing as true justice.

There are plenty of other cinematic examples, but I'm pushing my agreed wordage, and it's time for the sum-up.

That Mr. Lansdale is full of doodoo?

Likely. Yet, while I have you trapped mid-paragraph, let me conclude with a summary as to why I, and people like me, have a hard-on, or stiff nipples, for this stuff:

1. It's primal.

2. For many of us, it's nostalgic.

3. It's forbidden—less so these days, but that element remains.

4. It's something to do that's more interesting than polishing the silverware or vacuuming the carpet.

5. A few of us make our living from writing about this kind of stuff, because like the drive-in movies, we want to separate you from your buck, and I suppose if you're reading this—unless you've borrowed it—mission accomplished.

And you know what? It may not be any of these things.

For Russ Ansley

IN THE COLD, DARK TIME

It was the time of the Icing, and the snow and razor-winds blew across the lands and before and behind them came the war and the war went across the lands worse than the ice, like a plague, and there were those who took in the plague and died by it, or were wounded deeply by it, and I was one of the wounded, and at first I wished I was one of the dead.

I lay in bed hour on hour in the poorly heated hospital and watched the night come, then the day, then the night, then the day, and no time of night or day seemed lost to me, for I could not sleep, but could only cough out wads of blood-tainted phlegm and saliva that rose from my injured lungs like blobby, bubbly monsters to remind me of my rendering flesh. I lay there and prayed for death, for I knew all my life had been lost to me, and that my job in the war was no longer mine, and when the war was over, if it was ever over, I would never return to civilized life to continue the same necessary job I had pursued during wartime. The job with the children. The poor children. Millions of them. Parentless, homeless, forever being pushed onward by the ice and the war. It was a horror to see them. Little, frost-bitten waifs without food or shelter or good coats and there was no food or shelter or good coats to give them. Nothing to offer them but the war and a cold, slow death.

There were more children than adults now, and the adults were about war and there were only a few like myself there to help them. One of the few that could be spared for the Army's Children Corp. And now I could help no one, not even myself.

In the bed beside me in the crumbling, bomb-shook hospital, was an old man with his arm blown off at the elbow and his face splotched with the familiar frost-bite of a front-line man. He lay turned toward me, staring, but not speaking. And in the night, I would turn, and there would be his eyes, lit up by the night-lamp or by the moonlight, and that glow of theirs would strike me and I would imagine they contained the sparks of incendiary bombs for melting ice, or the red-hot destruction of rockets and bullets. In the daylight the sunlight toured the perimeters of his eyes like a firefight, but the night was the worst, for then they were the brightest, and the strangest.

I thought I should say something to him, but could never bring myself to utter a word because I was too lost in my misery and waiting for the change of day to night, night to day, and I was thinking of the children. Or I tell myself that now. My thoughts were mostly on me and how sad it was that a man like me had been born into a time of war and that none of what was good in me and great about me could be given to the world.

The children crossed my mind, but I must admit I saw them less as my mission in life, than as crosses I had borne on my back while climbing Christlike toward the front lines. Heavy crosses that had caused me to fall hard to the ground, driving the pain into my lungs, putting me here where I would die in inches far from home.

"Why do you fret for yourself," the old man said one morning. I turned and looked at him and his eyes were as animal bright as ever and there was no expression on his crunched, little face.

"I fret for the children."

"Ah," he said. "The children. Your job in the Corp."

I said nothing in reply and he said not another word until the middle of the night when I drifted into sleep momentarily, for all my sleep was momentary, and opened my eyes to the lamp light and the cold hospital air. I pulled a kleenex from the box beside my bed and coughed blood into it.

"You are getting better," he said.

"I'm dying," I said.

"No. You are getting better. You hardly cough at all. Your sleep is longer. You used to cough all night."

"You're a doctor I suppose?"

"No, but I am a soldier. Or was. Now I am a useless old man with no arm."

"In the old days a man your age would have been retired or put behind a desk. Not out on the front lines."

"I suppose you're right. But this is not the old days. This is now, and I'm finished anyway because of the arm."

"And I'm finished because of my wound."

"The lungs heal faster than anything. You are only finished if you are too bitter to heal. To be old and bitter is all right. It greases the path to the other side. To be young and bitter is foolish."

"How do you know so much about me?"

"I listen to the nurses and I listen to you and I observe."

"Have you nothing else to do but meddle in my affairs?"

"No."

"Leave me be."

"I would if I could, but I'm an old man and will not live long anyway, wounded or not. I have the pains of old age and no family and nothing I would be able to do if I leave here. All I know is the life of a soldier. But you will recover if you believe you will recover. It is up to you now."

"So you are a doctor?"

"An old soldier has seen wounds and sickness, and he knows a man that can get well if he chooses to get well. A coward will die. Which are you?"

I didn't answer and he didn't repeat the question. I turned my back to him and went to sleep and later in the night I heard him calling.

"Young man."

I lay there and listened but did not move.

"I think you can hear me and this may be the last I have to say on the matter. You are getting better. You sleep better. You cough less. The wound is healing. It may not matter what your attitude is now, you may heal anyway, but let me tell you this, if you heal, you must heal with your soul intact. You must not lose your love for the children, no matter what you've seen. It isn't your wound that aches you, makes you want to die, it's the war. There are few who are willing to do your job, to care for the children. They need you. They run in hungry, naked packs, and all that is between them and suffering is the Children's Corp and people like you. The love of children, the need not to see them hungry and in pain is a necessary human trait if we are to survive as a people. When, if, this war is over, it must not be a war that has poisoned our hopes for the future. Get well. Do your duty."

I lay there when he was finished and thought about all I had done for the children and thought about the war and all that had to be done afterwards, knew then that my love for the children, their needs, were the obsessions of my life. They were my reason to live, more than just living to exist. I knew then that I had to let their cause stay with me, had to let my hatred of the world and the war go, because there were the children.

The next day they came and took the old man away. He had pulled the bandage off of the nub of his arm during the night and chewed the cauterized wound open with the viciousness of a tiger and had bled to death. His sheets were the color of gun-metal rust when they came for him and pulled the stained sheet over his head and rolled him away.

They brought in a young, wounded pilot then, and his eyes were cold and hard and the color of grave dirt. I spoke to him and he wouldn't speak back, but I kept at it, and finally he yelled at me, and said he didn't want to live, that he had seen too much terror to want to go on, but I kept talking to him, and soon he was chattering like a machine gun and we had long conversations into the night about women and chess and the kind of beers we were missing back home. And he told me his hopes for after the war, and I told him mine. Told him how I would get out of my bed and go back to the front lines to help the refugee children, and after the war I would help those who remained.

A month later they let me out of the bed to wander.

I think often of the old man now, especially when the guns boom about the camp and I'm helping the children, and sometimes I think of the young man and that I may have helped do for him with a few well-placed words what the old man did for me, but mostly I think of the old one and what he said to me the night before he finished his life. It's a contradiction in a way, him giving me life and taking his own, but he knew that my life was important to the children. I wish I had turned and spoken to him, but that opportunity is long gone.

Each time they bring the sad little children in to me, one at a time, and I feed them and hold them, I pray the war will end and there will be money for food and shelter instead of the care of soldiers and the making of bullets, but wishes are wishes, and what is, is.

And when I put the scarf around the children's necks and tighten it until I have eased their pain, I am overcome with an even simpler wish for spare bullets or drugs to make it quicker, and I have to mentally close my ears to the drumming of their little feet and shut my nose to the smell of their defecation, but I know that this is the best way; a warm meal, a moment of hope, a quick, dark surrender, the only mercy available to them, and when I take the scarf from their sad, little necks and lay them aside, I think again of the old man and the life he gave me back and the mercy he gives the children through me.

For Neal Barrett

INCIDENT ON AND OFF A MOUNTAIN ROAD

When Ellen came to the moonlit mountain curve, her thoughts, which had been adrift with her problems, grounded, and she was suddenly aware that she was driving much too fast. The sign said CURVE: 30 MPH, and she was doing fifty.

She knew too that slamming on the brakes was the wrong move, so she optioned to keep her speed and fight the curve and make it, and she thought she could.

The moonlight was strong, so visibility was high, and she knew her Chevy was in good shape, easy to handle, and she was a good driver.

But as she negotiated the curve a blue Buick seemed to grow out of the ground in front of her. It was parked on the shoulder of the road, at the peak of the curve, its nose sticking out a foot too far, its rear end against the moon-wet, silver railing that separated the curve from a mountainous plunge.

Had she been going an appropriate speed, missing the Buick wouldn't have been a problem, but at her speed she was swinging too far right, directly in line with it, and was forced, after all, to use her brakes. When she did, the back wheels slid and the brakes groaned and the front of the Chevy hit the Buick and there was a sound like an explosion and then for a dizzy instant she felt as if she were in the tumblers of a dryer.

Through the windshield came: Moonlight. Blackness. Moonlight.

One high bounce and a tight roll and the Chevy came to rest upright with the engine dead, the right side flush against the railing. Another inch of jump or greater impact against the rail, and the Chevy would have gone over.

Ellen felt a sharp pain in her leg and reached down to discover that during the tumble she had banged it against something, probably the gear shift, and had ripped her stocking and her flesh. Blood was trickling into her shoe. Probing her leg cautiously, with the tips of her fingers, she determined the wound wasn't bad and that all other body parts were operative.

She unfastened her seat belt, and as a matter of habit, located her purse and slipped its strap over her shoulder. She got out of the Chevy feeling wobbly, eased around front of it, and saw the hood and bumper and roof were crumpled. A wisp of radiator steam hissed from beneath the wadded hood, rose into the moonlight and dissolved.

She turned her attention to the Buick. Its tail end was now turned to her, and as she edged alongside it, she saw the front left side had been badly damaged. Fearful of what she might see, she glanced inside.

The moonlight shone through the rear windshield bright as a spotlight and revealed no one, but the backseat was slick with something dark and wet and there was plenty of it. A foul scent seeped out of a partially rolled down back window.

210

It was a hot coppery smell that gnawed at her nostrils and ached her stomach.

God, someone had been hurt. Maybe thrown free of the car, or perhaps they had gotten out and crawled off. But when? She and the Chevy had been airborne for only a moment, and she had gotten out of the vehicle instants after it ceased to roll. Surely she would have seen someone get out of the Buick, and if they had been thrown free by the collision, wouldn't at least one of the Buick's doors be open? If it had whipped back and closed, it seemed unlikely that it would be locked, and all the doors of the Buick were locked, and all the glass was intact, and only on her side was it rolled down, and only a crack. Enough for the smell of the blood to escape, not enough for a person to slip through unless they were thin and flexible as a feather.

On the other side of the Buick, on the ground, between the back door and the railing, there were drag marks and a thick swath of blood, and another swath on the top of the railing; it glowed there in the moonlight as if it were molasses laced with radioactivity.

Ellen moved cautiously to the railing and peered over.

No one lay mangled and bleeding and oozing their guts. The ground was not as precarious there as she expected it. It was pebbly and sloped out gradually and there was a trail going down it. The trail twisted slightly and as it deepened the foliage grew dense on either side of it. Finally it curlicued its way into the dark thicket of a forest below, and from the forest, hot on the wind, came the strong turpentine tang of pines and something less fresh and not as easily identifiable.

Now she saw someone moving down there, floating up from the forest like an apparition; a white face split by silver—braces perhaps. She could tell from the way this someone moved that it was a man. She watched as he climbed the trail and came within examination range. He seemed to be surveying her as carefully as she was surveying him.

Could this be the driver of the Buick?

As he came nearer Ellen discovered she could not identify the expression he wore. It was neither joy nor anger nor fear nor exhaustion nor pain. It was somehow all and none of these.

When he was ten feet away, still looking up, that same odd expression on his face, she could hear him breathing. He was breathing with exertion, but not to the extent she thought him tired or injured. It was the sound of someone who had been about busy work.

She yelled down, "Are you injured?"

He turned his head quizzically, like a dog trying to make sense of a command, and it occurred to Ellen that he might be knocked about in the head enough to be disoriented.

"I'm the one who ran into your car," she said. "Are you all right?"

His expression changed then, and it was most certainly identifiable this time. He was surprised and angry. He came up the trail quickly, took hold of the top railing, his fingers going into the blood there, and vaulted over and onto the gravel.

Ellen stepped back out of his way and watched him from a distance. The guy made her nervous. He looked like some kind of spook.

He eyed her briefly, glanced at the Chevy, turned to look at the Buick.

"It was my fault," Ellen said.

He didn't reply, but turned his attention to her and continued to cock his head in that curious dog sort of way.

Ellen noticed that one of his shirt sleeves was stained with blood, and that there was blood on the knees of his pants, but he didn't act as if he were hurt in any way. He reached into his pants pocket and pulled out something and made a move with his wrist. Out flicked a lock-blade knife. The thin edge of it sucked up the moonlight and spat it out in a silver spray that fanned wide when he held it before him and jiggled it like a man working a stubborn key into a lock. He advanced toward her, and as he came, his lips split apart and pulled back at the corners, exposing, not braces, but metal-capped teeth that matched the sparkle of his blade.

It occurred to her that she could bolt for the Chevy, but in the same mental flash of lightning, it occurred to her she wouldn't make it.

Ellen threw herself over the railing, and as she leapt, she saw out of the corner of her eye, the knife slashing the place she had occupied, catching moonbeams and throwing them away. Then the blade was out of her view and she hit on her stomach and skidded onto the narrow trail and slid downward, feet first. The gravel and roots tore at the front of her dress and ripped through her nylons and gouged her flesh. She cried out in pain and her sliding gained speed. Lifting her chin, she saw that the man was climbing over the railing and coming after her at a stumbling run, the knife held before him like a wand.

Her sliding stopped, and she pushed off with her hands to make it start again, not knowing if this was the thing to do or not, since the trail inclined sharply on her right side, and should she skid only slightly in that direction, she could hurtle off into blackness. But somehow she kept slithering along the trail and even spun around a corner and stopped with her head facing downward, her purse practically in her teeth.

She got up then, without looking back, and began to run into the woods, the purse beating at her side. She moved as far away from the trail as she could, fighting limbs that conspired to hit her across the face or hold her, vines and bushes that tried to tie her feet or trip her.

Behind her, she could hear the man coming after her, breathing heavily now, not really winded, but hurrying. For the first time in months, she was grateful to Bruce and his survivalist insanity. His passion to be in shape and for her to be in shape with him was paying off. All that jogging had given her the lungs of an ox and strengthened her legs and ankles. A line from one of Bruce's survivalist books came to her: *Do the unexpected.*

She found a trail amongst the pines, and followed it, then, abruptly broke from it and went back into the thicket. It was harder going, but she assumed her pursuer would expect her to follow a trail.

The pines became so thick she got down on her hands and knees and began to crawl. It was easier to get through that way. After a moment, she stopped scuttling and eased her back against one of the pines and sat and listened. She felt reasonably well hidden, as the boughs of the pines grew low and drooped to the ground. She took several deep breaths, holding each for a long moment. Gradually, she began breathing normally. Above her, from the direction of the trail, she could hear the man running, coming nearer. She held her breath.

The running paused a couple of times, and she could imagine the man, his strange, pale face turning from side to side, as he tried to determine what had happened to her. The sound of running started again and the man moved on down the trail.

Ellen considered easing out and starting back up the trail, making her way to her car and driving off. Damaged as it was, she felt it would still run, but she was reluctant to leave her hiding place and step into the moonlight. Still, it seemed a better plan than waiting. If she didn't do something, the man could always go back topside himself and wait for her. The woods, covering acres and acres of land below and beyond, would take her days to get through, and without food and water and knowledge of the geography, she might never make it, could end up going in circles for days.

Bruce and his survivalist credos came back to her. She remembered something he had said to one of his self-defense classes, a bunch of rednecks hoping and praying for a commie takeover so they could show their stuff. He had told them: "Utilize what's at hand. Size up what you have with you and how it can be put to use."

All right, she thought. All right, Brucey, you sonofabitch. I'll see what's at hand.

One thing she knew she had for sure was a little flashlight. It wasn't much, but it would serve for her to check out the contents of her purse. She located it easily, and without withdrawing it from her purse, turned it on and held the open purse close to her face to see what was inside. Before she actually found it, she thought of her nail file kit. Besides the little bottle of nail polish remover, there was an emery board and two metal files. The files were the ticket. They might serve as weapons; they weren't much, but they were something.

She also carried a very small pair of nail scissors, independent of the kit, the points of the scissors being less than a quarter inch. That wouldn't be worth much, but she took note of it and mentally catalogued it.

She found the nail kit, turned off the flashlight and removed one of the files and returned the rest of the kit to her purse. She held the file tightly, made a little jabbing motion with it. It seemed so light and thin and insignificant.

She had been absently carrying her purse on one shoulder, and now to make sure she didn't lose it, she placed the strap over her neck and slid her arm through.

Clenching the nail file, she moved on hands and knees beneath the pine boughs and poked her head out into the clearing of the trail. She glanced down it first, and there, not ten yards from her, looking up the trail, holding his knife by his side, was the man. The moonlight lay cold on his face and the shadows of the wind-blown boughs fell across him and wavered. It seemed as if she were leaning over a pool and staring down into the water and seeing him at the bottom of it, or perhaps his reflection on the face of the pool.

She realized instantly that he had gone down the trail a ways, became suspicious of her ability to disappear so quickly, and had turned to judge where she might have gone. And, as if in answer to the question, she had poked her head into view.

They remained frozen for a moment, then the man took a step up the trail, and just as he began to run, Ellen went backwards into the pines on her hands and knees.

She had gone less than ten feet when she ran up against a thick limb that lay close to the ground and was preventing her passage. She got down on her belly and squirmed beneath it, and as she was pulling her head under, she saw Moon Face crawling into the thicket, making good time; time made better when he lunged suddenly and covered half the space between them, the knife missing her by fractions.

Ellen jerked back and felt her feet falling away from her. She let go of the file and grabbed out for the limb and it bent way back and down with her weight. It lowered her enough for her feet to touch ground. Relieved, she realized she had fallen into a wash made by erosion, not off the edge of the mountain.

Above her, gathered in shadows and stray strands of moonlight that showed through the pine boughs, was the man. His metal-tipped teeth caught a moonbeam and twinkled. He placed a hand on the limb she held, as if to lower himself, and she let go of it.

The limb whispered away from her and hit him full in the face and knocked him back.

Ellen didn't bother to scrutinize the damage. Turning, she saw that the wash ended in a slope and that the slope was thick with trees growing out like great, feathered spears thrown into the side of the mountain.

She started down, letting the slant carry her, grasping limbs and tree trunks to slow her descent and keep her balance. She could hear the man climbing down and pursuing her, but she didn't bother to turn and look. Below she could see the incline was becoming steeper, and if she continued, it would be almost straight up and down with nothing but the trees for support, and to move from one to the other, she would have to drop, chimpanzee-like, from limb to limb. Not a pleasant thought.

Her only consolation was that the trees to her right, veering back up the mountain, were thick as cancer cells. She took off in that direction, going wide, and began plodding upwards again, trying to regain the concealment of the forest.

She chanced a look behind her before entering the pines, and saw that the man, who she had come to think of as Moon Face, was some distance away.

Weaving through a mass of trees, she integrated herself into the forest, and as she went the limbs began to grow closer to the ground and the trees became so thick they twisted together like pipe cleaners. She got down on her hands and knees and crawled between limbs and around tree trunks and tried to lose herself among them.

To follow her, Moon Face had to do the same thing, and at first she heard him behind her, but after a while, there were only the sounds she was making.

She paused and listened.

Nothing.

Glancing the way she had come, she saw the intertwining limbs she had crawled under mixed with penetrating moon-beams, heard the short bursts of her breath and the beating of her heart, but detected no evidence of Moon Face. She decided the head start she had, all the weaving she had done, the cover of the pines, had confused him, at least temporarily.

It occurred to her that if she had stopped to listen, he might have done the same, and she wondered if he could hear the pounding of her heart. She took a deep breath and held it and let it out slowly through her nose, did it again. She was breathing more normally now, and her heart, though still hammering furiously, felt as if it were back inside her chest where it belonged.

Easing her back against a tree trunk, she sat and listened, watching for that strange face, fearing it might abruptly burst through the limbs and brush, grinning its horrible teeth, or worse, that he might come up behind her, reach around the tree trunk with his knife and finish her in a bloody instant.

She checked and saw that she still had her purse. She opened it and got hold of the file kit by feel and removed the last file, determined to make better use of it than the first. She had no qualms about using it, knew she would, but what good would it do? The man was obviously stronger than she, and crazy as the pattern in a scrap quilt.

Once again, she thought of Bruce. What would he have done in this situation? He would certainly have been the man for the job. He would have relished it. Would probably have challenged old Moon Face to a one-on-one at the edge of the mountain, and even with a nail file, would have been confident that he could take him.

Ellen thought about how much she hated Bruce, and even now, shed of him, that hatred burned bright. How had she gotten mixed up with that dumb, macho bastard in the first place? He had seemed enticing at first. So powerful. Confident. Capable. The survivalist stuff had always seemed a little nutty, but at first no more nutty than an obsession with golf or a strong belief in astrology. Perhaps had she known how serious he was about it, she wouldn't have been attracted to him in the first place.

No. It wouldn't have mattered. She had been captivated by him, by his looks and build and power. She had nothing but her own libido and stupidity to blame. And worse yet, when things turned sour, she had stayed and let them sour even more. There had been good moments, but they were quickly eclipsed by Bruce's determination to be ready for the Big Day, as he referred to it. He knew it was coming, if he was somewhat vague on who was bringing it. But someone would start a war of some sort, a nuclear war, a war in the streets, and only the rugged individualist, well-armed and well-trained and strong of body and will would survive beyond the initial attack. Those survivors would then carry out guerrilla warfare, hit and run operations, and eventually win back the country from . . . whoever. And if not win it back, at least have some kind of life free of dictatorship.

It was silly. It was every little boy's fantasy. Living by your wits with gun and knife. And owning a woman. She had been the woman. At first Bruce had been kind enough, treated her with respect. He was obviously on the male chauvinist side, but originally it had seemed harmless enough, kind of Old World charming. But when he moved them to the mountains, that charm had turned to domination, and the small crack in his mental state widened until it was a deep, dark gulf.

She was there to keep house and to warm his bed, and any opinions she had contrary to his own were stupid. He read survivalist books constantly and quoted passages to her and suggested she look the books over, be ready to stand tall against the oncoming aggressors.

By the time he had gone completely over the edge, living like a mountain man, ordering her about, his eyes roving from side to side, suspicious of her every move, expecting to hear on his shortwave at any moment World War Three had started, or that race riots were overrunning the U.S., or that a shiny probe packed with extraterrestrial invaders brandishing ray guns had landed on the White House lawn, she was trapped in his cabin in the mountains with him holding the keys to her Chevy and his jeep.

For a time she feared he would become paranoid enough to imagine she was one of the "bad guys" and put a .357 round through her chest. But now she was free of him, escaped from all that . . . only to be threatened by another man; a moon-faced, silver-toothed monster with a knife.

She returned once again to the question, what would Bruce do, outside of challenging Moon Face in hand-to-hand combat? Sneaking past him would be the best bet, making it back to the Chevy. To do that Bruce would have used guerrilla techniques. "Take advantage of what's at hand," he always said.

Well, she had looked to see what was at hand, and that turned out to be a couple of fingernail files, one of them lost up the mountain.

Then maybe she wasn't thinking about this in the right way. She might not be able to outfight Moon Face, but perhaps she could outthink him. She had outthought Bruce, and he had considered himself a master of strategy and preparation.

She tried to put herself in Moon Face's head. What was he thinking? For the moment he saw her as his prey, a frightened animal on the run. He might be more cautious because of that trick with the limb, but he'd most likely chalk that one up to accident—which it was for the most part . . . But what if the prey turned on him?

There was a sudden cracking sound, and Ellen crawled a few feet in the direction of the noise, gently moved aside a limb. Some distance away, discerned faintly through a tangle of limbs, she saw light and detected movement, and knew it was

Moon Face. The cracking sound must have been him stepping on a limb.

He was standing with his head bent, looking at the ground, flashing a little pocket flashlight, obviously examining the drag path she had made with her hands and knees when she entered into the pine thicket.

She watched as his shape and the light bobbed and twisted through the limbs and tree trunks, coming nearer. She wanted to run, but didn't know where to.

"All right," she thought. "All right. Take it easy. Think."

She made a quick decision. Removed the scissors from her purse, took off her shoes and slipped off her panty hose and put her shoes on again.

She quickly snipped three long strips of nylon from her damaged panty hose and knotted them together, using the sailor knots Bruce had taught her. She cut more thin strips from the hose—all the while listening for Moon Face's approach—and used all but one of them to fasten her fingernail file, point out, securely to the tapered end of one of the small, flexible pine limbs, then she tied one end of the long nylon strip she had made around the limb, just below the file, and crawled backwards, pulling the limb with her, bending it deep. When she had it back as far as she could manage, she took a death grip on the nylon strip, and using it to keep the limb's position taut, crawled around the trunk of a small pine and curved the nylon strip about it and made a loop knot at the base of a sapling that crossed her knee-drag trail. She used her last strip of nylon to fasten to the loop of the knot, and carefully stretched the remaining length across the trail and tied it to another sapling. If it worked correctly, when he came crawling through the thicket, following her, his hands or knees would hit the strip, pull the loop free, and the limb would fly forward, the file stabbing him, in an eye if she were lucky.

Pausing to look through the boughs again, she saw Moon Face was on his hands and knees, moving through the thick foliage toward her. Only moments were left.

She shoved pine needles over the strip and moved away on her belly, sliding under the cocked sapling, no longer concerned that she might make noise, in fact hoping noise would bring Moon Face quickly.

Following the upward slope of the hill, she crawled until the trees became thin again and she could stand. She cut two long strips of nylon from her hose with the scissors, and stretched them between two trees about ankle high.

That one would make him mad if it caught him, but the next one would be the corker.

She went up the path, used the rest of the nylon to tie between two saplings, then grabbed hold of a thin, short limb and yanked at it until it cracked, worked it free so there was a point made from the break. She snapped that over her knee to form a point at the opposite end. She made a quick mental measurement, jammed one end of the stick into the soft ground, leaving a point facing up.

At that moment came evidence her first snare had worked—a loud swishing sound as the limb popped forward and a cry of pain. This was followed by a howl as Moon Face crawled out of the thicket and onto the trail. He stood slowly, one hand to his face. He glared up at her, removed his hand. The file had struck him in the cheek; it was covered with blood. Moon Face pointed his blood-covered hand at her and let out an accusing shriek so horrible she retreated rapidly up the trail. Behind her, she could hear Moon Face running.

The trail curved upward and turned abruptly. She followed the curve a ways, looked back as Moon Face tripped over her first strip and hit the ground, came up madder, charged even more violently up the path. But the second strip got him and he fell forward, throwing his hands out. The spike in the trail hit him low in the throat.

She stood transfixed at the top of the trail as he did a push-up and came to one knee and put a hand to his throat. Even from a distance, and with only the moonlight to show it to her, she could see that the wound was dreadful.

Good.

Moon Face looked up, stabbed her with a look, started to rise. Ellen turned and ran. As she made the turns in the trail the going improved and she theorized that she was rushing up the trail she had originally come down.

This hopeful notion was dispelled when the pines thinned and the trail dropped, then leveled off, then tapered into nothing. Before she could slow up, she discovered she was on a sort of peninsula that jutted out from the mountain and resembled an irregular shaped diving board from which you could leap off into night-black eternity.

In place of the pines on the sides of the trail were numerous scarecrows on poles, and out on the very tip of the peninsula, somewhat dispelling the diving board image, was a shack made of sticks and mud and brambles.

After pausing to suck in some deep breaths, Ellen discovered on closer examination that it wasn't scarecrows bordering her path after all. It was people.

Dead people. She could smell them.

There were at least a dozen on either side, placed upright on poles, their feet touching the ground, their knees slightly bent. They were all fully clothed, and in various states of deterioration. Holes had been poked through the backs of their heads to correspond with the hollow sockets of their eyes, and the moonlight came through the holes and shined through the sockets, and Ellen noted with a warm sort of horror that one wore a white sun dress and pink, plastic shoes, and through its head she could see stars. On the corpse's finger was a wedding ring, and the finger had grown thin and withered and the ring was trapped there by knuckle bone alone.

The man next to her was fresher. He too was eyeless and holes had been drilled through the back of his skull, but he still wore glasses and was fleshy. There was a pen and pencil set in his coat pocket. He wore only one shoe.

There was a skeleton in overalls, a wilting cigar stuck between his teeth. A fresh UPS man with his cap at a jaunty angle, the moon through his head, and a clipboard tied to his hand with string. His legs had been positioned in such a way it seemed as if he were walking. A housewife with a crumpled, nearly disintegrated grocery bag under her arm, the contents having long fallen through the worn, wet bottom to heap at her feet in a mass of colorless boxes and broken glass. A withered corpse in a ballerina's tutu and slippers, rotting grapefruits tied to her chest with cord to simulate breasts, her legs arranged in such a way she seemed in mid-dance, up on her toes, about to leap or whirl.

The real horror was the children. One pathetic little boy's corpse, still full of flesh and with only his drilled eyes to show death, had been arranged in such a way that a teddy bear drooped from the crook of his elbow. A toy metal tractor and a plastic truck were at his feet.

There was a little girl wearing a red, rubber clown nose and propeller beanie. A green plastic purse hung from her shoulder by a strap and a doll's legs had been taped to her palm with black electrician's tape. The doll hung upside down, holes drilled through its plastic head so that it matched its owner.

Things began to click. Ellen understood what Moon Face had been doing down here in the first place. He hadn't been in the Buick when she struck it. He was disposing of a body. He was a murderer who brought his victims here and set them up on either side of the pathway, parodying the way they were in life, cutting out their eyes and punching through the backs of their heads to let the world in.

Ellen realized numbly that time was slipping away, and Moon Face was coming, and she had to find the trail up to her car. But when she turned to run, she froze.

Thirty feet away, where the trail met the last of the pines, squatting dead center in it, arms on his knees, one hand loosely holding the knife, was Moon Face. He looked calm, almost happy, in spite of the fact a large swath of dried blood was on his cheek and the wound in his throat was making a faint whistling sound as air escaped it.

He appeared to be gloating, savoring the moment when he would set his knife to work on her eyes, the gray matter behind them, the bone of her skull.

A vision of her corpse propped up next to the child with the teddy bear, or perhaps the skeletal ballerina, came to mind; she could see herself hanging there, the light of the moon falling through her empty head, melting into the path.

Then she felt anger. It boiled inside her. She determined she was not going to allow Moon Face his prize easily. He'd earn it.

Another line from Bruce's books came to her.

Consider your alternatives.

She did, in a flash. And they were grim. She could try charging past Moon Face, or pretend to, then dart into the pines. But it seemed unlikely she could make the trees before he overtook her. She could try going over the side of the trail and climbing down, but it was much too steep there, and she'd fall immediately. She could make for the shack and try and find something she could fight with. The last idea struck her as the correct one, the one Bruce would have pursued. What was his quote? "If you can't effect an escape, fall back and fight with what's available to you."

She hurried to the hut, glancing behind her from time to time to check on Moon Face. He hadn't moved. He was observing her calmly, as if he had all the time in the world.

When she was about to go through the doorless entryway, she looked back at him one last time. He was in the same spot, watching, the knife held limply against his leg. She knew he thought he had her right where he wanted her, and that's exactly what she wanted him to think. A surprise attack was the only chance she had. She just hoped she could find something to surprise him with.

She hastened inside and let out an involuntary gasp of breath.

The place stank, and for good reason. In the center of the little hut was a folding card table and some chairs, and seated in one of the chairs was a woman, the flesh rotting and dripping off her skull like candle wax, her eyes empty and holes in the back of her head. Her arm was resting on the table and her hand was clamped around an open bottle of whiskey. Beside her, also without eyes, suspended in a standing position by wires connected to the roof, was a man. He was a fresh kill. Big, dressed in khaki pants and shirt and work shoes. In one hand a doubled belt was taped, and wires were attached in such a way that his arm was drawn back as if ready to strike. Wires were secured to his lips and pulled tight behind his head so that he was smiling in a ghoulish way. Foil gum wrappers were fixed to his teeth, and the moonlight gleaming through the opening at the top of the hut fell on them and made them resemble Moon Face's metal-tipped choppers.

Ellen felt queasy, but fought the sensation down. She had more to worry about than corpses. She had to prevent herself from becoming one.

She gave the place a quick pan. To her left was a rust-framed roll-away bed with a thin, dirty mattress, and against the far wall was a baby crib, and next to that a camper stove with a small frying pan on it.

She glanced quickly out the door of the hut and saw that Moon Face had moved onto the stretch of trail bordered by the bodies. He was walking very slowly, looking up now and then as if to appreciate the stars.

Her heart pumped another beat.

She moved about the hut, looking for a weapon.

The frying pan.

She grabbed it, and as she did, she saw what was in the crib. What belonged there. A baby. But dead. A few months old. Its skin thin as plastic and stretched tight over pathetic, little rib bones. Eyes gone, holes through its head. Burnt match stubs between blackened toes. It wore a diaper and the stink of feces wafted from it and into her nostrils. A rattle lay at the foot of the crib.

A horrible realization rushed through her. The baby had been alive when taken by this mad man, and it had died here, starved and tortured. She gripped the frying pan with such intensity her hand cramped.

Her foot touched something.

She looked down. Large bones were heaped there—discarded Mommies and Daddies, for it now occurred to her that was who the corpses represented.

Something gleamed amongst the bones. A gold cigarette lighter.

Through the doorway of the hut she saw Moon Face was halfway down the trail. He had paused to nonchalantly adjust the UPS man's clipboard. The geek had made his own community here, his own family, people he could deal with—dead people—and it was obvious he intended for her to be part of his creation.

Ellen considered attacking straight-on with the frying pan when Moon Face came through the doorway, but so far he had proven strong enough to take a file in the cheek and a stick in the throat, and despite the severity of the latter wound, he had kept on coming. Chances were he was strong enough to handle her and her frying pan.

A back-up plan was necessary. Another one of Bruce's pronouncements. She recalled a college friend, Carol, who used to use her bikini panties to launch projectiles at a teddy bear propped on a chair. This graduated to an apple on the bear's head. Eventually, Ellen and her dorm sisters got into the act. Fresh panties with tight elastic and marbles for ammunition were ever ready in a box by the door, the bear and an apple were in constant position. In time, Ellen became the best shot of all. But that was ten years ago. Expertise was long gone, even the occasional shot now and then was no longer taken ... Still ...

Ellen replaced the frying pan on the stove, hiked up her dress and pulled her bikini panties down and stepped out of them and picked up the lighter.

She put the lighter in the crotch of the panties and stuck her fingers into the leg loops to form a fork and took hold of the lighter through the panties and pulled it back, assured herself the elastic was strong enough to launch the projectile.

All right. That was a start.

She removed her purse, so Moon Face couldn't grab it and snare her, and tossed it aside. She grabbed the whiskey bottle from the corpse's hand and turned and smashed the bottom of it against the cook stove. Whiskey and glass flew. The result was a jagged weapon she could lunge with. She placed the broken bottle on the stove next to the frying pan.

Outside, Moon Face was strolling toward the hut, like a shy teenager about to call on his date.

There were only moments left. She glanced around the room, hoping insanely at the last second she would find some escape route, but there was none.

Sweat dripped from her forehead and ran into her eye and she blinked it out and half-drew back the panty sling with its golden projectile. She knew her makeshift weapon wasn't powerful enough to do much damage, but it might give her a moment of distraction, a chance to attack him with the bottle. If she went at him straight on with it, she felt certain he would disarm her and make short work of her, but if she could get him off guard . . .

She lowered her arms, kept her makeshift slingshot in front of her, ready to be cocked and shot.

Moon Face came through the door, ducking as he did, a sour sweat smell entering with him. His neck wound whistled at her like a teapot about to boil. She saw then that he was bigger than she first thought. Tall and broad shouldered and strong.

He looked at her and there was that peculiar expression again. The moonlight from the hole in the roof hit his eyes and teeth, and it was as if that light was his source of energy. He filled his chest with air and seemed to stand a full two inches taller. He looked at the woman's corpse in the chair, the man's corpse supported on wires, glanced at the playpen.

He smiled at Ellen, squeaked more than spoke, "Bubba's home, Sissie."

I'm not Sissie yet, thought Ellen. Not yet.

Moon Face started to move around the card table and Ellen let out a blood-curdling scream that caused him to bob his head high like a rabbit surprised by headlights. Ellen jerked up the panties and pulled them back and let loose the lighter. It shot out of the panties and fell to the center of the card table with a clunk.

Moon Face looked down at it.

Ellen was temporarily gripped with paralysis, then she stepped forward and kicked the card table as hard as she could. It went into Moon Face, hitting him waist high, startling, but not hurting him.

Now! thought Ellen, grabbing her weapons. Now!

She rushed him, the broken bottle in one hand, the frying pan in the other. She slashed out with the bottle and it struck him in the center of the face and he let out a scream and the glass fractured and a splash of blood burst from him and in that same instant Ellen saw that his nose was cut half in two and she felt a tremendous throb in her hand. The bottle had broken in her palm and cut her.

She ignored the pain and as Moon Face bellowed and lashed out with the knife cutting the front of her dress but not her flesh, she brought the frying pan around and caught him on the elbow and the knife went soaring across the room and behind the roll-away bed.

Moon Face froze, glanced in the direction the knife had taken. He seemed empty and confused without it.

Ellen swung the pan again. Moon Face caught her wrist and jerked her around and she lost the pan and was sent hurtling toward the bed, where she collapsed on the mattress. The bed slid down and smashed through the thin wall of sticks and a foot of the bed stuck out into blackness and the great drop below. The bed tottered slightly, and Ellen rolled off of it, directly into the legs of Moon Face. As his knees bent, and he reached for her, she rolled backwards and went under the bed and her hand came to rest on the knife. She grabbed it, rolled back toward Moon Face's feet, reached out quickly and brought the knife down on one of his shoes and drove it in as hard as she could.

A bellow from Moon Face. His foot leaped back and it took the knife with it. Moon Face screamed, "Sissie! You're hurting me!"

Moon Face reached down and pulled the knife out, and Ellen saw his foot come forward, and then he was grabbing the bed and effortlessly jerking it off of her and back, smashing it into the crib, causing the child to topple out of it and roll across the floor, the rattle clattering behind it. He grabbed Ellen by the back of her dress and jerked her up and spun her around to face him, clutched her throat in one hand and held the knife close to her face with the other, as if for inspection; the blade caught the moonlight and winked.

Beyond the knife, she saw his face, pathetic and pained and white. His breath, sharp as the knife, practically wilted her. His neck wound whistled softly. The remnants of his nose dangled wet and red against his upper lip and cheek and his teeth grinned a moon-lit, metal good-bye.

It was all over, and she knew it, but then Bruce's words came back to her in a rush. "When it looks as if you're defeated, and there's nothing left, try anything."

She twisted and jabbed at his eyes with her fingers and caught him solid enough that he thrust her away and stumbled backwards. But only for an instant. He bolted forward, and Ellen stooped and grabbed the dead child by the ankle and struck Moon Face with it as if it were a club. Once in the face, once in the mid-section. The rotting child burst into a spray of desiccated flesh and innards and she hurled the leg at Moon Face and then she was circling around the roll-away bed, trying to make the door. Moon Face, at the other end of the bed, saw this, and when she moved for the door, he lunged in that direction, causing her to jump back to the end of the bed. Smiling, he returned to his end, waited for her next attempt.

She lurched for the door again, and Moon Face jerked back too, but this time Ellen bent and grabbed the end of the bed and hurled herself against it. The bed hit Moon Face in the knees, and as he fell, the bed rolled over him and he let go of the knife and tried to put out his hands to stop the bed's momentum. The impetus of the roll-away carried him across the short length of the dirt floor and his head hit the far wall and the sticks cracked and hurtled out into blackness, and Moon Face followed and the bed followed him, then caught on the edge of the drop and the wheels buried up in the dirt and hung there.

Ellen had shoved so hard she fell face down, and when she looked up, she saw the bed was dangling, shaking, the mattress slipping loose, about to glide off into nothingness.

Moon Face's hands flicked into sight, clawing at the sides of the bed's frame. Ellen gasped. He was going to make it up. The bed's wheels were going to hold.

She pulled a knee under her, cocking herself, then sprang forward, thrusting both palms savagely against the bed. The wheels popped free and the roll-away shot out into the dark emptiness.

Ellen scooted forward on her knees and looked over the edge. There was blackness, a glimpse of the mattress falling free, and a pale object, like a white-washed planet with a great vein of silver in it, jetting through the cold expanse of space. Then the mattress and the face were gone and there was just the darkness and a distant sound like a water balloon exploding.

Ellen sat back and took a breather. When she felt strong again and felt certain her heart wouldn't tear through her chest, she stood up and looked around the room. She thought a long time about what she saw.

She found her purse and panties, went out of the hut and up the trail, and after a few wrong turns, she found the proper trail that wound its way up the mountainside to where her car was parked. When she climbed over the railing, she was exhausted.

Everything was as it was. She wondered if anyone had seen the cars, if anyone had stopped, then decided it didn't matter. There was no one here now, and that's what was important.

She took the keys from her purse and tried the engine. It turned over. That was a relief.

She killed the engine, got out and went around and opened the trunk of the Chevy and looked down at Bruce's body. His face looked like one big bruise, his lips were as large as sausages. It made her happy to look at him.

A new energy came to her. She got him under the arms and pulled him out and managed him over to the rail and grabbed his legs and flipped him over the railing and onto the trail. She got one of his hands and started pulling him down the path, letting the momentum help her. She felt good. She felt strong. First Bruce had tried to dominate her, had threatened her, had thought she was weak because she was a woman, and one night, after slapping her, after raping her, while he slept a drunken sleep, she had pulled the blankets up tight around him and looped rope over and under the bed and used the knots he had taught her, and secured him.

Then she took a stick of stove wood and had beat him until she was so weak she fell to her knees. She hadn't meant to kill him, just punish him for slapping her around, but when she got started she couldn't stop until she was too worn out to go on, and when she was finished, she discovered he was dead.

That didn't disturb her much. The thing then was to get rid of the body somewhere, drive on back to the city and say he had abandoned her and not come back. It was weak, but all she had. Until now.

After several stops for breath, a chance to lie on her back and look up at the stars, Ellen managed Bruce to the hut and got her arms under his and got him seated in one of the empty chairs. She straightened things up as best as she could. She put the larger pieces of the baby back in the crib. She picked Moon Face's knife up off the floor and looked at it and looked at Bruce, his eyes wide open, the moonlight from the roof striking them, showing them to be dull as scratched glass.

Bending over his face, she went to work on his eyes. When she finished with them, she pushed his head forward and used the blade like a drill. She worked until the holes satisfied her. Now if the police found the Buick up there and came down the trail to investigate, and found the trail leading here, saw what was in the shack, Bruce would fit in with the rest of Moon Face's victims. The police would probably conclude Moon Face, sleeping here with his "family," had put his bed too close to the cliff and it had broken through the thin wall and he had tumbled to his death.

She liked it.

She held Bruce's chin, lifted it, examined her work.

"You can be Uncle Brucey," she said, and gave Bruce a pat on the shoulder. "Thanks for all your advice and help, Uncle Brucey. It's what got me through." She gave him another pat.

She found a shirt—possibly Moon Face's, possibly a victim's—on the opposite side of the shack, next to a little box of Harlequin Romances, and she used it to wipe the knife, pan, all she had touched, clean of her prints, then she went out of there, back up to her car.

For Jo Foshee

BY BIZARRE HANDS
The Play Version

Lights up on a rural scene. East Texas. Fall. Late afternoon. A ramshackle house with a sagging front porch. Living room, except for an open window on the side opposite the porch, is a cut away and it's furnished simply. Couch. Coffee table. End-table with a wooden hula-girl lamp on it. An old Sylvania TV set with foil-covered rabbit ears on top. A faded, framed embroidery on the wall that reads: GOD WATCHES OVER THIS HOUSE. Outside, in the yard, is an old fashioned rock well with a roof over it and a pulley with a rope and bucket. A woman, THE WIDOW CASE, is at the well. She's in her forties, whipped by sun, wind and ignorance, wearing a colorless sundress and a man's shoes without socks. She's slowly and painfully cranking the heavy well bucket up. CINDERELLA is nearby on her knees in the dirt, one eye close to the ground. She has a little stick in one hand and is using it to work something on the ground not quite visible to the audience. Cinderella is about twenty, but has the mind of a not too bright three-year-old. She's twenty pounds over-weight, barefoot, dressed in a short, little-girl dress with white panties stained by dirt. The panties are visible to the audience as she wiggles on her knees and cocks her butt up and makes grunting sounds and moves the stick; now and then she lifts the stick up, picks something from it with her free hand and puts it in her mouth.

CINDERELLA: (To herself.) Ant.

SOUND OF A CAR stopping nearby. The Widow Case takes notice. Cinderella doesn't, continues to twist the stick.

CAR DOOR SLAMS. Enter PREACHER JUDD. He's decked out in black suit, white shirt, string tie and black loafers. Has on a short-brimmed black hat. Wears an alligator smile. As he enters he takes off his hat. He glances now and then in Cinderella's direction. Cinderella still has not taken notice. She is back at work with her stick.

WIDOW CASE: (Placing the bucket of drawn water on the well-curbing.) Reckon you've come far enough. You look like one of them Jehovah Witnesses or such.

PREACHER JUDD: No, I ain't, ma'am.

WIDOW CASE: If you're here to take up money for them starving African niggers, I can tell you now, I don't give to the niggers around here, and I sure ain't giving to no hungry foreign niggers can't even speak English.

PREACHER JUDD: Ain't collecting money for nobody. Not even myself.

WIDOW CASE: Well, I ain't seen you around here before, and don't know you from white rice. You might be one of them *mash* murderers for all I know.

PREACHER JUDD: No ma'am. I ain't a *mash* murderer, and I ain't from around here. I'm from East Texas. I'm traveling through here, so I can talk to white folks about God.

Preacher Judd puts on his hat and stares at Cinderella who is still twisting her stick, starting to move to the side on her knees. As she does, we see that what she's been playing with is a small dead dog and she has the stick stuck into one of its eye sockets, twirling it as though mixing a recipe. There is the SOUND OF FLIES BUZZING. Widow Case notes Preacher Judd's interest in Cinderella's activities.

WIDOW CASE: I don't normally let her play with no dead dog like that, but way she is, I can't hardly watch her all the time and get things done. She'll drag dead stuff off the road if she sees it. It's the ants interest her the most. She eats 'em.

Preacher Judd watches as Cinderella deftly uses her free hand to snag something off her arm and deliver the prize to her mouth.

CINDERELLA: Ant.

PREACHER JUDD: I think that there was a fly.

WIDOW CASE: She'll eat them too. She calls all bugs ants.

They stare at Cinderella. She pulls the stick from the dog's eye socket and watches intently as the messy remains of the stirred eyeball, like thick semi-hard snot, drip to the ground.

CINDERELLA: Eye.

PREACHER JUDD: It sure ain't sanitary. That dog could have some germs.

Cinderella uses the stick to push the eyeball goop around on the ground.

WIDOW CASE: She don't know no better. Ain't got no sense at all. All she does is play around all day, eat bugs and drool. Finds something dead, she'll mess with it for hours. Kind of keeps her out of my hair, though . . . Case you ain't noticed, she's simple.

PREACHER JUDD: Yes ma'am, I noticed. In fact, that's one of the reasons I'm here. I heard about her in town.

WIDOW CASE: There's people talking about her in town? (Sharply to Cinderella as the girl re-snags the eyeball on her stick and moves it toward her mouth.) DON'T EAT THAT!

Cinderella turns, looks at the Widow Case as if the old woman has wounded her. She reluctantly pops the goopy eye off the stick and onto the ground.

WIDOW CASE: Now, you said they was talking about Cinderella?

PREACHER JUDD: It was friendly talk. I did a little preaching outside a honky-tonk there, trying to save a few sinners, and this one fella, he prayed with me and told me he has a simple-headed little boy and how bad he used to hate going home on account of it. Said he thought about trying to run over the boy with his car. Had all kinds of bad thoughts. Finally he and his wife had to put the boy in a home. Said they go to see him Christmases. Anyway, we talked on and he mentioned you having a daughter same way as his boy.

WIDOW CASE: That has to be Old Man Favor. I don't reckon he came to Jesus.

PREACHER JUDD: I think maybe he did. He said he did.

WIDOW CASE: Go back by that honky-tonk on your way out, and see if he ain't back in there on a stool. Come tomorrow, he won't remember you or Jesus.

PREACHER JUDD: That just might be . . . But the thing got me interested in your daughter here is the fact that they don't usually get God training. Retards, I mean. They get looked over. You see, I had a sister same way. Retarded, like your girl. She got killed on Halloween, ten years ago to this night. She was raped and murdered and had her trick-or-treat candy stolen, and it was done, the sheriff said, by bizarre hands.

WIDOW CASE: No kiddin'?

PREACHER JUDD: No kiddin'. Figure she went on to hell cause she didn't have any God talk in her. And retard or not, she deserved some so she wouldn't have to cook for eternity. I mean, think on it. How hot it must be down there. Her boiling in her own sweat, and she didn't do nothing, and it's mostly my fault she's down there 'cause I didn't teach her a thing about the Lord Jesus and his daddy, God.

WIDOW CASE: Took her Halloween candy too, huh?

PREACHER JUDD: Whole kitandkaboodle. Rape, murder and candy theft, one fatal swoop. That's why I hate to see a young'n like yours who might not have no word of God in her. And come Halloween, I think on it more than ever. (Looking at Cinderella.) Is she without training?

WIDOW CASE: She ain't even toilet trained. You couldn't perch her on the outdoor convenience if she was sick and her manage to hit the hole. Old man Favor's boy can at least do that. He can talk about the weather some. Cinderella, she can't talk much or do nothing that don't make a mess. Can't teach her a thing. Just runs them ants with that stick all day. Half the time she don't even know her name. You don't yell at her, she don't pay you any mind at all. (To Cinderella in a normal tone of voice.) Cindereller.

Cinderella pays no attention. She continues to rock and twirl her stick. Suddenly she raises up and thrashes her stick in the air as if striking an invisible opponent or conducting an important musical movement, then she begins to run around in a circle, her knuckles practically dragging. She makes little hooting sounds. She resumes her former position, starts twirling her stick in the hollow of the dog's eye.

WIDOW CASE: See? She's worse than any little ole baby, and it ain't no easy row to hoe with her here and me not having a man around to do the heavy work.

PREACHER JUDD: I can see that. Woman like you has got her work cut out for her. It takes some real courage and dedication to do what you have to do . . . By the way, call me Preacher Judd . . . And can I help you tote that bucket up to the house there?

WIDOW CASE: Well now, I'd appreciate that kindly.

Preacher Judd goes to the well smiling, takes the bucket.

WIDOW CASE: Come on into the house. (She starts toward the house, pauses.) You got to watch the porch and walk on the far side. It's starting to rot through in the middle. You don't want to fall through there cause there's a big hole where a old well used to be underneath.

PREACHER JUDD: You don't mind me saying so, you ought to get that fixed.

WIDOW CASE: I get the time and money and a man willing to swing a hammer, I will. (She bends and picks up a little rock, chunks it softly at Cinderella, hits her in the head. Cinderella looks up.) Leave that ole mutt alone! Get on in the house! And mind that porch! (To Preacher Judd) Only thing I've taught that she knows good, and that's to watch for them rotten boards. Good thing too, big as she is she'd drop through there like a stone. They'd find her in China.

Cinderella drops her stick, jumps up and runs in circles with her back bent and her knuckles dragging, hooting as she goes.

PREACHER JUDD: Now ain't that cute.

WIDOW CASE: When you're trying to get her to do something, it gets a mite less cute. (To Cinderella) Come on here, now. Get on up to the house!

Preacher Judd follows the Widow Case onto the porch. He observes how carefully she mounts the porch. He follows her lead through the front door. Cinderella, like a little duck following bigger ducks, comes in after them, carefully staying away from the rotted lumber. Once in the living room, she forgets about them. She sits in the middle of the floor and rocks and looks up and about, as if observing the stars.

WIDOW CASE: (As she takes the bucket from Preacher Judd.) Thank you. I'll take it now. Good to see the world ain't empty of gentlemen yet.

Cinderella is now pulling her dress up. Picking something off her knee. She puts it in her mouth.

WIDOW CASE: (Glaring at Cinderella.) Pull your dress down, girl. And don't eat them ants. They ain't good for you.

Cinderella pays absolutely no attention, continues to search for ants on her person.

PREACHER JUDD: Figure them ants will make her sick.

WIDOW CASE: Figure not. You took all the ants she's et, there'd be enough to tote off a good sized cow. I'm gonna pour this water up.

PREACHER JUDD: (Takes a Bible from his coat pocket.) You don't mind if I try and read a verse or two to Cindy, do you?

WIDOW CASE: You make an effort on that while I fix us some tea. You're hungry, I'll bring some things for ham sandwiches.

PREACHER JUDD: Now that's right nice of you. I could use a bite.

Widow Case smiles, exits with her bucket. Cinderella has pulled her dress up to expose her panties. Preacher Judd studies Cinderella for a long moment, watching her look for more ants.

PREACHER JUDD: (Softly to Cinderella.) You know tonight's Halloween, Cindy?

Cinderella pays no attention. She's found another ant and she darts her fingers to her mouth to dispose of it.

PREACHER JUDD: (As much to himself as to Cinderella.) Halloween is my favorite time of the year. That may be strange for a preacher to say, considering it's a devil thing, but

I've always loved it. It just does something to my blood. It's like a tonic for me, you know?

Cinderella gets up, wanders over to the TV and turns it on, sits on the floor in front of it. Banal TV prattle is heard.

PREACHER JUDD: Let's don't run the TV just now, sugar baby. Let's you and me talk about God.

Preacher Judd goes over and turns the set off. Cinderella continues to stare at it. Preacher Judd opens his Bible and lets it lie open in one hand while he raises the other as if pointing to God. He reads.

PREACHER JUDD: "For God so loved the world, he gave his only begotten son." (Lowers his hand and uses a finger to find the next verse he wants.) Let's see, blah, blah, blah, "I have need to be baptized of thee, and comest thou to me?" Amen.

CINDERELLA: Uhman.

Preacher Judd jumps with happy surprise, slams the Bible shut and dunks it in his pocket.

PREACHER JUDD: Well, well, now, that does it. You got some Bible training.

Widow Case enters with a tray of sandwich fixings: a small ham on the bone, tomatoes, a huge butcher knife, a mustard jar and two glasses of iced tea.

WIDOW CASE: What's that you're saying?

PREACHER JUDD: (Happy as if he'd just been jacked off.) She said some of a prayer. God don't expect much from retards, and that ought to do for keeping her from burning in hell. (Practically skips over to the Widow Case and dunks two fingers into a glass of tea, whirls and flicks the drops on Cinderella's confused, upturned face.) I pronounce you seriously baptized. In the name of God, the Son, and the Holy Ghost. Amen.

WIDOW CASE: Well, I'll swan. That there tea works for baptizing? (She sits the tray on the coffee table.)

PREACHER JUDD: It ain't the tea water. It's what's said and who says it makes it take. Consider that gal legal baptized... Now, she ought to have some fun too, don't you think? Since she's baptized, she ought to celebrate a little. Not having a full head of brains don't mean she shouldn't have some fun.

WIDOW CASE: (Defensively) She likes what she does with them ants. (She sits on the couch, begins to cut slices of ham.)

PREACHER JUDD: I know, but I'm talking about something special. It's Halloween. Time for young folks to have fun, even if they are retards. In fact, retards like it better than anyone. They *love* this stuff... A thing my sister enjoyed was dressing up like a ghost.

WIDOW CASE: (Preparing the sandwiches.) Ghost?

PREACHER JUDD: (Excited) We took this sheet, you see, cut some mouth and eye holes in it, then we wore it and went trick-or-treatin'.

WIDOW CASE: I don't know I got an old sheet. And there ain't a house close enough for trick-or-treatin' at.

PREACHER JUDD: I could take her around in my car. That would be fun, I think. I'd like to see her have fun, wouldn't you? She'd be real scary too under that sheet, big as she is and liking to run stooped down with her knuckles dragging.

Preacher Judd makes his point by hunching over and running around in a circle, knuckles dragging, making hooting noises as he goes.

WIDOW CASE: (Laughs) She would be scary, I admit . . . Though that sheet over her head would take away from it some. Sometimes she scares me when I don't got my mind on her, you know? Like if I'm napping in there on the bed, and I sorta open my eyes, *and there she is,* looking at me like she does them ants. I declare, she looks like she'd like to take a stick and whirl it around on me.

PREACHER JUDD: Whatd'ya say?

WIDOW CASE: I don't know . . .

PREACHER JUDD: She'd get so much candy you and her could eat on it for a week.

WIDOW CASE: Well now, I like candy. . . . Maybe it would be nice for Cindereller to go out and have some fun.

PREACHER JUDD: Good. It's decided. You need a sheet. A white one, for a ghost suit.

WIDOW CASE: (Slightly hesitant.) I'll see what I can find.

Widow Case exits into a "bedroom." Preacher Judd picks up one of the sandwiches and takes a bite out of it. He looks at Cinderella. She's staring at him as if she just now discovered him. He hands the sandwich to her. She promptly takes the bread off, lays the mustard-swathed bread on her knees and eats the meat by tilting her head and lowering it into her mouth. She smacks and gobbles loudly, starts in on the bread.

PREACHER JUDD: That good, sugar?

Cinderella smiles mustard bread as Widow Case enters carrying a sheet and a pair of scissors.

WIDOW CASE: This do?

PREACHER JUDD: (Taking the sheet and scissors.) Just the thing! (To Cinderella) Come on, sugar. Let's you and me go in the back room there and get you fixed up and surprise your mama.

WIDOW CASE: You got to take her by the arm. Lead her around like a dog.

PREACHER JUDD: (Taking Cinderella's arm) Come on, Cindy. (As he walks her to the bedroom, calls to the Widow Case.) You're gonna like this. This'll be fun.

Preacher Judd exits into the bedroom. Widow Case sits down on the couch and goes back to making sandwiches, casting an eye now and then toward the bedroom. From in there we hear CINDERELLA GRUNTING, SCISSORS SNIPPING and the MUMBLE OF PREACHER JUDD'S VOICE, but we can't make out what he's saying. A few moments of silence, and—

—the bedroom door flies open and out darts Cinderella wearing the sheet with mouth and eye-holes cut in it. She has her arms out in front of her and she runs around the room in circles yelling.

CINDERELLA: Wooo, wooo, goats! Wooo, wooo, goats!

Cinderella hits the coffee table, sends it and the sandwich makings flying, trips, goes tumbling across the floor. Widow Case pulls herself into a defensive position. Preacher Judd enters and he goes over and helps Cinderella up. He has something white draped in the crook of an arm.

PREACHER JUDD: That's ghosts, Cindy. Not goats.

CINDERELLA: Goats! Goats!

PREACHER JUDD: We'll work on that.

WIDOW CASE: (Recovering from Cinderella's entrance.) Damn you, Cinderella . . . (Noticing what Preacher Judd has on his arm.) What's that you got there?

PREACHER JUDD: One of your piller cases. For a trick-or-treat sack.

WIDOW CASE: (Stiffly.) Oh.

Widow Case eases off the couch and rights the coffee table. She's reaching for the ham on the floor when—

PREACHER JUDD: I think we've got to go now.

WIDOW CASE: (Surprised. Straightening up.) But you ain't et yet.

PREACHER JUDD: I can eat some trick-or-treat candy.

WIDOW CASE: A sandwich will do you a mite better for supper. I can wipe this ham off with a rag and it'll be good as new.

PREACHER JUDD: It'll be ambrosia, I'm sure. But we ought to run on and get started good. Get to the houses late they quit giving you candy and start sticking apples and bananas and stuff like that in your bag. We'll be back in a few hours, just long enough to run the houses around here.

WIDOW CASE: Whoa, whoa! Trick-or-treatin' I can go for, but I can't let my daughter go off with no strange man.

PREACHER JUDD: I ain't strange. I'm a preacher.

WIDOW CASE: You strike me as an all right fella that wants to do things right, but I can't let you take my daughter off without me going. People will talk. You can understand that.

PREACHER JUDD: I'll pay you some money to let me take her.

WIDOW CASE: I don't like the sound of that none, you offering me money.

PREACHER JUDD: I just want her for the night. (He puts his arm around Cinderella and pulls her close.) She'd have fun.

WIDOW CASE: I don't like the sound of that no better. Maybe you ain't as right thinking as I thought. (She grabs the butcher knife off the floor and points it at Preacher Judd.) I reckon you better just let go of her and run on out to that car of yours and take your ownself trick-or-treatin'. And without my piller case.

PREACHER JUDD: No ma'am can't do that. I've come for Cindy and that's the thing God expects of me, and I'm gonna do it. I got to do it. I didn't do my sister right and she's burning in hell. I'm doing Cindy right. She said some of a prayer and she's baptized. Anything happened to her, wouldn't be on my conscious.

Cinderella lifts up her ghost suit and looks at herself. She's naked underneath. The Widow Case's mouth falls open.

WIDOW CASE: You pervert! Let go of her right now! And drop that piller case. Toss it on the couch would be better. It's clean.

Preacher Judd doesn't move. Beat.

PREACHER JUDD: I won't do that. I'm taking her.

WIDOW CASE: (Gritting her teeth.) Hell you are!

Widow Case slashes at Preacher Judd with the knife. He dodges, drops the pillow case. Cinderella breaks away, runs about the room, yelling, "Wooo, wooo, goats," in nervous agitation.

Another slash from the Widow Case. Preacher Judd isn't fast enough. It cuts his coat sleeve.

PREACHER JUDD: (Leaping back.) You Jezebel! You just ruined a J.C. Penney's suit.

They start to circle, like wrestlers preparing for the run together. Preacher Judd stops abruptly. Holds out his left hand and sticks up two fingers and wiggles them like rabbit ears.

PREACHER JUDD: Lookee here!

Widow Case is snookered. She looks. Preacher Judd grabs her wrist and tries to wrestle the knife away. They fall over

249

the coffee table and roll around on the floor, grunting. Cinderella is still zipping about, yelling, "Wooo, wooo, goats!" She hits one of the rabbit ears on the television set, knocks it winding.

Preacher Judd gets hold of the ham with his free hand and strikes Widow Case a couple of greasy blows in the head with it. He loses the ham, applies both of his hands to her knife hand, twists the knife away. Widow Case screams and tries to roll out from under him and crawl away on her hands and knees. Preacher Judd grabs the knife and leaps at her and puts an arm around her neck and brings the knife high up and down into the center of her back.

Cinderella has stopped whipping about the room and is standing in one place bobbing up and down and waving her arms as if preparing to fly. Widow Case has gone down on her belly and is moaning and crawling. Preacher Judd still has hold of the hilt of the knife, and as Widow Case crawls, he is pulled after her. He's working frantically to free the knife, wiggling it up and down, but it won't come free. He turns his attention to the frantic, moaning Cinderella.

PREACHER JUDD: (To Cinderella) It's okay, sugar. Everything's gonna be all right, now.

WIDOW CASE: Help! Help! Bloody murder!

PREACHER JUDD: (To Widow Case.) Shut up, goddamn it! (Jerking his face heavenward, he speaks calmly.) Forgive me my language, oh Lord. (To Cinderella.) Ain't nothing wrong, baby chile. Not a thing.

WIDOW CASE: Oh Lordy Mercy! Mercy! I'm being kilt.

PREACHER JUDD: Die you stupid cow!

Cinderella is in a blind panic. She has started stepping from side to side and is going "Uhuhuhuhuhuh." Widow Case struggles to rise, dragging Preacher Judd, who is still clinging to the knife, up with her. As she struggles up, she whips an elbow around and hits Preacher Judd in the ribs. He is knocked back. Knife remains in her back. She stumbles forward and falls against the wall, slides into the end-table and knocks over the hula-girl lamp, popping the shade free. She falls to the floor on her stomach, lies there panting like a dog.

Preacher Judd leaps forward and grabs the hula-girl lamp and hits Widow Case in the head with it. She tries to get up and he pops her again. She falls out flat. He hits her again. Then again.

Cinderella has begun climbing out the window.

Preacher Judd turns from beaning the Widow Case just as Cinderella makes it "outside," and exits the stage running.

PREACHER JUDD: Cindy! Wait! (Still carrying the hula-girl lamp, he moves weak and wobbly to the window and looks in the direction of her exit.) Don't run off. Come on back. Preacher Judd'll be nice to you. I promise. (Hand cupped to his mouth.) Cinderella! Come on back, honey! I got something for you. I ain't gonna hurt you ... *You little bitch! Come here!*

He starts to climb out the window, but goes limp. He takes in several deep breaths. Deflated, he leans on the window. After a moment, he looks at the heavens and drops to his knees and lays the hula-girl aside and pushes his hands together, props his elbows on the window sill, closes his eyes and prays.

PREACHER JUDD: God. All the talking I do in your name, you're supposed to make things work out better for me. But you don't. Why's that? (He opens his eyes as if watching for God, waiting for an answer. No sign from the heavens. He closes his eyes and continues.) Night I took my sister trick-er-treatin', that didn't work out. It could have, but you didn't let it ... Her naked under that sheet, it got to me, God. I had to have her, but you let her scream and ... (He lets it hang.) I had to eat her trick-or-treat candy so it'd look like theft. Can't touch a Tootsie Roll to this day ... It was kind of a relief, her being dead. She was lots of trouble. Messed the bed. Embarrassed us around sensible people. Drank straight out of the water jar in the 'frigerator ... Her dying was no real crime. 'Cept she wasn't baptized. (Long beat.) This here girl, Cindy. She's been baptized, so it don't matter she lives or not. What's she gonna accomplish? Brain surgery? She couldn't sort rocks from peas. So, God, can't you show love to your humble servant, this once. I got some needs to satisfy ... Won't you help me, God? Won't you—

CINDERELLA: (OS) Wooooo, woooo, goats! Wooooo, wooooo, goats!

Preacher Judd looks and sees Cinderella run by the window still wearing the ghost suit.

CINDERELLA: (As she runs by.) Woooo, wooo, goats! (She goes around the front of the house and disappears behind it. But she can still be heard OS.) Wooooooo, woooo, goats! Wooooo, woooo, goats!

Preacher Judd lifts his face to the heavens again and mouths AMEN. He pops up with the hula-girl in hand and darts for the front door, tugs it open. Cinderella has reversed and is coming around front of the porch again.

CINDERELLA: (As she passes, not noting Preacher Judd.) Woooo, woooo, goats!

PREACHER JUDD: (Stepping forward enthusiastically with his club cocked.) Cindy, baby! Wait up!

Cinderella is halfway around the house now.

Preacher Judd, in his haste to catch her, steps in the wrong spot and boards shatter beneath him and he goes through the flooring, drops the hula-girl lamp and catches himself at armpit level. He screams and writhes, trying to pull himself up.

PREACHER JUDD: Oh, God, you're doing it again! You're starting on me! I'm hurt here, Ol' Man. You hear me, hurt? Something's sticking in me . . . God, for the love of mercy, help me!

Cinderella comes around the edge of the house again. She's strolling now. She finally takes note of Preacher Judd. She watches him in a curious dog way, turning her sheet-covered head from side to side.

PREACHER JUDD: (Spots her, turns friendly, but it's obvious he's in serious pain.) Cindy! Oh, girl, am I glad you came back. Old Preacher Judd, he's hurt here. I got something stuck in me, sugar. Hurts awful bad. Give me a hand, will you, honey?

CINDERELLA: (Staring at Preacher Judd, speaking softly) Woooo, woooo, goats.

PREACHER JUDD: (Smiling) That's right, you little fool. Woooo, wooo, goats. Now get Ol' Preacher Judd out, will you?

Cinderella has already lost interest. She stops looking at Preacher Judd, spots the dead dog and starts for it.

PREACHER JUDD: Cindy! Cindy! You brainless bitch! Come back here! Come here!

She reaches the dog, squats down by the corpse and recovers her stick. She begins working the stick against the corpse.

PREACHER JUDD: Now you come here! You mind your elders, you hear me!

CINDERELLA: (Holding up her stick, examining it.) Ant. (Her tongue snakes out of the mouth hole in the sheet and licks the ant off the stick, then she goes back to work on the dog.) Puppy.

Preacher Judd struggles painfully, and after some major effort, manages himself out of the hole and onto the solid remains of the porch. He lays panting with his legs toward us, and we see that a long sliver of board has broken off and gone straight into his crotch. It is long enough and wide enough to look like a small, bloody, beaver tail.

PREACHER JUDD: (Looking down at his injury.) Oh, sweet Jesus, I'm ruined! . . . Ruined!

Cinderella continues to capture ants onto her stick and lick it clean.

Preacher Judd takes hold of the broken board and yanks and screams. Cinderella lifts her head at the sound of the scream, but seems unable to locate its source. She goes back to her ants. Preacher Judd falls back in agony on the porch and lays there for a long moment, puffing like a busted steam engine. Finally, he comes up on one elbow and looks at Cindy. There is no love in his eyes.

He looks about, locates the hula-girl lamp, grabs it, tries to stand and can't. He begins crawling off the porch, toward Cinderella.

PREACHER JUDD: (As he crawls.) Then don't come. I'll come to you. I got a little present for you, retard. Something nice. Something solid.

Cinderella pays no attention to Preacher Judd. She might as well be on the moon. She's totally absorbed in her play and ant eating.

Preacher Judd draws closer, pauses with pain, begins to crawl again, blood trailing behind him like slug slime.

Closer.

Closer.

Closer.

And now he's right behind her. He rises painfully to his knees, cocks the lamp and swings—

—and about that time Cinderella sees an ant to her left and—

CINDERELLA: (Leaning to the left, almost touching her head to the ground.) Ooooooh, big ant.

Preacher Judd's swing is brutal and it carries him forward, hard, and with his victim moving at just the wrong moment, his blow strikes the dead dog with a sound like a bag of mud being thumped, and he falls forward on top of the dog with a cry of pain.

Cinderella, unaware, licks the ant off the ground, sits up and sees Preacher Judd beside her. His hat has finally fallen off, and that catches her eye. As Preacher Judd struggles unsuccessfully to get up, Cinderella picks up his hat and puts it on over her sheeted head. She rises, runs in a circle around him and the dog, spanking her butt with the stick.

CINDERELLA: Wooooo, wooooo, goats!

Preacher Judd can't get up. He's spent. He twists instead and rolls onto his back, the dead dog for a pillow. He puts a hand between his legs and holds himself. He lifts the hand and looks at it. It's covered in blood.

PREACHER JUDD: Insult to injury, God. Insult to injury.

CINDERELLA: (Still circling.) Wooooo, woooo, goats!

PREACHER JUDD: (Angrily to Cinderella.) *It's ghosts! Ghosts! You imbecile!*

Preacher Judd's head nods to the side and the hand holding the hula-girl lamp fans out and strikes the ground with a thump and the lamp rolls away. That's all for Preacher Judd, but the rolling lamp attracts Cinderella, and she looks first at it, then at Preacher Judd. She turns her head from side to side. She goes cautiously to her knees and bends over Preacher Judd, the brim of the hat almost touching his face. She watches him for a time, scanning from one ear to the next, her eyes following something.

CINDERELLA: (Casually poking his face with the stick.) Ant ... Ant. (She pokes into his eye and tries to pull the stick back, but it doesn't come. She tugs harder, begins to stir it around and around, grunting as she does. She finally draws the stick out, and as we see what is now on the end of it, she says ...) Eye. Eye. (And as the lights dim around her, she puts the tip

256

of the stick and the morsel into the mouth, and at that moment she says—) Eye. Eye. (—and the lights go down and we have—)

CURTAIN

GODZILLA'S TWELVE STEP PROGRAM

ONE: Honest Work

Godzilla, on his way to work at the foundry, sees a large building that seems to be mostly made of shiny copper and dark, reflecting solar glass. He sees his image in the glass and thinks of the old days, wonders what it would be like to stomp on the building, to blow flames at it, kiss the windows black with his burning breath, then dance rapturously in the smoking debris.

One day at a time, he tells himself. One day at a time.

Godzilla makes himself look at the building hard. He passes it by. He goes to the foundry. He puts on his hard hat. He blows his fiery breath into the great vat full of used car parts, turns the car parts to molten metal. The metal runs through pipes and into new molds for new car parts. Doors. Roofs. Etc.

Godzilla feels some of the tension drain out.

TWO: Recreation

After work Godzilla stays away from downtown. He feels tense. To stop blowing flames after work is difficult. He goes over to the BIG MONSTER RECREATION CENTER.

Gorgo is there. Drunk from oily seawater, as usual. Gorgo talks about the old days. She's like that. Always the old days.

They go out back and use their breath on the debris that is deposited there daily for the center's use. Kong is out back. Drunk as a monkey. He's playing with Barbie dolls. He does that all the time. Finally, he puts the Barbies away in his coat pocket, takes hold of his walker and wobbles past Godzilla and Gorgo.

Gorgo says, "Since the fall he ain't been worth shit. And what's with him and the little plastic broads anyway? Don't he know there's real women in the world."

Godzilla thinks Gorgo looks at Kong's departing walker-supported ass a little too wistfully. He's sure he sees wetness in Gorgo's eyes.

Godzilla blows some scrap to cinders for recreation, but it doesn't do much for him, as he's been blowing fire all day long and has, at best, merely taken the edge off his compulsions. This isn't even as satisfying as the foundry. He goes home.

THREE: Sex and Destruction

That night there's a monster movie on television. The usual one. Big beasts wrecking havoc on city after city. Crushing pedestrians under foot.

Godzilla examines the bottom of his right foot, looks at the scar there from stomping cars flat. He remembers how it was to have people squish between his toes. He thinks about all of that and changes the channel. He watches twenty minutes of "Mr. Ed," turns off the TV, masturbates to the images of burning cities and squashing flesh.

Later, deep into the night, he awakens in a cold sweat. He goes to the bathroom and quickly carves crude human figures from bars of soap. He mashes the soap between his toes, closes his eyes and imagines. Tries to remember.

FOUR: Beach Trip and The Big Turtle

Saturday, Godzilla goes to the beach. A drunk monster that looks like a big turtle flies by and bumps Godzilla. The turtle calls Godzilla a name, looking for a fight. Godzilla remembers the turtle is called Gamera.

Gamera is always trouble. No one liked Gamera. The turtle was a real asshole.

Godzilla grits his teeth and holds back the flames. He turns his back and walks along the beach. He mutters a secret mantra given him by his sponsor. The giant turtle follows after, calling him names.

Godzilla packs up his beach stuff and goes home. At his back he hears the turtle, still cussing, still pushing. It's all he can do not to respond to the big dumb bastard. All he can do. He knows the turtle will be in the news tomorrow. He will have destroyed something, or will have been destroyed himself.

Godzilla thinks perhaps he should try and talk to the turtle, get him on the twelve step program. That's what you're supposed to do. Help others. Maybe the turtle could find some peace.

But then again, you can only help those who help themselves. Godzilla realizes he can not save all the monsters of the world. They have to make these decisions for themselves.

But he makes a mental note to go armed with leaflets about the twelve step program from now on.

Later, he calls in to his sponsor. Tells him he's had a bad day. That he wanted to burn buildings and fight the big turtle. Reptilicus tells him it's okay. He's had days like that. Will have days like that once again.

Once a monster always a monster. But a recovering monster is where it's at. Take it one day at a time. It's the only way to be happy in the world. You can't burn and kill and chew up humans and their creations without paying the price of guilt and multiple artillery wounds.

Godzilla thanks Reptilicus and hangs up. He feels better for awhile, but deep down he wonders just how much guilt he really harbors. He thinks maybe it's the artillery and the rocket-firing jets he really hates, not the guilt.

FIVE: Off The Wagon

It happens suddenly. He falls off tho wagon. Coming back from work he sees a small dog house with a sleeping dog sticking halfway out of a doorway. There's no one around. The dog looks old. It's on a chain. Probably miserable anyway. The water dish is empty. The dog is living a worthless life. Chained. Bored. No water.

Godzilla leaps and comes down on the dog house and squashes dog in all directions. He burns what's left of the dog house with a blast of his breath. He leaps and spins on tip-toe through the wreckage. Black cinders and cooked dog slip through his toes and remind him of the old days.

He gets away fast. No one has seen him. He feels giddy. He can hardly walk he's so intoxicated. He calls Reptilicus, gets his answering machine. "I'm not in right now. I'm out doing good. But please leave a message, and I'll get right back to you."

The machine beeps. Godzilla says, "Help."

SIX: His Sponsor

The dog house rolls around in his head all the next day. While at work he thinks of the dog and the way it burned. He thinks of the little house and the way it crumbled. He thinks of the dance he did in the ruins.

The day drags on forever. He thinks maybe when work is through he might find another dog house, another dog.

On the way home he keeps an eye peeled, but no dog houses or dogs are seen.

When he gets home his answering machine light is blinking. It's a message from Reptilicus. Reptilicus's voice says, "Call me."

Godzilla does. He says, "Reptilicus. Forgive me, for I have sinned."

SEVEN: Disillusioned. Disappointed.

Reptilicus's talk doesn't help much. Godzilla shreds all the twelve step program leaflets. He wipes his butt on a couple and throws them out the window. He puts the scraps of the others in the sink and sets them on fire with his breath. He burns a coffee table and a chair, and when he's through, feels bad for it. He knows the landlady will expect him to replace them.

He turns on the radio and lies on the bed listening to an Oldies station. After a while, he falls asleep to Martha and the Vandellas singing "Heat Wave."

EIGHT: Unemployed

Godzilla dreams. In it God comes to him, all scaly and blowing fire. He tells Godzilla he's ashamed of him. He says he should do better. Godzilla awakes covered in sweat. No one is in the room.

Godzilla feels guilty. He has faint memories of waking up and going out to destroy part of the city. He really tied one on, but he can't remember everything he did. Maybe he'll read about it in the papers. He notices he smells like charred lumber and melted plastic. There's gooshy stuff between his toes, and something tells him it isn't soap.

He wants to kill himself. He goes to look for his gun, but he's too drunk to find it. He passes out on the floor. He dreams of the devil this time. He looks just like God except he has one eyebrow that goes over both eyes. The devil says he's come for Godzilla.

Godzilla moans and fights. He dreams he gets up and takes pokes at the devil, blows ineffective fire on him.

Godzilla rises late the next morning, hung over. He remembers the dream. He calls into work sick. Sleeps off most of the day. That evening, he reads about himself in the papers. He really did some damage. Smoked a large part of the city. There's a very clear picture of him biting the head off of a woman.

He gets a call from the plant manager that night. The manager's seen the paper. He tells Godzilla he's fired.

NINE: Enticement

Next day some humans show up. They're wearing black suits and white shirts and polished shoes and they've got badges. They've got guns, too. One of them says, "You're a problem. Our government wants to send you back to Japan."

"They hate me there," says Godzilla. "I burned Tokyo down."

"You haven't done so good here either. Lucky that was a colored section of town you burned, or we'd be on your ass. As it is, we've got a job proposition for you."

"What?" Godzilla asks.

"You scratch our back, we'll scratch yours." Then the men tell him what they have in mind.

TEN: Choosing

Godzilla sleeps badly that night. He gets up and plays the monster mash on his little record player. He dances around the room as if he's enjoying himself, but knows he's not. He goes over to the BIG MONSTER RECREATION CENTER. He sees Kong there, on a stool, undressing one of his Barbies, fingering the smooth spot between her legs. He sees that Kong has drawn a crack there, like a vagina. It appears to have been drawn with a blue ink pen. He's feathered the central line with ink-drawn pubic hair. Godzilla thinks he should have got someone to do the work for him. It doesn't look all that natural.

God, he doesn't want to end up like Kong. Completely spaced. Then again, maybe if he had some dolls he could melt, maybe that would serve to relax him.

No. After the real thing, what was a Barbie? Some kind of form of Near Beer. That's what the debris out back was. Near Beer. The foundry. The Twelve Step Program. All of it. Near Beer.

ELEVEN: Working for the Government

Godzilla calls the government assholes. "All right," he says. "I'll do it."

"Good," says the government man. "We thought you would. Check your mail box. The map and instructions are there."

Godzilla goes outside and looks in his box. There's a manila envelope there. Inside are instructions. They say: "Burn all the spots you see on the map. You finish those, we'll find others. No penalties. Just make sure no one escapes. Any rioting starts, you finish them. To the last man, woman and child."

Godzilla unfolds the map. On it are red marks. Above the red marks are listings: *Nigger Town. Chink Village. White Trash Enclave. A Clutch of Queers. Mostly Democrats.*

Godzilla thinks about what he can do now. Unbidden. He can burn without guilt. He can stomp without guilt. Not only that, they'll send him a check. He has been hired by his adopted country to clean out the bad spots as they see them.

TWELVE: The Final Step

Godzilla stops near the first place on the list: *Nigger Town.* He sees kids playing in the streets. Dogs. Humans looking up at him, wondering what the hell he's doing here.

Godzilla suddenly feels something move inside him. He knows he's being used. He turns around and walks away. He heads toward the government section of town. He starts with the governor's mansion. He goes wild. Artillery is brought out, but it's no use, he's rampaging. Like the old days.

Reptilicus shows up with a megaphone, tries to talk Godzilla down from the top of the Great Monument Building, but Godzilla doesn't listen. He's burning the top of the building off with his breath, moving down, burning some more, moving down, burning some more, all the way to the ground.

Kong shows up and cheers him on. Kong drops his walker and crawls along the road on his belly and reaches a building and pulls himself up and starts climbing. Bullets spark all around the big ape.

Godzilla watches as Kong reaches the summit of the building and clings by one hand and waves the other, which contains a Barbie doll.

Kong puts the Barbie doll between his teeth. He reaches in his coat and brings out a naked Ken doll. Godzilla can see that Kong has made Ken some kind of penis out of silly putty or something. The penis is as big as Ken's leg.

Kong is yelling, "Yeah, that's right. That's right. I'm AC/DC, you sonsofabitches."

Jets appear and swoop down on Kong. The big ape catches a load of rocket right in the teeth. Barbie, teeth and brains decorate the greying sky. Kong falls.

Gorgo comes out of the crowd and bends over the ape, takes him in her arms and cries. Kong's hand slowly opens, revealing Ken, his penis broken off.

The flying turtle shows up and starts trying to steal Godzilla's thunder, but Godzilla isn't having it. He tears the top off the building Kong had mounted and beats Gamera with it. Even the cops and the army cheer over this.

Godzilla beats and beats the turtle, splattering turtle meat all over the place, like an overheated poodle in a microwave. A few quick pedestrians gather up chunks of the turtle meat to take home and cook, cause the rumor is it tastes just like chicken.

Godzilla takes a triple shot of rockets in the chest, staggers, goes down. Tanks gather around him.

Godzilla opens his bloody mouth and laughs. He thinks: If I'd have gotten finished here, then I'd have done the black people too. I'd have gotten the yellow people and the white trash and the homosexuals. I'm an equal opportunity destroyer. To hell with the twelve step program. To hell with humanity.

Then Godzilla dies and makes a mess on the street. Military men tip-toe around the mess and hold their noses.

Later, Gorgo claims Kong's body and leaves.

Reptilicus, being interviewed by television reporters, says, "Zilla was almost there, man. Almost. If he could have completed the program, he'd have been all right. But the pressures of society were too much for him. You can't blame him for what society made of him."

On the way home, Reptilicus thinks about all the excitement. The burning buildings. The gunfire. Just like the old days when he and Zilla and Kong and that goon-ball turtle were young.

Reptilicus thinks of Kong's defiance, waving the Ken doll, the Barbie in his teeth. He thinks of Godzilla, laughing as he died.

Reptilicus finds a lot of old feelings resurfacing. They're hard to fight. He locates a lonesome spot and a dark house and urinates through an open window, then goes home.

DRIVE-IN DATE

The line into the Starlite Drive-In that night was short. Monday nights were like that. Dave and Merle paid their money at the ticket house and Dave drove the Ford to a spot up near the front where there were only a few cars. He parked in a space with no one directly on either side. On the left, the first car was four speakers away, on the right, six speakers.

Dave said, "I like to be up close so it all looks bigger than life. You don't mind do you?"

"You ask me that every time," Merle said. "You don't never ask me that when we're driving in, you ask when we're parked."

"You don't like it, we can move."

"No, I like it. I'm just saying, you don't really care if I like it. You just ask."

"Politeness isn't a crime."

"No, but you ought to mean it."

"I said we can move."

"Hell no, stay where you are. I'm just saying when you ask me what I like, you could mean it."

"You're a testy motherfucker tonight. I thought coming to see a monster picture would cheer you up."

"You're the one likes 'em, and that's why you come. I don't believe in monsters, so I can't enjoy what I'm seeing. I like something that's real. Cop movies. Things like that."

"I tell you, Merle, there's just no satisfying you, man. You'll feel better when they cut the lot lights and the movie starts. We can get our date then."

"I don't know that makes me feel better."

"You done quit liking pussy?"

"Watch your mouth. I didn't say that. You know I like pussy. I like pussy fine."

"Whoa. Aren't we fussy? Way you talk, you're trying to convince me. Maybe it's butt holes you like."

"Goddamnit, don't start on the butt holes."

Dave laughed and got out a cigarette and lipped it. "I know you did that one ole gal in the butt that night." Dave reached up and tapped the rearview mirror. "I seen you in the mirror here."

"You didn't see nothing," Merle said.

"I seen you get in her butt hole. I seen that much."

"What the hell you doing watching? It ain't good enough for you by yourself, so you got to watch someone else get theirs?"

"I don't mind watching."

"Yeah, well, I bet you don't. You're like one of those fucking perverts."

Dave snickered, popped his lighter and lit his cigarette. The lot lights went out. The big lights at the top of the drive-in screen went black. Dave rolled down the window and pulled the speaker in and fastened it to the door. He slapped at a mosquito on his neck.

"Won't be long now," Dave said.

"I don't know I feel up to it tonight."

"You don't like this first feature, the second's some kind of mystery. It might be like a cop show."

"I don't mean the movies."

"The girl?"

"Yeah. I'm in a funny mood."

Dave smoked for a moment. "Merle, this is kind of a touchy subject, but you been having trouble, you know, getting a bone to keep, I'll tell you, that happens. It's happened to me. Once."

"I'm not having trouble with my dick, okay?"

"If you are, it's no disgrace. It'll happen to a man from time to time."

"My tool is all right. It works. No problem."

"Then what's the beef?"

"I don't know. It's a mood. I feel like I'm going through a kind of, I don't know . . . mid-life crisis or something."

"Mood, huh? Let me tell you, when she's stretched out on that backseat, you'll be all right, crisis or no crisis. Hell, get her butt hole if you want it, I don't care."

"Don't start on me."

"Who's starting? I'm telling you, you want her butt hole, her ear, her goddamn nostril, that's your business. Me, I'll stick to the right hole, though."

"Think I don't know a snide remark when you make it?"

"I hope you do, or I wouldn't make it. You don't know I'm making one, what's the fun of making it?" Dave reached over and slapped Merle playfully on the arm. "Lighten up, boy. Let's see a movie, get some pussy. Hey, you feel better if I went and got us some corn and stuff . . . That'd do you better, wouldn't it?"

Merle hesitated. "I guess."

"Back in a jiffy."

Dave got out of the car.

Fifteen minutes and Dave was back. He had a cardboard box that held two bags of popcorn and some tall drinks. He set the box on top of the car, opened the door, then got the box and slid inside. He put the box on the seat between them.

"How much I owe you?" Merle said.

"Not a thing. You get it next time . . . Think how much more expensive this would be, we had to pay for her to eat too."

"A couple or three dollars. So what? That gonna break us?"

"No, but it's beer money. You think about it."

Merle sat and thought about it.

The big white drive-in screen was turned whiter by the projector light, then there was a flicker and images moved on the screen: Ads for the concession. Coming attractions.

Dave got his popcorn, started eating. He said, "I'm getting kind of horny thinking about her. You see the legs on that bitch?"

"Course I seen the legs. You don't know from legs. A woman's got legs is all you care, and you might not care about that. Couple of stumps would be all the same to you."

"No, I don't care for any stumps. Got to be feet on one end, pussy on the other. That's legs enough. But this one, she's got some good ones. Hell, you're bound to've noticed how good they were."

"I noticed. You saying I'm queer or something? I noticed. I noticed she's got an ankle bracelet on the right leg and she wears about a size ten shoe. Biggest goddamn feet I've ever seen on a woman."

"Now, it comes out. You wanted to pick the date, not me?"

"I never did care for a woman with big feet. You got a good-looking woman all over and you get down to them feet and they look like something goes on either side of a water plane . . . Well, it ruins things."

"She ain't ruined. Way she looks, big feet or not, she ain't ruined. Besides, you don't fuck the feet ... Well, maybe *you* do. Right after the butt hole."

"You gonna push one time too much, Dave. One time too much."

"I'm just kidding, man. Lighten up. You don't ever lighten up. Don't we deserve some fun after working like niggers all day?"

Merle sighed. "You got to use that nigger stuff? I don't like it. It makes you sound ignorant. Will, he's colored and I like him. He's done me all right. Man like that, he don't deserve to be called nigger."

"He's all right at the plant, but you go by his house and ask for a loan."

"I don't want to borrow nothing from him. I'm just saying people ought to get their due, no matter what color they are. Nigger is an ugly word."

"You like boogie better, Martin Luther? How about coon or shine? I was always kind of fond of burrhead or woolly, myself."

"There's just no talking to you, is there?"

"Hell, you like niggers so much, next date we set up, we'll make it a nigger. Shit, I'd fuck a nigger. It's all pink on the inside, ain't that what you've heard?"

"You're a bigot is what you are."

"If that means I'm not wanting to buddy up to coons, then, yeah, that's what I am." Dave thumped his cigarette butt out the window. "You got to learn to lighten up, Merle. You don't, you'll die. My uncle, he couldn't never lighten up. Gave him a spastic colon, all that tension. He swelled up until he couldn't wear his pants. Had to get some stretch pants, one of those running suits, just so he could have on clothes. He eventually got so bad they had to go in and operate. You can bet he wishes he didn't do all that worrying now. It didn't get him a thing but sick. He didn't get a better life on account of that worry, now did he? Still lives over in that apartment where he's been living, on account of he got so sick from worry he couldn't work. They're about to throw him out of there, and him a grown man and sixty years old. Lost his good job, his wife—which he ought to know is a good thing—and now he's doing little odd shit here and there to make ends meet. Going down to catch the day work truck with the winos and niggers— Excuse me. Afro-Americans, Colored Folks, whatever you prefer.

"Before he got to worrying over nothing, he had him some serious savings and was about ready to put some money down on a couple of acres and a good double-wide.

"I was planning on buying me a double-wide, that'd make me worry. Them old trailers ain't worth a shit. Comes a tornado, or just a good wind, and you can find those fuckers at the bottom of the Gulf of Mexico, next to the regular trailers. Tornado will take a double-wide easy as any of the others."

Dave shook his head. "You go from one thing to the other, don't you? I know what a tornado can do. It can take a house, too. Your house. That don't matter. I'm not talking about mobile homes here, Merle. I'm talking about living. It's a thing you better attend to. You're forty goddamn years old. Your life's half over . . . I know, that's a cold thing to say, but there you have it. It's out of my mouth. I'm forty this next birthday, so I'm not just putting the doom on you. It's a thing every man's got to face. Getting over the hill. Before I die, I'd like to think I did something fun with my life. It's the little things that count. I want to enjoy things, not worry them away. Hear what I'm saying, Merle?"

"Hard not to, being in the goddamn car with you."

"Look here. Way we work, we deserve to lighten up a little. You haul your ashes first. That'll take some edge off."

"Well . . ."

"Naw, go on."

"All right . . . But one thing . . . "

"What?"

"Don't do me no more butt hole jokes, okay? One friend to another, Dave, no more butt hole jokes."

"It bothers you that bad, okay. Deal."

Merle climbed over the seat and got on his knees on the floorboard. He took hold of the backseat and pulled. It was rigged with a hinge. It folded down. He got on top of the folded-down seat and bent and looked into the exposed trunk. The young woman's face was turned toward him, half of her cheek was hidden by the spare tire. There was a smudge of grease on her nose.

"We should have put a blanket back here," Merle said. "Wrapped her in that. I don't like 'em dirty."

"She's got pants on," Dave said. "You take them off, the part that counts won't be dirty."

"That part's always dirty. They pee and bleed out of it don't they? Hell, hot as it is back here, she's already starting to smell."

"Oh, bullshit." Dave turned and looked over the seat at Merle. "You can't get pleased, can you? She ain't stinking. She didn't even shit her pants when she checked out. And she ain't been dead long enough to smell, and you know it. Quit being so goddamn contrary." Dave turned back around and shook out a cigarette and lit it.

"Blow that out the window, damnit," Merle said. "You know that smoke works my allergies."

Dave shook his head and blew smoke out the window. He turned up the speaker. The ads and commercials were over. The movie was starting.

"And don't be looking back here at me neither," Merle said.

Merle rolled the woman out of the trunk, across the seat, into the floorboard and up against him. He pushed the seat back into place and got hold of the woman and hoisted her onto the backseat. He pushed her tee-shirt over her breasts. He fondled her breasts. They were big and firm and rubbery cold. He unfastened her shorts and pulled them over her shoes and ripped her panties apart at one side. He pushed one of her legs onto the floorboard and gripped her hips and pulled her ass down a little, got it cocked to a position he liked. He unfastened and pulled down his jeans and boxer shorts and got on her.

Dave roamed an eye to the rearview mirror, caught sight of Merle's butt bobbing. He grinned and puffed at his cigarette. After a while, he turned his attention to the movie.

When Merle was finished he looked at the woman's dead eyes. He couldn't see their color in the dark, but he guessed blue. Her hair he could tell was blond.

"How was it?" Dave asked.

"It was pussy. Hand me the flashlight."

Dave reached over and got the light out of the glove box and handed it over the seat. Merle took it. He put it close to the woman's face and turned it on.

"She's got blue eyes," Merle said.

"I noticed that right off when we grabbed her," Dave said. "I thought you'd like that, being how you are about blue eyes."

Merle turned off the flashlight, handed it to Dave, pulled up his pants and climbed over the seat. On the screen a worm-like monster was coming out of the sand on a beach.

"This flick isn't half bad," Dave said. "It's kind of funny, really. You don't get too good a look at the monster though. That all the pussy you gonna get?"

"Maybe some later," Merle said.

"You feeling any better?"

"Some."

"Yeah, well, why don't you eat some popcorn while I get me a little. Want a cigarette? You like a cigarette after sex, don't you?"

"All right."

Dave gave Merle a cigarette, lit it. Merle sucked the smoke in deeply.

"Better?" Dave asked.

"Yeah, I guess."

"Good." Dave thumbed his cigarette out the window. "I'm gonna take my turn now. Don't let nothing happen on the movie. Make it wait."

"Sure."

Dave climbed over the seat. Merle tried to watch the movie. After a moment, he quit. He turned and looked out his window. Six speakers down he could see a Chevy rocking.

"Got to be something more to life than this," Merle said without turning to look at Dave.

"I been telling you," Dave said. "This is life, and you better start enjoying. Get you some orientation before it's too late and it's all over but the dirt in the face . . . Talk to me later. Right now this is what I want out of life. Little later, I might want a drink."

Merle shook his head.

Dave lifted the woman's leg and hooked her ankle over the front seat. Merle looked at her foot, the ankle bracelet dangling from it. "I bet that damn foot's more a size eleven than a size ten," Merle said. "Probably buys her shoes at the ski shop."

Dave hooked her other ankle over the backseat, on the package shelf. "Like I said, it's not the feet I'm interested in."

Merle shook his head again. He rolled down his window and thumped out some ash and turned his attention to the Chevy again. It was still rocking.

Dave shifted into position in the backseat. The Ford began to rock. The foot next to Merle vibrated, made little dead hops.

From the backseat, Dave began to chant: "Give it to me, baby. Give it to me. Am I your Prince, baby? Am I your goddamn King? Take that anaconda, bitch. Take it!"

"For heaven's sake," Merle said.

Five minutes later, Dave climbed into the front seat, said, "Damn. Damn good piece."

"You act like she had something to do with it," Merle said.

"Her pussy, ain't it?"

"We're doing all the work. We could cut a hole in the seat back there and get it that good."

"That ain't true. It ain't the hole does it, and it damn sure ain't the personality, it's how they look. That flesh under you. Young. Firm. Try coming in an ugly or fat woman and you'll see what I mean. You'll have some troubles. Or maybe you won't."

"I don't like 'em old or fat."

"Yeah, well, I don't see the live ones like either one of us all that much. The old ones or the fat ones. Face it, we've got no way with live women. And I don't like the courting. I like to know that I see one I like, I can have her if I can catch her."

Merle reached over and shoved the woman's foot off the seat. It fell heavily onto the floorboard. "I'm tired of looking at that slat. Feet like that, they ought to have paper bags over them."

When the second feature was over, they drove to Dave's house and parked out back next to the tall board fence. They killed the lights and sat there for a while, watching, listening.

No movement at the neighbors.

"You get the gate," Dave said. "I'll get the meat."

"We could just go on and dump her," Merle said. "We could call it a night."

"It's best to be careful. The law can look at sput now and know who it comes from. We got to clean her up some."

Merle got out and opened the gate and Dave got out and opened the trunk and pulled the woman out by the foot and let her fall on her face to the ground. He reached in and got her shorts and put them in the crook of his arm, then bent and ripped her torn panties the rest of the way off and stuffed them in a pocket of her shorts and stuffed the shorts into the front of his pants. He got hold of her ankle and dragged her through the gate.

Merle closed the gate as Dave and the corpse came through. "You got to drag her on her face?" he said.

"She don't care," Dave said.

"I know, but I don't like her messed up."

"We're through with her."

"When we let her off, I want her to be, you know, okay."

"She ain't okay now, Merle. She's dead."

"I don't want her messed up."

Dave shrugged. He crossed her ankles and flipped her on her back and dragged her over next to the house and let go of her next to the water hose. He uncoiled the hose and took the nozzle and inserted it up the woman with a sound like a boot being withdrawn from mud, and turned the water on low.

When he looked up from his work, Merle was coming out of the house with a six-pack of beer. He carried it over to the redwood picnic table and sat down. Dave joined him.

"Have a Lone Star," Merle said.

Dave twisted the top off one. "You're thinking on something. I can tell."

"I was thinking we ought to take them alive," Merle said.

Dave lit a cigarette and looked at him. "We been over this. We take one alive she might scream or get away. We could get caught easy enough."

"We could kill her when we're finished. Way we're doing, we could buy one of those blow-up dolls, put it in the glove box and bring it to the drive-in."

"I've never cottoned to something like that. Even jacking off bothers me. A man ought to have a woman."

"A dead woman?"

"That's the best kind. She's quiet. You haven't got to put up with clothes and makeup jabber, keeping up with the Jones' jabber, getting that promotion jabber. She's not gonna tell you *no* in the middle of the night. Ain't gonna complain about how you put it to her. One stroke's as good as the next to a dead bitch."

"I kind of like hearing 'em grunt, though. I like being kissed."

"Rape some girl, think she'll want to kiss you?"

"I can make her."

"Dead's better. You don't have to worry yourself about how happy she is. You don't pay for nothing. If you got a live woman, one you're married to even, you're still paying for pussy. If you don't pay in money, you'll pay in pain. They'll smile and coo for a time, but stay out late with the boys, have a little financial stress, they all revert to just what my mamma was. A bitch. She drove my daddy into an early grave, way she nagged, and the old sow lived to be ninety. No wonder women live longer than men. They worry men to death.

"Like my uncle I was talking about. All that worry . . . Hell, that was his wife put it on him. Wanting this and wanting that. When he got sick, had that operation and had to dip into his savings, she was out of there. They'd been married thirty years, but things got tough, you could see what those thirty years meant. He didn't even come out of that deal with a place to put his dick at night."

"Ain't all women that way."

"Yeah, they are. They can't help it. I'm not blaming them. It's in them, like germs. In time, they all turn out just the same."

"I'm talking about raping them, though, not marrying them. Getting kissed."

"You're with the kissing again. You been reading Cosmo or something? What's this kiss stuff? You get hungry, you eat. You get thirsty, you drink. You get tired, you sleep. You get horny, you kill and fuck. You use them like a product, Merle, then when you get through with the product, you throw out the package. Get a new one when you need it. This way, you always got the young ones, the tan ones, no matter how old or fat or ugly *you* get. You don't have to see a pretty woman get old, see that tan turn her face to leather. You can keep the world bright and fresh all the time. You listen to me, Merle. It's the best way."

Merle looked at the woman's body. Her head was turned toward him. Her eyes looked to have filled with milk. Water was running out of her and pooling on the grass and starting to spurt from between her legs. Merle looked away from her, said, "Guess I'm just looking for a little romance. I had me a taste of it, you know. It was all right. She could really kiss."

"Yeah, it was all right for a while, then she ran off with a sand nigger."

"Arab, Dave. She ran off with an Arab."

"He was here right now, you'd call him an Arab?"

"I'd kill him."

"There you are. Call him an Arab or a sand nigger, you'd kill him, right?"

Merle nodded.

"Listen," Dave said. "Don't think I don't understand what you're saying. Thing I like about you, Merle, is you aren't like those guys down at the plant, come in do your job, go home, watch a little TV, fall asleep in the chair dreaming about some magazine model cause the old lady won't give out, or you don't want to think about her giving out on account of the way she's got ugly. Thing is, Merle, you know you're dissatisfied. That's the first step to knowing there's more to life than the old grind. I appreciate that in you. It's a kind of sensitivity some men don't like to face. Think it makes them weak. It's a strength, is what it is, Merle. Something I wish I had more of."

"That's damn nice of you to say, Dave."

"It's true. Anybody knows you, knows you feel things deeply. And I don't want you to think that I don't appreciate romance, but you get our age, you got to look at things a little straighter. I can't see any romance with an old woman anyway, and a young one, she ain't gonna have me . . . Unless it's the way we're doing it now."

Merle glanced at the corpse. Water was spewing up from between her legs like a whale blowing. Her stomach was a fat, white mound.

"We don't get that hose out of her," Merle said, "she's gonna blow the hell up."

"I'll get it," Dave said. He went over and turned off the water and pulled the hose out of her and put his foot on her stomach and began to pump his leg. Water gushed from her and her stomach began to flatten. "She was all right, wasn't she, Merle?"

"'Cept for them feet, she was fine."

They drove out into the pines and pulled off to the side of a little dirt road and parked. They got out and went around to the trunk, and with her legs spread like a wishbone, they dragged her into the brush and dropped her on the edge of an incline coated in blackberry briars.

"Man," Dave said. "Taste that air. This is the prettiest night I can remember."

"It's nice," Merle said.

Dave put a boot to the woman and pushed. She went rolling down the incline in a white moon-licked haze and crashed into the brush at the bottom. Dave pulled her shorts from the front of his pants and tossed them after her.

"Time they find her, the worms will have had some pussy, too," Dave said.

They got in the car and Dave started it up and eased down the road.

"Dave?"

"Yeah?"

"You're a good friend," Merle said. "The talk and all, it done me good. Really."

Dave smiled, clapped Merle's shoulder. "Hey, it's all right. I been seeing this coming in you for a time, since the girl before last . . . You're all right now, though. Right?"

"Well, I'm better."

"That's how you start."

They drove a piece. Merle said, "But I got to admit to you, I still miss being kissed."

Dave laughed. "You and the kiss. You're some piece of work buddy . . . I got your kiss. Kiss my ass."

Merle grinned. "Way I feel, your ass could kiss back, I just might."

Dave laughed again. They drove out of the woods and onto the highway. The moon was high and bright.

STORY NOTES

Mister Weed-Eater is one of my all-time favorites of my own work. I like it because I feel it's in touch with what I do best, yet, it's somehow different. I hesitate to say it's less dark than a lot of my work, because in some ways, I suppose it is dark. I tend to see it more as white humor than black humor, and I hope it's clear those terms have nothing to do with Negroes or Caucasians. But, just in case, pardon me while I give a little lecture on the off chance someone reading this isn't familiar with the terms.

Black humor is of the gallows variety. Dark and dreadful, funny on an immediate level, but brutally frightening on another. White humor is a term I first heard associated with Charles Portis. Actually, I suppose you could make a racial thing out of white humor and call it Honky Humor, or Ignorant Honkey's In Jeopardy Humor, because most white humor I've read is about Honkeys In Jeopardy. I know that is certainly part of my intent when I write this sort of thing. To take a close-up look at the happily ignorant. But what was meant by the term when referring to Portis, and I think it's a term that can be applied to one of my heroes as well, Mark Twain, is that the humor is biting, ironic, but less dark. It's humor that comes from innocence and ignorance.

Weirdly enough, and I swear, I am not making this up, the background of this story is 100 percent true. The basic premise for it is based on an event that happened to me personally. Obviously, it didn't go this far and didn't work out this way, but I swear, the initiating circumstance here really happened. I wrote about it in an article for *Iniquities* Magazine, which, by the way, I've somehow lost. If anyone has a spare copy, hey, I could use it. In fact, I could use copies of both the issues I was in.

Anyway, the amazing circumstance that initiated the story lay in the back of my mind for years, but I could never quite figure out how to make it into a story. I finally had to take myself out of the picture, create one of life's honkey innocents, or rather design him from the artifacts of my memory, meaning Job Harold is based on many people I know, with a little of myself thrown in. After creating a character, and having the initiating circumstance for my story given to me by real life, I just let the story run from there, having no idea where it was going—I rarely do—and finding the story jerking me along as if I were tied on the end of a rope being dragged by a run-away mule. Which is something that actually happened to me, too. Being dragged by a run-away mule, I mean. But that's another story.

Steppin' Out, Summer 68. This story isn't based on any single fact, but it's based on a number of minor incidents, attitudes, and such that I experienced growing up in Gladewater, Texas. I've added in the normal problems that males experience while coming of age. Like a surge of hormones and a need for sex. This makes a fella stupid, trust me, and no one is immune. But then again, what if you're pretty goddam stupid to begin with? What will it do to you then?

I got to thinking about that. Got to thinking about a few idiots I grew up with, people like them, and this began to boil.

It's a favorite story of mine. My finest moment with this story, at least for me, came when I gave a reading of it at *The Little Bookshop of Horrors* in Arvada, Colorado. I like that bookstore. Tomi and Doug Lewis, the owners of the bookstore, are good people.

And hey, did you know I'm responsible for the bookstore being in business? You see, Doug had a hard time finding a copy of my novel *The Nightrunners*, a book he'd heard about and wanted to read, so he opened a store that catered to that sort of thing. He finally got *The Nightrunners*, by the way, read it, and liked it.

How about that?

Love Doll. This little short-short is a favorite of mine, and was originally written for the Dark Harvest *Night Vision's* series. I turned it in with four other stories. Paul Mikol, publisher at Dark Harvest, felt thematically, it was too much like the other stories I had written.

This was correct. All of the stories I had written were supposed to be, in one way or another, about sexual obsession, power, control. It was just something I decided to do as a thematic linking to the stories, since in all other ways they were completely different. Oddly enough, this one struck me in tone and attitude as the most different of all, not one that was like the others.

But, I said nothing, agreed, and withdrew this one and let the other four stand as my contribution. I'm not saying Paul was wrong. I'm just saying it didn't matter to me at all. I turned around and sold it to Tom Monteleone to appear in one of his *Borderlands* anthology series books.

It was a throwback, in some ways to the old days when I wrote mostly absurdist short-shorts. I thought it was the best short-short I had written in years. It was wild, entertaining, and it actually had something to say about the war between the sexes, about the roles we adopt for ourselves, and the roles we expect others to perform. But let's let the story cover that instead of my mouth.

Bubba Ho-Tep. This is a story I have mixed feelings about. In 1992 I had a very bad year. Not the worst year of my life, as that could have been 1993, and certainly I don't remember 1983 as a cheery time either, but this one was different in that it was just one day after the other that was wearing me down. It wasn't the sort of stuff we all deal with. The things we can't control in life. Deaths of loved ones. Disintegration of friendships. It was somehow more bone weary than that, because at the center of these problems was the back-of-the-head feeling that you can't quite figure what the problem is, but if you could, you could fix it.

The other things, like loss of loved ones, can't be fixed. They can be dealt with, but they can't be fixed. Dead is dead. And friendships once gone astray are sometimes impossible to repair as well, but this . . . . Well, I knew once I sorted it out, whatever it was, I'd be okay. Only problem was, I couldn't sort it out.

This is not to say I was unhappy all the time in 1992. Though, on the other hand, it's not to say I was constantly delirious with pleasure either. Life is a series of events, and happiness is neither a moment nor a constant, it's an attitude, an ability to roll with the bad times and come up on your feet, and, if you're fortunate, and you've got your nose forward and your ears laid back, you can move ahead and find that on the whole, life is pretty goddamn enjoyable.

But 1992. Wheeee. I was suffering soul exhaustion. I was changing as a writer and going in all directions at once. I was being offered all sorts of things not available to me before. Being given greater chances for success, new avenues in which to express my talent. It was dizzying, and not nearly as delightful as it should have been.

I spent ten months on a novel that disappointed me. I tried to do something I couldn't pull off. It wasn't intentional, but what had happened was this: unconsciously, I had tried to write a novel for others instead of myself. Something I'd sworn never to do. You do this, it's like the worst of television, which tries to please everyone and ends up pleasing no one.

Upon completion of the book, I knew it had problems. But I was fooled by the good stuff in it. My editor, rightfully, was disappointed in it, and so was I. I was more disappointed than he was. They felt work could be done to improve it. I felt it could be improved in another way. I withdrew it, and in four months wrote another that was much better, and more the sort of book I wanted to write. When I turned it in my editor was surprised and delighted. He thought I was revising the original novel, but I turned in a totally different book, and one he liked very much.

Part of what happened was this: I had been pushed to write a bestseller by a lot of folks close to me, and someone in particular. It wasn't that they said, "Write a Bestseller," but they were, in subtle ways, trying to push me in directions already taken by others. Trying to help me find a comfortable niche. This person is a good person. A friend. Someone who had always supported me and understood what I was doing and liked me as Joe R. Lansdale, his ownself, but somehow they changed. I could no longer touch base with them. Our phone talks were often punctuated by me saying something, asking a question, and then from the other end . . . Silence. Not a moment of silence, but loooooonnnngggg moments. Then this person, as if having just returned from an astral trip to Antares, would tune back into the conversation and the tone of their voice would be as hollow as an empty oil drum. If I said something positive, they always found a negative. If I sold a story, a book, a comic, this was always offset by a story of industry woe. Got so I went outside, I constantly looked to see if the sky was falling.

Anyway, what this person was doing, without meaning to, was wearing me down. Since they were someone I respected, I listened on a deeper level than I realized. I felt obligated to write, if not a Bestseller, then, my "break-out book," as they like to refer to it in the industry. I kept getting the subtle message that I had to not write like I had written before. Apparently, what I was doing before was all wrong. Now that I was in the big time, (notice big with small letters, and not BIG TIME, which is another league altogether) I had to create a more acceptable sort of book.

I think the person who gave me these feelings meant well. I think I may even be doing them a bit of an injustice in making these conclusions, but I don't think it's much of one. I think this individual was tired too, disappointed with life, and just plain burned out.

Now, let me explain something. I've nothing against Bestsellers. I'd love to have one. *I am a commercial writer.* But I have artistic pride, meaning if I write a Batman book, it's because I like the money, the crossover opportunities, but most of all, I have to want to do it, and my way.

There may come a day when I have to write whatever is out there, and if it's between that and my family going hungry, well, I'll peck shit with the chickens. But as long as I don't have to do that, and as long as my artistic pride allows me to play at all sorts of things and make a living, I'll follow it.

Maybe someday it'll lead me into a Bestseller, or a comfortable niche. Or to the chicken yard where the chicken shit is. But I know this, I don't want to chase after success like a dog chasing a car. I might catch one and not like it when I do. I want to create something that will draw success to me. In other words, I write what I write.

Do I blame this unnamed person for my writing a disappointing novel? Nope. I made the decision, even if it was on a subconscious level, to do what I did, and I knew I was getting bad advice, and I knew I was getting this advice from a person who was depressed and unhappy and who was beginning to see their career—and maybe their life—as a dead end. And maybe it was just dealing with me that was wearing them down. I can't say.

Anyway, I made the choice to respond with the ten month disaster, and, thankfully, I also made the choice to correct this by writing a new book. One I'm considerably more satisfied with.

And what of this person? I still care for them, but I no longer listen to their advice. That part of my life has changed. I just don't have room for negative attitudes all the time. I've eliminated that sort of thing. I stepped back, started over, and the world got brighter and I grew an inch taller. I began to feel like myself again.

I don't want to live in a Pollyanna universe, but I do know this. Love and enthusiasm for what I do has always carried me through, and I hope to goodness it continues to do so. And, hey, if that love and enthusiasm leads me to a Bestseller, I can deal with that. So my motto is the same as always. Be true to yourself. Do what you love and the good things in life will come to you. But don't ask me for a loan.

So now, Joe R., you ask, since you got that off your chest, what does this have to do with "Bubba Ho-Tep"?

"Bubba Ho-Tep" was written during that period of emotional adjustment. Meaning 1992. Everything written during that time is colored by my experiences concerning the novel and my career. I wrote this story originally for a book that will now be called *The King Is Dead*, or maybe it's *Elvis Is Dead*. I don't remember. It has changed titles a lot. Anyway, that book's publication date has dragged on and on. So, I present the story here for the first time. I like a lot of things about it, but again, that bad year weighs heavily on me. So much, in fact, it's hard to look at anything I wrote during that period with less than a mild form of nausea. "Bubba" was inspired not only by Elvis, of course, but the fact that my mother had been in a rest home for some years after an accident that disabled her. I always hated her having to be there, but it wasn't a matter of her age, it was a matter of the type of medical attention she had to have, and the around the clock supervision. Something neither my brother or I could accomplish at home.

Every time I went there to visit, or to take Mom out for a while, the place depressed me more and more. It was actually a pretty good home, and my mother was as happy as she could be there, given the circumstances of her condition. We hoped she would improve enough to leave some day. But she didn't, and when she finally was able to leave, it was to be buried.

With this nursing home in mind, and the story to be written, and having always wanted to write some goofy sort of Mummy story called "Bubba Ho-Tep," something I had already decided should be placed in a nursing home, well, this came out.

Even though everything written during that time seems a little suspect to me, I did have fun writing this, and I especially like the stuff with the hieroglyphics, thanks to Mark A. Nelson, a wonderful artist who understood what I was doing immediately and ran with it.

Man With Two Lives. This story is an old one. Possibly the oldest story in the book, but I have a soft spot for it. It's simple but, believe it or not, sweet. At one time, I came close to being a full-time Western writer. Fate, however, conspired against me. That was okay. I've also almost been a full-time Young Adult writer—or rather I wanted to be—and I was almost a full-time Horror writer, and . . . . Well, if you've followed my career at all, you can see that to some extent I've done all those things, but not just one of these things.

I was writing a lot of pen-name novels then, not selling them, doing a little ghost work, and I got the opportunity to do this and relished the break. I don't think the writers even got paid for their stories in this book, which was called *The Roundup*, and was designed to boost the Western Writers of America.

I wanted to help, and I wanted a story in print, so I wrote this out of my passions for Wild Bill Hickok, the West in general, and even mysteries. It also contained another of my passions, Nacogdoches, Texas, which is where I now live, and have for nearly twenty years. Another interest, if not a passion, is Sheriff Spradley, who I mention in passing here. He was a real lawman. And an interesting one. Not quite the saint he's often been portrayed in local legend and writings, but interesting. Recently, on a visit to the Texas Ranger Museum in Waco, Texas, site of David Koresh's demise—Waco, not the museum—I saw a collection of Spradley's guns and badges and the little book I read about him so many years ago. The one I used as a basis for my research when I wrote a non-fiction article on him for one of the Old West Magazines. Since that was one of my earliest works, and I was at the museum to do research on a couple of future projects, I sort of felt warm, as if I'd come full-circle.

Course, since I had a fever at the time and was circling the glass cases in the museum like a buzzard, this feeling of warmth and coming full-circle only seems natural.

Another note. After I donated this story to the *Roundup* anthology, I later went on to edit two Western Writers of America anthologies, *Best of the West* and *New Frontiers*. From these, I donated money to the Western Writers of America—a large percentage of the book's earnings, actually—paid the writers' advances and even some minor royalties. The books were well reviewed and were noted as ground breakers because they combined off-beat Westerns along with more traditional fare. A number of anthologies were inspired by these volumes.

The year of *Best of the West*, all three Spur-nominated stories came from that book. Loren Estleman won for "The Bandit," a very good story.

The year *New Frontiers* came out, two of the nominees came from the book. One of the stories, "The Indian Summer of Nancy Redwing," by Harry W. Paige won the Spur.

Neal Barrett, Jr.'s "Winter on the Belle Fourche," which was one of the Spur nominees, by the way, was picked up for a science fiction Best of the Year volume. The first unpublished story by Max Brand in years appeared in *New Frontiers*. There were many great stories in these two volumes. Award winners, nominees, stories that have been reprinted numerous times, and stories that have started careers. I'm proud of that. I don't want a pat on the back for it. That's just evolution, but I'm proud of it.

But . . . The Western Writers of America never said thank you for your financial contribution or kiss my ass. They just took the money and deposited it in their bank account.

Guess what? Next western-related anthology I did was not a Western Writers of America volume, and I didn't send them shit.

Pilots (With Dan Lowry). This is an old story, and one of the handful of collaborations I've done. I've done two with Dan. The first was titled "This Little Piggy," and it appeared in an issue of *Skullduggery*, a small magazine that mixed horror and crime stories. It didn't last many issues. I had two or three stories there, counting "Piggy."

Anyway, "This Little Piggy" has its moments, but ultimately, it's not so great. This one, however, I like. Intellectual it ain't, but it's a perfect Weird Menace pulp story, and that was our aim.

Dan used to come over to the house and tell me about all the stories he wanted to write. Course, he's never gotten around to but one on his own, but heck, he might do those others someday.

He's a great idea man, and he knows about mood. His problem is, dagnabit, he never quite gets around to stuff. He told me about this idea he had, about this car shooting trucks down on the highway, about using CB radios as the backbeat, trucker language, which was hot then, and about having the main character be a Viet Nam Vet. I said something like, "Man that sounds like fun. I'd like to read that."

Next time I saw him, as with all of Dan's stories, it hadn't progressed beyond the idea part. I finally couldn't take it anymore. I suggested a collaboration. He agreed. I put him at the kitchen table with a pen, and I got my electric portable, and we started kicking it around. Dan wrote a few lines, and I typed them up, modified them, added a bit, and we talked our way through about half the story. He went home. I cleaned up what we had, wrote a little more, according to our game plan.

He came back over another day and we finished it up, except for the ending. He went home, I rewrote, and wrote the last seven or eight pages in a white-hot flash.

He came back another day, we reworked the whole thing. He went home. I typed it up and gave it to him. He made changes and additions, I did another draft, and out it went.

Nobody bought it.

This perplexed me. I was selling a number of stories, and this one, though not an intellectual feast, always struck me as more than professional. T.E.D. Klein at *Twilight Zone* told us he liked it and it would make a great movie, but . . . . That was about as excited as anyone got.

Years went by. The ink on the manuscript began to fade.

Then Ed Gorman and Marty Greenberg did an anthology called *Stalkers* and invited me in. They bought it, and since that time *Stalkers* has been in hardback, paperback, audio, and foreign editions. "Pilots" also has a life of its own outside of that anthology, and will soon appear in a comic book, as well as find itself reprinted again. There's even been a film nibble.

Go figure.

The Phone Woman. Like "Mister Wood Eater," "The Phone Woman" is also based on a true story. The true event was recorded in an article I wrote for *Iniquities*, which I hope to reprint. I've twisted the facts here to meet my thematical needs, but the initiating premise is real.

The inspiration for this story occurred at what we call our "old house," or "old neighborhood." Place where my wife and I were living at the time of this event was a conductor for weirdness. At least four of my stories owe their existence to my neighbors. "Pentecostal Punk Rock," "Mister Weed-Eater," "The Fat Man And The Elephant," and this one. A number of other stories and novels, though not as directly influenced, also owe my neighbors much credit.

We sold that house, moved out of the neighborhood to the other side of town. It's less weird over here, more pleasant, but you know what? Sometimes I miss that old house. How many places you gonna live where people hire blind grounds keepers? Where weird people come to use your phone then try to lodge themselves securely in your hallway? Where weird people appear in your yard you've never seen before? Appear like smoke, and disappear even more rapidly. I tell you, on that side of town there was some kind of hole into the universe, a hole into which someone, or something, was constantly pouring strange ingredients, people and events.

Maybe I'll just go back over there and hang around, get a few story ideas.

Naw.

The Diaper. I wanted to write a story in an experimental manner, but as I started writing, the story got sillier and the experiment became a parody of experimental writing. The inspiration for the story was my son, Keith. I was a house husband for years. The first six years of my son's life, the first eighteen months or so of my daughter's. Keith was born four years before Kasey. Back then, our financial situation was pretty tight, my work schedule was a wreck, because Keith *did not sleep.* Twenty minute stretches for three years. I swear. My wife worked at the Fire Department, and when she was away for twenty-four hours, well, it was a nightmare. No reprieve. And again, Keith didn't sleep.

Back then I'd changed so many diapers, stayed up so many nights with that kid, well, I was a little crazy. And Keith, man, he's a character. One of the most special human beings in the universe and I love him dearly, but he was a challenge.

So challenging, I hardly ever got any writing time. I wrote so much stuff in fifteen and twenty minute spurts over a period of several years, I don't know how I managed to get anything done. What I did for reading pleasure was I read short-shorts.

I'd always liked them, and had to some extent—and I say this with all humility—mastered them. I sold a lot of them. But the main reason I was reading them then was they were all I had the time or energy to read. Novels were rarely read, or longer short stories. It was hard to even get through a movie.

Still, I wrote. I'd write for a few minutes here, a few minutes there, and then when Karen was home she'd arrange for me to steal a few hours to create. In this manner I wrote *The Magic Wagon*, edited *Best of the West* and *The Way The West Was* (this has a co-editor, Tom Knowles, and has just been released in hardback; it's a non-fiction work about the Old West, and has sat on a shelf for nearly nine years for reasons too complicated to go into here), as well as managed a lot of short stories.

But I'm getting ahead of myself. This was written when Keith was very young, long before *The Magic Wagon* and the others. It was a lot of fun. I read it at a writer's meeting, giving a chuckle to those there, then I put it away. I think I tried it out a few times, but no takers. Later, *Nova Express* asked to see something by me, and I gave them this. It's lightweight, and I meant it to be, but, hey, I still like it. The experimentation is a parody of William S. Burroughs, if you're wondering. Burroughs is one of those writers who I find interesting and sometimes inspiring, but I can't honestly say I like his stuff. It's sort of like too much rich chocolate. A taste will do me. He's the sort of writer that strikes sparks, however, and I think he's great for younger writers to read to excite them about language, but I can't say as I'd take anything by him to a deserted island. Or for that matter, to read while waiting for the dentist. Still, I like to get his books down now and then, flip them open and read sections from them.

The best Burroughs pastiche ever, because it not only rings the bells of William S. Burroughs, but of Edgar Rice Burroughs as well, is "The Jungle Rot Kid On The Nod" by

Philip Jose Farmer. In fact, I think his story beats anything I've ever read by Burroughs, but then again, without William S., it couldn't have existed. Very clever. Look it up.

Everybody Plays the Fool. This was supposed to be the beginning of a novel, but that didn't pan out. It was too whacked an opening for me to continue in this vein. And when finished, I realized something. It stood by itself.

It was inspired by a popcorn dream. I've talked about this before. Popcorn is a favorite food of mine, but it often gives me bad dreams. I think it stirs my stomach up so I can't sleep well and I remember my dreams, and the dreams I have while under the influence of P.C. are *out there*. They also tend to make good stories and the stories sell. I like good stories. I like money. I like popcorn. Who could ask for anything more?

A Hard-On For Horror. This one is an article, but since I do a moderate amount of non-fiction, I like to have it represented whenever possible.

After my love for prose, movies are my greatest passion, along with martial arts, comics, and Lipton Ice Tea, preferably unsweetened, so, it's only natural that I should write about them from time to time.

I grew up on Universal films. Roger Corman productions. Hammer films, and then later, the low-budget boom of horror films from the middle seventies that rode hell-bent-for-leather through the early eighties. They made some good ones during that period—they made *more* bad ones, but that's beside the point—and I can't say the number of interesting ones since has maintained. The low-budget horror film, at least as far as my tastes go, is pretty much in the toilet.

Course, what you like one year may not be something you're proud of liking years later. As a child, I spent many an hour watching low-budget extravaganzas. Some of the worst back then seemed fun. Like *Reptilicus*. I saw this again when I was adult, and couldn't believe it. This was the movie I'd seen as a kid? The beginning was just how I remembered it, but after a great and spooky opening concerning a drill bit bringing up a piece of meat from the depths of the earth, the film quickly turned into a mad puppet show. The puppet was the monster, Reptilicus, of course, and all you got to see of it was it's neck rising up behind a hill, and when it wanted to wreck stuff, well, it just brought its neck down on cardboard buildings and tore them up with the weight of its neck.

It's neck! Can you believe that? I've seen more exciting sock puppet presentations.

So, time does wreck a lot of perceptions. My mind had maintained that original spooky opening and I guess, as a kid, I had just filled in the blanks from there. And my blanks were better than anything the film makers could come up with.

But some old favorites when seen again, like *Alligator People*, though certainly ripe with its cheap moments, have aged well and have something inexplicable going for them. You can't quite put your finger on it, but it's got it.

And what about Tourneau's *The Cat People*? Here was a brilliant film saddled with a title out of kiddie land, and no one has yet topped it. The remake was absolutely stupid, and a waste of film. Back when the original was made, they could have taken the money blown on the wardrobe for the stars of the remake and made three pictures. Each one better than the remade *Cat People*. The remake was certainly an example of how more money and more artistic freedom did not result in a better film. Just one with tits and ass. Old isn't always better. But sometimes it is.

On the other hand. Who asked me? That's not really what my article is about, but sometimes I can't help myself. But the article is on low-budget films, and I hope you get a kick out of it.

In The Cold Dark Time. I don't remember much about this. Gary Raisor asked me for a story for his anthology *Obsessions,* and I told him I didn't think I had time. And then I ate popcorn, which always upsets my stomach and gives me bad dreams, and well, I came up with this and wrote it in about twenty minutes and sent it to him. Andrew Vachss called it a prose poem. That made me feel good, because I sort of saw it that way myself. But, as I said, I don't remember much about it. No idea what inspired it. I just woke up with it. I hadn't expected a story to come out—I was working on something else at the time—and this was handed to me. A gift from the gods.

Or the devils.

Incident On And Off A Mountain Road. This is one of the stories I wrote for the *Night Visions* series, and I wanted for one of the stories to just be an old fashioned crime/suspense story with a dollop of weirdness. Sort of an episode of *Alfred Hitchcock Presents* for the nineties. Or did I do this in the late eighties? Boy, time flies when you're having a good time.

This one was what I considered to be one of my "professional" stories. Meaning something that was a good read, but not particularly special when you added it to the pool of my other work. I felt the same way about "The Steel Valentine" which first appeared in *By Bizarre Hands,* which, by the way, I wrote for a Valentine anthology. The story was accepted by the editors of the anthology, but their editor had a shit fit, and tossed it back. I got to keep the money, though, and it appeared in *By Bizarre Hands*, and since, every goddamn where. I was surprised that story stirred anyone up that bad, and I was surprised at how many people have liked it as well as they do. That's not to say I wasn't proud of it, I just never expected the response it got.

Ditto on this one.

By Bizarre Hands—The Play. This is based on one of my more popular short stories, *By Bizarre Hands*. The story has been reprinted many times, and the title of the story has been used as the title of my first short story collection, *By Bizarre Hands*, as well as the title of a comic book series based on my work, which should by the appearance of this book, debut from Dark Horse Comics.

Not long ago, I, as well as several other writers, were approached to write plays for an Off-Broadway production of One-Act Plays with horror as its theme. It was supposed to be a revival of the Grand Guignol. I liked the idea. I had been reading a lot of plays just about then, and was looking for an excuse to write one.

I wrote two. Both based on short stories of mine, one, "Drive-In Date," which was written while under the influence of reading and watching a lot of plays.

"By Bizarre Hands" required more work to turn into a play than I had anticipated. I also found the ending of the short story, though perfect for a short story, and still my preferred ending, just didn't cut it on stage. It sort of . . . I guess the word died isn't appropriate here . . . but, it fizzled.

It also struck me that it might be fun to alter the story some to have a slightly different version of the story, so I set to work and came out with this.

My two plays were paid for, but alas, never produced. This one appeared in a volume of crime/suspense stories title *Cold*

Blood, edited by Richard Chizmar, and the "Drive-In Date" play ended up being reprinted in *Cemetery Dance* magazine. But I wasn't happy. I wanted more people to see it.

If you liked the story, you should enjoy this—as I think my method of writing plays make them quite readable, or so I like to think—and if you feel as if you already know the story, well, this version varies enough to make it interesting, especially toward the end.

Godzilla's Twelve Step Program. This one came from reading about all those twelve step programs for losing weight, stopping smoking, stopping drinking, stopping sex, whatever.

I had also been reading something about Godzilla, and I got to thinking. Godzilla can't help himself, this eating folks and wrecking cities. It's in his blood. But that's no reason for it to continue. It's not social, and since the military is always trying to drive a nuclear warhead up his ass, it ain't healthy either.

What if he wanted to quit?

What if there were other monsters, like Kong, or Reptilicus who wanted to quit? Or had? What kind of help, support groups, would be available to them?

Important questions like that brought this about. I tell you, you got to keep reading matter away from me. It gives me ideas.

Drive-In Date. This one comes from a dream, which comes from reading about Henry Lee Lucas and his pal Otis, whose last name won't come to me right now. Not sure, it's either Toole, or O' Toole, or something like that. But that isn't important. Those two guys were scary. Serial killers, and probably not responsible for a quarter of the crimes they claimed, but hey, they were scumbags and dangerous just the same. I got to tell you, if they throw the switch on these fuckers, stick needles in their arms, you can bet I won't lose sleep over it. They were cancers in society and I'm glad they're behind bars, and truthfully, I wish those assholes were in the ground with dirt in their faces, meat for the worms, fertilizer for roses, which would be the only beauty they could bring into this life.

Anyway, I read about those guys, and they scared me, and at the time I was reading a lot of plays and planning to write one, and this story came to me in play-like structure, if not format. Single set. Simple situation. Two actors. Lots of dialogue.

I hesitated writing it. It struck me as too much on the money and too scary. I didn't want to write something that was just mean or crude. I wanted to awaken in others the kind of horror I had felt about these guys, if for no other reason than to assure myself that others felt the terror of such things as well. Misery loves company, maybe. Whatever, I knew I had to go ahead with it, and I felt better the moment I finished. I flushed Otis and Henry out of my system, like working out a big, slow-to-digest Italian dinner.

A final note on my feelings about the story. I think this is the most disturbing story I've ever written. Maybe not my favorite, but certainly the most disturbing. As for the stuff I said about writing a play, well, this was later turned into a play. By me. It's been printed, and I hope to reprint it at some future date, and I'd even like to see it performed. If performed well.

I think.